# THE BANK

BREACHING THE UNDERWORLD

A SASKIA VAN ESSEN CRIME THRILLER
BOOK 1

## MIRIAM VERBEEK

'The Bank' is a work of fiction. Names, characters, places and incidents are either the product of the author's imagination or used fictitiously. Any resemblance to an actual person, living or dead, events or locales is coincidental. AI was not used to create any part of this book.

Copyright © 2024 by Miriam Verbeek

Published by Miriam Verbeek, 2024

All rights reserved.

No part of this book may be reproduced in any form or by any electronic or mechanical means, including information storage and retrieval systems, without written permission from the author, except for the use of brief quotations in a book review.

ISBN 978-0-6488854-9-8 Ebook

ISBN 978-1-7638190-0-9 Trade paperback

Cover design by 100 Covers

Many thanks to the brilliant help of my cousin Thea, whose wonderful knowledge of languages helped me get foreign phrases right. Special thanks go to my terrific editor, Juliet Middleton.

❦ Created with Vellum

# ABOUT 'THE BANK'

Saskia loves her new dream job in Lyon, France, investigating financial systems for the Friendly Society Bank. In her free time, she indulges her second passion, bike riding.

She's astonished when a stranger accuses her of murder, and even more bewildered when Europe's top law enforcement agencies ask her to trace money trails that could lead to some of Europe's criminal masterminds. Somehow, she must learn how to present an innocent face to the criminals who begin to track her every move as she delves into the secrets they think are hidden in the cyber world.

When her family and friends receive death threats, she's terrified, but it's too late to stop her clandestine work. There's a small window of opportunity for her to save herself and those she loves while bringing down an evil network … and she has no way of knowing if her strategy will work.

# 1

## RANSOMWARE

Saskia sat up, one hand searching around in the dark for her buzzing phone.

She held the lit screen to her face.

*2am!*

"Schijt! Wie belt nou?" she muttered, frowning at the number on the screen. It had a +1 prefix. She did not recognise it and rejected the call.

Five seconds later, the phone vibrated to life again. Not a wrong number then. She swiped to answer and lifted the device to her ear. "Hallo?"

"Doctor van Essen? Is it you, Dr van Essen? I'm in deep trouble. You've got to help me!" The panicked male voice – speaking English in a pronounced southern American accent – was so loud that Saskia jerked the phone away from her ear.

"Who is this?"

"It's me, Doctor van Essen. It's Clint Bailey. I've done something really stupid, and you've got to help me!"

*Who is Clint Bailey?*

"Mr Bailey, please help me by telling me who you are and what your problem is."

"I'm Clint. You know? I spoke with you after your talk at the bank about cybersecurity. You know – I'm seconded to FSB for a couple of weeks. But, Doctor van Essen, I've done exactly what you warned us not to do."

Saskia dredged up a memory of a tall man with a broad middle, floppy brown hair, eyes behind rimless glasses that blinked too much and – yes! the same penetrating voice.

*Though maybe he's not so tall,* Saskia reflected, *I have to stop thinking of all adults as tall.*

She brought her attention back to the matter at hand. "How can I help, Mr Bailey?"

"There was a message from Mister Aubert telling me to attend urgently to a matter. There was a link, and I clicked on the link." At the last word, Clint Bailey's voice rose to a squeak. "It's not from Mister Aubert!"

"Where are you?" Saskia kicked off the bed cover and reached for her laptop on the small table jammed between the bedhead and wall of her cramped bedroom.

"I'm in the office – I know – it's a ridiculous time, but I wanted to get some stuff done, and it's the right time to talk to my American colleagues – you know? Time difference and all –"

"Mr Bailey, are you using the bank's computers?" Saskia put the phone on loudspeaker and set it on the table as she opened her laptop. Using her foot, she hooked a stool out from under the table and transferred herself on to it.

"I am! You know – you told us not to click on links unless we were sure about them – that some of them could infect systems. You know – worms and viruses and all –"

"Mr Bailey, when did you do this?"

"Just now. I mean. I realised I might be in trouble. There's no IT people here. You know, it's late –"

"Mr Bailey, disconnect your computer from its power source."

"What?"

"Disconnect your computer from its power source. Pull out the electricity plug now!"

"What? Oh! Oh! Yes. Okay. I've just – yeah – I see it! Okay. Done."

"Exactly how much time has passed since you clicked the link?"

"Uh? Ah? About ten minutes – maybe less. I had your number. You know – "

"I want you to unplug every computer in the bank."

"All of them?"

"All! Now, Mr Bailey! Call me again when you've done it." Saskia typed a password into her laptop, clicked into the bank's website and located the after-hours number. She tapped out the number for the security section.

"Oui?"

In French, she introduced herself and then said, "Monsieur, there is every possibility that the bank's computer system has been compromised. We may have time to stop the whole system from being infected, but I need you to switch off all the power in the building."

"That's impossible!"

"Monsieur, the bank may lose many millions of euros if this infection takes hold. Our computer system is linked to all other branches of the bank, and if you do not do this, it may cause problems worldwide."

As she negotiated with Security, Saskia searched her phone contacts for Ferdinand Fourvier, head of FSB's IT section.

"It is imperative you do this, Monsieur. I am working now to ensure that the power outage will be short, but it must happen now, or the consequences could be terrible."

She heard a muttered conversation offline. Another person came online. "Who are you?"

"I am Doctor Saskia van Essen. I'm with the Compliance Risk Management Unit of the bank. With whom am I speaking?"

"Alain Dubois."

"Monsieur Dubois, I met you when I first took up the position at the bank. To remind you, I am the small Dutch woman, and we discussed the issue of risk to your security protocols."

"I remember you."

"Good. Please act urgently on my request. The sooner this is done, the quicker I can resolve the matter. I will get back to you as soon as I can to further explain the situation. Please give me a mobile phone number where I can call you after you turn off the power. The line we are currently using may not work." Saskia struggled to keep her voice calm as waves of impatience threatened to close her throat. Her attention was only partly on the conversation, because she was scanning her email inbox to check if she had also received the email Clint Bailey had opened. Her scan stopped at a message from 'Antoine Aubert':

> This is an urgent matter that needs your attention immediately! Click here!
>
> Antoine Aubert
>
> Managing Director
>
> Friendly Society Bank Pty Limited (FSB)
>
> Lyon Branch

Saskia squinted at the screen. So, the same message had probably been sent to all bank staff in Lyon. How many others had clicked the link?

Alain Dubois finally made a decision. "Very well, Mademoiselle. Please hurry with a callback."

Saskia noted the mobile number he dictated and thanked him.

She tapped out a message to Clint Bailey:

> Power about to be switched off in building. Stay put. I'll call soon. S

Then she called Ferdinand Fourvier, who was as disgruntled at being woken as she had been until she explained what had happened and the action she had taken. "Do we know what the infection is?" he asked.

"Not yet. I don't even know if there is an infection. I'm currently in my parents' home in Holland, so I can only help remotely. If you can get to the bank for a hands-on, I'll have a look at the email Monsieur

Bailey opened and tell you as much as I can. How long will it take you to get to the bank?"

"Eh? Go to the – of course – thirty – maybe forty minutes."

"As soon as I know, I'll let you know whether this panic is for nothing or something."

She tapped out another message to Clint Bailey:

> Ferdinand Fourvier, Head of IT, will be at bank
> in about 30 mins. Stay put. S

All her attention was now focused on her laptop. Using the sandbox application on her computer, she began to investigate the nature of the link, quickly confirming that her panic was justified. The link was to install a trojan designed to make the computer – or, in this case, the computer system – inoperable. Within half-an-hour of infection, the screen of a compromised computer would display a demand for payment.

Saskia frowned as she scrolled through the code. There was something amateurish about it, but it was still beyond her capability to quickly interrogate.

She clicked into the private chat group she shared with her geek friends.

> #AllThere: URGENT. I need someone who
> can undo ransomware before it goes live.

She waited for a response, continuing to study the code, hoping to find something to make it inoperable.

"Ping!"

> #JackoFry: Try #CaseIt10 on gig.geeks.hire.
> New. Good reputation.

Saskia knew #JackoFry. It didn't surprise her that her friend was up at this ungodly hour. They rarely left off fiddling with his screens till dawn. Saskia did a quick search on the gig.geeks.hire site for #CaseIt10 and verified #JackoFry's recommendation, including the 'charge for services was always reasonable'.

She sent a note to #CaseIt10 via the website using her handle #All-There, which would allow #CaseIt10 to check her bonafides; then she sent a direct message in the faint hope she could get a quick answer – who knew where in the world #CaseIt10 lived.

Five minutes later, 'Ping!' #CaseIt10 responded.

> #CaseIt10: How can I help?
>
> #AllThere: My organisation has just had a ransomware attack. Hopefully we've checked the spread. Can you disable?
>
> #CaseIt10: Who shall I send the bill to?
>
> #AllThere: Me.
>
> #CaseIt10: Send me what you've got.

Saskia did as requested.

Not even a half hour had passed since she'd been woken. With the immediate panic over, she noticed that she was cold, and the only light in the room was from the laptop screen and her phone. She switched on a bedside lamp, climbed into her bed and under the cover of a doona. She propped herself up against the wall with a pillow tucked at her back, positioning the laptop before her. She messaged M. Fourvier the details he would need when he started investigating the spread of the infection. The bank's computer system operated on a hybrid network topology. Hopefully, that would work in his favour.

M. Fourvier replied:

> Have shut down computer network. Power back on. Have started tracing spread of infection. So far seems your actions have stopped it in its tracks.

Saskia dropped her head back against the wall.

*I'm not going to sleep!*

A message 'ping' from her computer shocked her awake.

#CaseIt10: EasyPeasy. Real amateur work this one. Bought the malware from the Dark Web for US$39.90 yesterday. IP's from a public site so it won't help you. But I've got the code to decrypt the malware. I'll send it separately.

#AllThere: Wonderful! Thank you!

#CaseIt10: No problem. Happy to help.

# 2

## BIRTHDAY PARTY

Saskia took a deep breath as she exited the back seat of her brother's new car. Sunday mornings at her grandparents' home were mostly a chore, alleviated by the excellent cakes and pies Ma van Essen served – especially the apple pie.

True to form, the broad figure of her grandmother greeted first her parents and brother at the front door, then announced loudly, "Onze kleine Saskia is bij ons!" (Our little Saskia is with us!) She tut-tutted that Saskia had not grown even a centimetre taller, and why was it that she only ever wore trousers and blouses?

Saskia dutifully stood on tiptoes to kiss her grandmother's soft, wrinkled cheek. "Happy birthday, Oma. I also have a coat, pyjamas and underclothes."

Ma van Essen tut-tutted some more while she ushered the family into the house and drew Saskia along by the arm. Three aunts, four uncles and six cousins stood up from their seats to welcome the newcomers, crowding around Saskia as if she had been absent for centuries rather than a mere few months. Clearly, they had not yet recovered from her decision to leave her professoriate position at the LMU Munich School of Management to work at a bank in France. The former, they argued, held prestige; the latter was a job anyone could master.

"I can't understand it!" shrilled Ma van Essen, sending an accusing stare in Saskia's father's direction as he plonked into a vacant armchair. "Theo, you told me she is a doctor. Trin from Bep and Nat Bengtson have bank jobs. They didn't go to university." To Saskia, she asserted, "You should live in the Netherlands. The French give bad jobs to Dutch people."

"Mother!" protested Tante Alice. "Trin is a bank teller. That might not be Saskia's job."

Ma van Essen huffed. "Banks are all crooks!"

Saskia was not called upon to comment, so she concentrated on eating apple pie as the conversation about whether she had a good job and whether all banks were 'crooks' and the evidence for such 'crookness' grew more heated. Even Saskia's mother, who ate her chocolate cake in small, delicate forkfuls, joined the fray with a gossiper's passion, repeating some of the complaints her café customers had made about banks.

Pa van Essen, who usually sat in silent contemplation at these family gatherings, surprised everyone by saying, "Let Saskia tell us."

Saskia jerked to attention, noting all eyes rested on her. "Er – tell you what?"

"Your mother said you've found a place to live," Tante Pauline said. "She wasn't sure where. Is it nice?"

"Um – yes. I think so. I have a few rooms in a house in the sixth arrondissement of Lyon."

"An apartment?"

"Sort of. It's a large old home owned by an elderly lady, and she's divided the space into a few apartments."

"And what about friends? Have you made any friends?"

"I've joined a mountain biking club and made friends."

"So, you're still bike crazy?" Ma van Essen inserted. "Have you learned to drive yet?"

Saskia shook her head.

"And rightly so! I never learned to drive. We have excellent public transport." Ma van Essen lifted her chin in the direction of Saskia's brother, Jan. "You're not like your silly brother who just wasted money buying a car."

"I need it to pick up girls," Jan responded cheerfully. He was tall and congenial like their father, though, like Saskia, he had inherited their Indonesian mother Sophia's black hair, brown eyes and brown skin. His ambitions in life ran little further than carving out a comfortable living by working in and one day taking over the running of his parents' café, finding a girl to marry and starting a family. He was three years younger than Saskia. She had doted on him from the moment he was born and, though he now towered over her, she still felt the instinct to mother him.

Ma van Essen took away Saskia's empty plate, replacing it with a mug of coffee.

"What's the name of your bank?" cousin Willem asked.

"The bank is called the Friendly Society Bank – FSB," Saskia said. "It's an investment bank."

"I know that bank!" Willem returned. "They took my money and disappeared it."

"Hey! What do you say now?" Ma van Essen demanded. Saskia could almost smell the avid interest in the possibility of scandal.

"Yes. It's true," Willem said, nodding his head, face pulling into a scowl.

Tante Tineke shifted to the edge of her seat, becoming animated. "It's true," she echoed. "He thought I sent him a message that I needed to pay an invoice and didn't have my credit card with me. So, he sent the money to an account. But it wasn't me."

"I soon worked out it was a scam, but I'd already paid the money," Willem said. "I tried to put a stop to the funds, but my bank said the money had already been transferred to another account at the FSB, and they couldn't retrieve it. I contacted the FSB, and they said there was nothing they could do because they didn't have the money either, and they didn't know where it went to."

"Is that possible?" Oom Joost asked. "Surely a bank knows where they send money. Isn't that the case, Saskia?"

"Er – yes – but maybe it's gone into another bank and sometimes it gets complicated tracing money."

"Can you do it now that you're at the FSB?"

"Um –"

"Don't be ridiculous, Willem," Oom Anton said. "The money's gone. It's probably in the hands of some shark in the Bahamas by now."

The conversation moved on to more family-important matters: who had married whom, who had separated from whom, deaths, births, funerals, problems with the gemeenteraad (municipal council) and the weather. Saskia made an effort to engage because, when all was said and done, she loved her comfortable, inward-looking family – especially if she could mostly enjoy them at a distance. However, her contributions to the conversation were mostly in the form of, "Really!" or "But how can that be?" "But I thought so and so was with such and such!".

When Saskia was finally released from the gathering and into Jan's car with her father in the front seat and mother in the back beside her, she took a deep breath and let it out with relief. Sophia folded Saskia's hand in her work-worn one, brown eyes twinkling with amusement behind thick-lensed glasses. "You them make happy you come for Ma's birthday," she said in her heavily accented and grammatically poor Dutch that had not improved even after living in the Netherlands for twenty-seven years – not that anyone cared how Sophia van Essen spoke, because she was funny, energetic, insightful and kind. "You good girl."

"Do you really have to go this afternoon?" Jan asked.

"I promised to give a guest lecture at the university in Rotterdam tomorrow morning, and then I need to return to Lyon."

"Ma is right," said her father, twisting to look into the back seat. "You would be better off taking a job with a bank closer to your family. Or will that university you're going to in Rotterdam give you a job? At least we would see more of you if you lived in Rotterdam."

"We suspect you are trying your hardest to get as far from us as you can," her brother added.

"Er – it's just where opportunities seem to fall," Saskia lied, and her mother's hand squeezed a little harder.

The family accompanied her to the railway station to say their goodbyes, father and brother still unhappy she was leaving them again. But her mother bent down to hug her and whispered in her ear, "Fly, my clever, independent daughter. Fly high."

# 3

## ROTTERDAM

Saskia unfolded her travel bike and set off from Rotterdam Station along back streets and lanes towards Schiekanaal, where her friends Nicolaas Bakker and his son Hans lived on their canal boat. She rode at a leisurely pace, enjoying the late afternoon mid-summer warmth.

The men greeted her enthusiastically, lifting her bike over the railings of the gangway and inviting her into their two-storey water home. Saskia settled in their comfortable kitchen, drinking coffee and catching up on the news. Unlike her family, Nicolaas and Hans understood her aims and ambitions and were eager to learn about her new job at the bank.

"Compliance risk management," Hans said. "What do you actually do?"

"So far, I've mostly been involved in identifying whether the bank's policies and IT systems are in line with EU legal and regulatory requirements."

"What does your family think of this?" Hans asked.

Saskia chuckled. "Most don't know what to think. They think I've become a bank teller."

One blond eyebrow lifted. "And you didn't try to put them straight?"

"Goodness, no! It's much easier letting them argue about what I do. Besides, they're mostly put out that I haven't moved back home and decided to live in France instead."

Nicolaas's lips twitched into a slight smile. He knew Saskia's family; understood their parochial ways. He had taught Saskia in her senior school years at Delft, recognised her talents and helped her to make good her dream of moving beyond the confines of her family's ambitions. That help included offering to give her a home in Rotterdam when she declared she wanted to study at the city's Erasmus University. "Well, Saskia, I hope the bureaucracy does not swallow you up. These large organisations can be a challenge, and you are not a forceful person."

"Oh!" Saskia said, grinning at his concern, "I'm a backroom person. I just have to research and present reports. I leave it to other people to actually implement recommendations ... Although perhaps not yesterday." She recounted the drama she'd been dragged into the previous night.

"Quick thinking," Hans praised. "They'll be thanking you when you get back to the bank. Maybe they'll promote you."

"I don't think so. But it does make me think that the bank needs to have a system in place that catches these sorts of things without having to wake some person on the other side of Europe in the vague hope they can help."

"How did this person know to call you anyway?"

"I gave a talk on staying cyber secure to the bank staff a few weeks ago. The IT manager was supposed to give it, but he said he hated talking to an audience, and since I'd brought up the issue, I should do it."

"So, did you just give out your phone number also?"

"Er – yes – that wasn't very smart of me. This person wanted to catch up with me again and so I invited him to call me to make a time."

"Hey! Hey!" Hans exclaimed. He put a possessive arm around her and drew her close. "Just remember, my sweetness, that if I can't have you, no one can." He pressed his lips first on one eyelid, then the other.

Saskia leaned into his familiar embrace, a comforting warmth stirring in her belly. She and Hans had been lovers throughout her university years in Rotterdam, but in the end she knew she did not want to be tied to any relationship. Not at this stage of her life. Maybe never. Her decision to move on had hurt Hans, but he remained her friend – her closest friend. And now, she knew, he had another lover and plans for marriage. She was happy for him.

"Come, love birds!" Nicolaas said, sliding off the bench seat, "we need to go, or we'll be late."

"Late for what?" Saskia asked.

"Claasen has a new game she wants us to break."

Saskia clapped her hands in glee. She could not have wished for a better way to spend an evening.

The sign on the café door read 'CLOSED', but Hans pushed the door open and a chorus of greetings filled the air. "Hey! Saskia! Surprise! Welcome!" Chairs scraped back and the café's twenty-three occupants surrounded her, some hugging her and others slapping her on the back. They were all sizes, shapes, sexualities and mental stabilities. Some wore Goth clothing, others simple tee shirts over baggy trousers, others alluring outfits. What tied their friendships together was a love of computing. Claasen, who owned the handle #JackoFry, had an androgynous figure and face. They had brightened their lips blood-red, and wore a long, raven black wig and a tightly fitting, sleeveless tube dress. The café's proprietor, Hendrik, a thin man in his late fifties with a shock of wild grey hair atop a long, deeply lined face, held up a welcoming hand, then went back to dressing pizzas ready for the oven.

Greetings over, it was down to business.

Claasen created computer games and gathered this group of nerds to test the games. The challenge was not only to master the game and score the most points but also to work out how to manipulate the game. The ultimate aim was to break the game. When that happened, the play was over and the debrief began. Sometimes these sessions extended into the small hours of the morning. If the game was not broken by the time Hendrik's wife arrived to prepare the café for opening to daylight customers, Claasen was declared 'the winner'.

Lost in the world of the game, Saskia hardly noticed the servings of pizza and coffee meted out by Hendrik as the hours swept by, punctuated by rapid clicks of fingers on keyboards and occasional exasperated or exhilarated utterances.

Two hours after midnight, a triumphant shout heralded that the game had been broken. Everyone crowded around the winner for the debrief, and Claasen made notes to help them improve the game.

Finally, it was time to relax and chat over beer and nuts. Saskia was wired up, adrenalin from the chase still surging through her system.

"Hey, Saskia, did you have any luck with hash CaseIt Ten?" Claasen asked.

"Yes. I did! Thanks."

"A trojan, eh?" Petrie said.

It barely surprised Saskia that someone in the group would have followed through on her urgent call and done their own search on the problem at FSB. Most members of this group were highly skilled computer hackers. They poked around in the nooks and crannies of the internet, sometimes out of curiosity and sometimes to find vulnerabilities. The group's rules were not to exploit weaknesses but to monitor them and, maybe, warn the individual or organisation about a potential threat. Many sold their services as white-hat hackers. Others had stable jobs – though not all in IT.

Do we know anything about hash CaseIt Ten?" Saskia asked.

But no one knew who #CaseIt10 might be – he, she or they knew how to hide their identity. "Formidable work!" was the general agreement. "Works fast – can work in the dark net, too."

"I'll tell you something for nothing, though, Saskia," Petrie said, his surprisingly effeminate voice crammed by the jowls folding around his neck, and somewhat indistinct as his mouth worked its way around a slice of cold pizza, "your bank's popular for funnelling money from Europe to abroad."

"Its systems are set up to do that," Saskia said. "What's the problem?"

Petrie smirked. "There are rules about what sort of money's allowed to go through. You sure the bank's not laundering money?" He waved around a partially eaten triangle of pizza and pitched his voice into something resembling spookiness. "Woooh ooooh, it's called money laundering."

"I hope not. The bank has steps in place to act on AML and CFT."

This answer caused others to smirk. Someone said, "What's with the acronyms?"

"Idiot!" Petrie sniffed. "They mean anti money laundering and countering the financing of terrorism."

Laughter. "Good luck with that." Claasen looked up from her note-making. "The whole AML CFT shit has holes big enough to fund ISIS without blinking."

"Hey! Leave the girl alone," Hans defended. "Saskia's only just started at the bank."

"Yeah!" Saskia said, but added, "All information about problems gratefully accepted, though."

Close to four in the morning, Saskia fell asleep in Hans's arms. Nicolaas woke her a few hours later to remind her she was due at the university soon to give her guest lecture.

# 4

## CHIDED

"Why weren't you at work on Monday?" Antoine Aubert demanded, leaning forward on sharp elbows over the vast oak desk in his office.

Saskia blinked, surprised by the censorious tone. "Er – I took the day off."

"You think you can just take any day off whenever you like? You're not at some cruisy university anymore. This is a business, and you are expected –" M. Aubert jabbed a finger at Saskia, the action causing a strand of hair on his head to dislodge from it oiled companions. "You are expected to earn your wage."

"Monsieur, I applied for leave and –"

M. Aubert leaned further over his desk, his lips rolling inward into a line. "Let me make it quite clear. In a crisis, staff are expected to contribute. You!" He jabbed his finger at Saskia again. "Caused the problem, and you," another finger jab, "chose to be absent. No doubt you hoped to avoid responsibility."

Saskia's jaw slackened a little. "R-responsibility?"

"Where were you on Monday?"

"I – I was in Rotterdam."

"In case it escaped your notice, Monday is a working day!"

"I – I was giving a guest lecture to students about – well – about my university research."

The FSB Lyon branch manager gave a derisive huff; his dark eyes seemed to glow. "University research! I had it right. Your brain is still there in that rarified world. I had grave misgivings about hiring you. Small frame. Small brain. Did it not occur to you ... no, let me rephrase that." He held one manicured index finger upright. "You are so stupid that you did not consider the repercussions of a total power shutdown to the building! You had no right!" M. Aubert slammed the flat palm of his hand on the desktop. "You had no right to demand such a shutdown!"

Saskia stared at the angry man, her own face heating with a mixture of confusion and anger.

"Well! What have you to say for yourself?"

Saskia looked up at Ferdinand Fourvier from IT, standing to her left. Clint Bailey was on her right. All three stood before Antoine Aubert's desk like naughty children in the headmaster's office. Ferdinand's gaze flickered towards her, then settled to studying the floor. Clearly, he was not going to speak up in her defence.

"Er – Monsieur, my aim was to stop a possible –"

"Possible!" yelled M. Aubert. He snatched up a page on his desk and waved it at her. "By your own misguided, utterly unnecessary investigation, there was no danger from what this idiot – " this time, the finger jab went in Clint Bailey's direction – "did!"

"You!" M. Aubert continued, addressing Clint, "precipitated this. You –" another jab, "should have called the right people. Namely, him!" He thrust the page in Ferdinand's direction.

"Mister Aubert," Clint said in English. "I don't understand French. I'm sorry. I don't know what you're saying or what's going on."

M. Aubert slumped back into his seat and heaved a great sigh. "You are an idiot," he said in heavily accented English. "By calling this – this –" he waved the page at Saskia, "you have lost this bank reputation."

"I apologise, Mister Aubert. I just knew I had to act quickly and that was – Dr van Essen's phone number was all I had straight away. I knew she understood English, and I was under the impression she did —"

Antoine Aubert lunged over his desk again, his glare falling full on Clint. "I fail to understand why they send someone like you to this bank. I will report your misjudgements. Get out of here, all three of you!"

No-one moved. Saskia and Clint continued to stare at the bank manager in disbelief; Ferdinand supplemented his floor-study with a troubled frown.

"Out!" M. Aubert shouted. "And do your jobs!" He thrust the page at Saskia. "Take this and pay for it yourself – or not. I don't care. It might teach you to consider the consequences of your actions next time and not presume you have authority to make decisions that impact this bank. And shut the door on your way out."

Ferdinand closed the door behind the three of them and let out a slow breath. "That wasn't pleasant," he said quietly.

"You said nothing!" Saskia blurted.

Ferdinand lifted his shoulders, his gaze avoiding hers. "What could I say? He is angry. I did not want to make our situation worse."

"Our – what?"

Again, a shrug. "Saskia, I am sorry it has landed on you, but the situation is out of my hands."

"Out of your –" Saskia stopped echoing his words and forced her jaw to set. Exploding at Ferdinand was not going to help.

"Don't worry. This will blow over," he said. Saskia ground her teeth.

Clint cleared his throat. "I'm sorry. I seem to have got you in a deal of trouble, Doctor van Essen. But I don't understand all the reasons why he was angry."

"Monsieur Aubert's major concern is that the power shutdown interrupted scheduled financial transfers, and some backups scrambled," Ferdinand said.

"But isn't that what would happen if there was a power outage?" Clint asked. "Don't you have a system in place to ensure backup integrity?"

"The system is not perfect. We are working on it."

"But you told me on the night that Dr van Essen did the right thing."

Ferdinand raised his eyes to the ceiling, the corners of his mouth down. "I suppose the fact is that you should have called IT first before calling Saskia, Mr Bailey. It would have been the right thing to do."

Saskia walked away. *Coward!* she fumed. *I didn't do anything wrong! I didn't do anything wrong!* She shut herself into her office, dropped the #CaseIt10 invoice on a corner of her desk and plonked into her office chair. Her shoulders barely cleared the top of her desk. Resentfully, she jammed her hand on to the lever to raise her to a reasonable height. "Naine!" she hissed, then jerked in shock at her self-admonishment. She had long ago ceased resenting her short stature, turning insults such as those flung at her by Antoine Aubert into insight into the character of the perpetrator rather than accepting the affront.

"He really did get under your skin!" she muttered. She glared at the top of her desk with its litter of books, papers and computer monitors. She'd been studying the European Union anti-money laundering regulations regarding beneficial trusts when she was summoned to M. Aubert's office. Researching complex legislation and rummaging in the codes of computers was what she was good at, not dealing with irate people!

*Maybe I should have shouted back at Monsieur Antoine Aubert! Maybe I should have told him that malware is a real danger to the bank and the repercussions would have been more than just a power outage. Why didn't I? Why didn't I?*

She buried her face in her hands. *Because you don't. Because you've never known how to react when someone shouts at you. It's why you're a backroom girl.*

A soft knock on the door interrupted her self-recriminations.

"Entrez," she said, working her voice past the tight lump in her throat.

Clint Bailey let himself in. "I'm sorry," he said. "I seem to have really landed you in the soup."

Saskia shrugged nonchalantly – or, at least, she hoped it appeared nonchalant. "I was surprised by Monsieur Aubert's reaction. I don't think you should blame yourself. Perhaps I should have reacted differently."

Clint shook his head, hair flopping over his forehead, eyes behind his glasses becoming intense under a frown. "But on the night, Ferdinand told me your actions saved the bank. Why didn't he say this to Mr Aubert?"

"I don't know what to think, Mr Bailey."

"Clint, please."

"I don't know what to think, Clint. As Ferdinand said, that was a most unpleasant interview."

"May I ask what this is for?" Clint indicated the #CaseIt10 invoice on the desk.

"I engaged a party to investigate the nature of the trojan you downloaded. It's their invoice."

Clint was silent for a while. "He wants you to pay it?"

Saskia nodded.

He picked up the page. "Mr Aubert may tell HQ about my actions, but I will also relate my side of the story. In the meantime, I will take this off your hands."

Saskia shook her head. "Clint, this is a favour I called in and I need to ensure I fulfil the commitment to pay."

Clint took a phone out of his pocket. He tapped at it, glancing from time to time at the invoice. "It's paid," he said. He took a pen from the top pocket of his shirt and wrote the payment details on the invoice. "It's the least I can do. I am due to fly back to New York tomorrow. I will report this incident there."

# 5

## SCAM REVIEW

After Clint left, Saskia swung in her chair, glowering at the mess of papers and books, mentally telling M. Aubert all the ways the bank could have suffered if the malware had succeeded. "What you should have done," she grumbled, "is told Ferdinand to take the information provided by hash CaseIt Ten and report it to the National Cyber Security Agency." She poked her tongue out at the door Clint had closed behind him and added, "Better still! Why don't you report it and make yourself out as a hero!" Remembering what her family in Delft and friends in Rotterdam had said about scams linked to the FSB, she grumbled further about the need for the bank to take all security seriously, including that of its customers.

Saskia paused in her tirade, her thoughts turning to the issue of scams. She logged into FSB's staff site and searched for procedures regarding scam reports.

She could find none that were specific to customer reports of scams. *Hmmm.* She wondered whom to ask for more information on the issue. There were several possibilities. Perhaps her supervisor could point her in the right direction and shortcut the search.

Madame Le Fèvre looked up from her desktop computer when Saskia knocked lightly on the open office door. She was a classically beautiful woman. Red lipstick enhanced her shapely lips, a touch of eyeliner defined her hazel eyes and mascara extended and darkened lashes. As usual, she wore a meticulously tailored suit, matched with stiletto heels. Next to her immediate superior, Saskia felt like a small frump, even though Mme Le Fèvre always treated her with the utmost respect and friendliness. She had, after all, wooed Saskia into her department.

"Come to my bank and help us internalise the organisational ethics and responsibility you have just lectured us about," Mme Le Fèvre had said after listening to a conference talk Saskia delivered in London on risk management in financial institutions.

It was a position more suited to Saskia's skills than the one she had held at the Maximilian University at Munich. She now spent her days in her office in the FSB building studying the bank's organisational systems and procedures. She loved her work. It gave her the opportunity to put into practice the ideas she'd worked with in her doctoral thesis at Erasmus University Rotterdam and furthered in her post-doctorate and teaching post in Munich. As a bonus, despite her decision to move into the corporate world, her academic colleagues continued to invite her to co-author articles and give talks at conferences and to students. Sometimes she felt as if she had two jobs: one performed in her office at the bank, and the other at the small dining table in her one-bedroom apartment.

"Entrez, Saskia. What can I do for you?"

"Good morning. I was wondering if you could tell me what the procedure is for dealing with people who notify the bank of scams? Or perhaps where I can look it up, because I can't find it online."

Mme Le Fèvre leaned against the back of her chair. "What do you mean by procedure?"

"Umm – scams strategy."

"Meaning?"

"Umm – what the bank's objectives are in relation to dealing with scams, and the procedures to achieve those objectives."

Mme Le Fèvre was quiet for some time. She pursed her lips. "This came up in a management meeting last year. You need to talk to

Phillip Quayle. Would you like me to ask him if you can meet with him?"

Ten minutes later, Saskia was sitting in Phillip Quayle's office in the bank's marketing department. He was in his late fifties, Saskia guessed, with thinning white hair that tufted about his ears, and a rotund stomach that the buttons of his shirt strained to contain.

"Scam notifications?" he quizzed, pushing dark-rimmed round glasses further up his nose, bushy eyebrows drawing together. "Why are you interested?"

"I'm generally looking for procedures – er – to do with customers and risk to the bank and customers."

"What are you going to do with the information?"

Taken aback by M. Quayle's apparent defensiveness, Saskia hesitated. "I don't know. At this point I'm just puzzled that I haven't been able to find procedures for dealing with customer scam notifications."

"They are recorded."

Saskia waited for elaboration while M. Quayle stared at her, perhaps waiting for her to slip off the uncomfortable chair and leave his office. She didn't. She was starting to wonder if he was a special friend of M. Aubert when he heaved a sigh.

"Mademoiselle. The increasing prevalence of scams and the funnelling of scam monies through banks – not only FSB – are a community concern. My section has implemented various modules to warn customers about the possibility of scams."

"What happens if someone contacts customer services and says that they might be a victim of a scam involving a transaction through this bank?"

"Of course, that depends how quickly the customer notifies the bank. It might be possible to put a stop to the transaction."

"How quickly does the customer have to do this?"

M. Quayle shrugged his broad shoulders. "As you know, funds move fast nowadays. But if the customer contacts the bank immediately, it may be possible."

"I assume by phone?"

"That would be the quickest way."

Saskia considered. Her experience with contacting any bank by phone involved being placed on hold for a long time, answering questions posed by a machine, and then possibly speaking to someone in a call centre. She was about to ask Monsieur Quayle what the average wait time for a response was, but changed tack. "What happens when a customer notifies the bank of a suspected scam transaction?"

"The customer is transferred to our IT security section, who would attempt to put a stop to the transaction if that's deemed appropriate."

"So, the customer service staff answering the call can't do it immediately?"

"No. They have limited access to customer accounts."

*So, another delay.*

*What are the average wait times, procedures for staff training in these matters and protection of customers? Hmmm, perhaps I should discuss this with Madame Le Fèvre.*

Saskia decided not to put Phillip Quayle further offside. She slipped to her feet. "Thank you for your help, Monsieur."

She was at the door when he said, "Mademoiselle, I submitted a document to senior management last year asking for more resources to deal with scam notifications. You may like to review that document."

# 6
## QUESTIONS

Saskia made it a point not to dwell on slights and injustices aimed at her. Throughout her life, her small stature, Asian appearance and intelligence often made her a target for bullies and overly protective people alike. Her mother had been the major influence in teaching her to ignore insults and concentrate on the task at hand. Mostly, she succeeded, but her encounter with M. Aubert, coupled with Ferdinand Fourvier's silence and Phillip Quayle's prickliness, rankled her. On Friday evening, a mountain biking friend invited her to join them on a ride the next day, but she declined, wanting time to work out her irritability alone. She rose early, dressed in her biking gear and set off on a long ride to Parc de la Tête d'Or, Lyon's zoo and botanic gardens, and thence along the Rhône River to Miribel-Jonage Park, touted as one of Europe's largest peri-urban nature parks.

Saskia had fallen in love with Lyon within hours of leaving Gare Part-Dieu, the busy central railway hub. The city exhibited layers of history, from early Roman times through the upheavals of the Middle Ages to modern times. Each layer intrigued her, giving her much to explore and discover. But the city's history, culture and architecture were secondary interests. Once she had settled into her apartment, she'd sought out the mountain biking community, partly to connect with like-minded people and partly to ensure she did not drown herself in her passion for studying patterns and tinkering with computer code. Over the months of her time in Lyon, her recreational home became the Lyon Bike Centre, where bikers gathered to enjoy each other's company and the excellent outdoor and indoor freestyle parks. She often joined her newfound friends on rides through the nearby mountains or the city's surrounding villages and agricultural lands, but not this day, or so was her intent.

The route she decided upon was one of her favourites. It had her climbing some 652 metres, enabling her to enjoy forests, lakeside, multiple birdsongs and glimpses of wildlife. However, this trail was also a favourite of others, and she was only an hour into her ride when she met a cheerful group of friends. Despite her initial intent, she let them persuade her to join them for a meal and drink at the Lyon Bike Centre Park. She was not long in the café when two children approached and begged her to teach them bike tricks. Laughingly, she promised them an hour of her time after she'd rested a little.

Danny Prendergast, the centre's co-owner, called out to her from the bar where he was serving drinks, "Job offer's still open!"

She grinned and waved him off. Almost every time she came, she ended up unofficially coaching children and he'd offer her a job. "You're good with the children, and you're good with the tricks," he enthused.

As she rode home after teaching several enthusiastic youngsters how to manipulate their bodies, BMX bikes and scooters into daring leaps and twists, she wondered whether she might be better off accepting Danny's job offer. It would mean she could stay in Lyon and do the occasional freelance computer hack, as so many of her geeky friends did, and continue her research associations with academia.

When she pushed open the garden gate into the grounds of the grand home containing her apartment, Madame Claire's large, hairy, black German shepherd Rufus shoved his nose into her waist, demanding a pat. "Let me get in the gate first, you brute," she grunted, pushing past him. The spring-hinged gate slammed shut behind her.

"You have thunder on your brow."

Saskia, one hand steadying her bike, the other giving Rufus the attention he demanded, turned at the sound of Mme Claire's voice.

The elderly woman sat on her heels at the edge of a garden bed, freshly dug earth among colourful sprays of flowers displaying her labours. Saskia appreciated the carefully tended garden of the home. She could see it when seated at the dining table in her apartment, often noting her petite landlady, always accompanied by Rufus, sitting reading at the table in the shade of the one large tree in a corner of the yard, or digging, planting, weeding or pruning.

Mme Claire tipped her head slightly to one side, resting the small trowel she held in a gloved hand on her thigh. "Did something happen on your bike ride?"

Saskia shook her head. "No, I had a good ride."

"And the thunder?"

"Office stuff," she said. "I thought I might ride it out, but it's staying stubbornly stuck in my brain."

Mme Claire scrunched up her nose sympathetically. She stood up. "That is unfortunate." Brushing dirt off her skirt, she said, "Well, I can do nothing about office stuff, but would you like to join me for a cup of tea?" She pointed to the garden table. "I have a thermos."

"Thank you. Let me just put away my bike." Saskia shoved against Rufus, who seemed determined to extract as much fondling as possible. "Let me pass, you great beast," she grumbled affectionately.

The garden shed door was open. Its availability was one of the reasons Saskia had chosen the apartment, other reasons being Mme Claire's unfussy friendliness, the pleasant neighbourhood lined with grand houses, and proximity to parks. The three-storey home had been in Mme Claire's family for generations, and she had modified the second floor into two apartments. Saskia had the apartment overlooking the garden; Mme Claire's nephew had the apartment on the opposite side of the hallway. Saskia had not met the nephew. He had been abroad for a year and would likely remain away for a while longer. The third floor of the home was set aside to accommodate Mme Claire's children and grandchildren when they visited.

Mme Claire had moved all her garden tools and machines to one side of the garden shed to make room for Saskia's bikes: a touring bike, a mountain bike, a BMX, a travel folding bike and a road bike.

Rufus stood at the door of the shed as if checking to ensure Saskia packed away the bikes in their correct order, then walked so close to her in his insistence to gain yet more attention that he all but tripped her up as she made her way back to the garden table.

"Your dog is a pest," Saskia said as she hitched herself up on to a chair and roughed the dog's thick neck fur. Rufus grinned, his tail sweeping lazily through the air. Saskia laughed. "And he has a stupid grin."

"You are right on both counts," Mme Claire smiled. She poured tea into the thermos lid. "I hope you don't mind drinking out of the lid. I only brought out one cup, but I can go in and fetch another."

"Of course, I don't mind. I've drunk out of much less wholesome vessels in my time. Do you always bring tea out to the garden?"

Mme Claire chuckled; her intelligent, bright blue eyes sparkling. "I used to live in Scotland and the weather there somehow drove me to always prepare a thermos upon venturing outdoors."

"I didn't know you'd lived in Scotland."

"Oh, yes. That's where I learned to speak English."

"I also didn't know that you speak English." *In fact, thought Saskia, in the time I've lived here, I've not had many conversations with you... Though I know I like you.*

"I do. Such an easy language to learn. No silliness with gendered words and difficult declensions. How many languages do you speak?"

"Dutch, German, English and French," Saskia said. "And a working knowledge of Spanish. My family owns a café in Delft and we had a lot of tourists visiting. So, I started early hearing different languages and then I went to an international school."

"Clever. And you are also physically clever, I think." Mme Claire indicated the garden shed with a lift of her chin. "I see that you took your mountain bike today. Did you ride with friends?"

"Half-half. I started off solo but met friends along the way."

"Did you intend to go solo all the way?"

"Mmm. I thought it best to grind out my chagrin solo."

*THE BANK*

"And did you succeed – I mean to grind out your chagrin?"

"Not really." Saskia shrugged. Though she liked Mme Claire, she didn't think discussing personal problems with her would be appropriate. "I'm sure I'll get over being grumpy. But I'm really interested in learning that you lived in Scotland. It's a place I'd like to visit."

"Worth a visit." Mme Claire used her small, blue-veined hands with their knobby arthritic joints as a cradle to lift the mug of tea to her thin lips.

"And may I ask, why did you – er – live in Scotland?"

"My husband was a Scot. He came from Edinburgh, and that's where we lived till he died. One of my children still lives in Edinburgh."

"Oh." Saskia was even less sure whether it was appropriate to venture into Mme Claire's personal details than it was to talk about her own office woes.

Mme Claire, however, seemed relaxed about continuing. "When Albert – that was my husband's name – died, I decided to return here to help my aging parents. They were beginning to need help. My sister and her husband had died in a traffic accident and left my nephew in their care. My eldest son wanted to stay in Scotland and was old enough to look after himself. The other two children returned to Lyon with me, though they did not stay here long. One lives in London, the other in Geneva, and my nephew travels the world as a diplomat." Mme Claire sipped more tea, blue eyes taking in the garden before coming to rest again on Saskia. "I find it interesting in these modern times how so many people are fluid in moving from one place to another. In my parents' time, very few people did so. I was branded a rebel for moving to Scotland. And you? I think you have done much moving around. Do you think you will move again?"

"I don't know," Saskia said. "I like Lyon – probably more than any other place I've lived in so far."

"Will you tell me what has unsettled you?"

Saskia shrugged. *Why not?* It would be good to share her thoughts with someone, especially someone likely to be neutral. She thought to simply sketch an outline of being on the wrong end of office politics, but the interested blue eyes teased out the whole story, from being woken up to deal with a malware crisis to her unhappy encounter with Antoine Aubert and the unsatisfactory interaction with Phillip Quayle. "I'm a small person, not a stupid person," Saskia finished irritably. "Last week, my friend said he hoped the bureaucracy at the bank would not get me down. I thought I'd learnt all about bureaucracies at the university. But maybe he's right to caution me."

Mme Claire studied Saskia quietly for some breaths, then asked, "Does being small upset you?"

"Being small?" Saskia shook her head. "No. It doesn't. But sometimes it's a battle to get people to take me seriously because I don't top their armpits." Saskia wrinkled her nose, disappointed at the bitterness in her voice.

"Then don't start your sentence with 'I am a small person'. Just say, 'I am not a stupid person'." Mme Claire rose, gathering up the emptied mug, lid and thermos. The evening had settled darkness on the garden, though the air was still pleasantly warm. "I think it would be good for you to vent a little more to a friend. Some emotions are better shared than stewed."

Saskia slid off her chair. "Er – thank you. I didn't mean to sound off at you."

"I enjoyed spending a little time with you," Mme Claire said. "We haven't spoken very much in the months you have been here. Come, Rufus, it's time for us to settle for the evening."

After a shower and a meal, Saskia sat on her bed and called Hans. "I want to vent," she told him as soon as she determined he had time to speak with her. "I got into a lot of trouble for taking control of that incursion last weekend."

"Wait. I'll put you on speaker. Father is here, and he'll want to hear," Hans said.

Saskia repeated her tale of woe regarding M. Aubert.

Hans scoffed when she'd finished. "Why do you think he reacted like that? Do you think he might be trying to hide something?"

"Hide?" Saskia's eyes blinked rapidly as she considered his ques-

*THE BANK*

tion. "Why do you think he'd have anything to hide? I think he just didn't understand what might've happened."

"Hmmf. Maybe." Hans sounded unconvinced. "Do you know anything about him?"

"N–no. I mean he's the bank's senior manager. I mean, what's there to know? I mean, why is it important?"

"It just seems strange to me that he reacted the way he did. What do you think, Papa?"

"Whoa!" Nicolaas's voice held a note of amusement. "That sort of suspicion is way beyond my pay grade! I'm with Saskia. Let it go, Saskia. If anything, I think that this Ferdinand person is the real deplorable. Go ask him why he didn't back you up."

"I don't think so," Saskia sighed. "I think I'll just get on with my job and forget this ever happened."

"On to more pleasant things," Hans said. "Melanie and I are planning a road trip in three weeks. Shall we come to visit you?"

"Of course! That would be lovely. And I would love to meet Melanie. Tell me about her."

"Well. She's about one point six metres tall. She has straight blonde hair, which she mostly holds off her face with a clip. She has freckles, hazel eyes and plucks her eyebrows. She's unhappy about her weight because she thinks she's too fat. I, of course, tell her I like the softness. She doesn't like wearing trousers… "

"Stop! Stop!" Saskia laughed. "I mean about her. Not what she looks like."

"Oh, about her. She works as a checkout person at the local supermarket. She has no interest whatsoever in computers or bikes – unlike a previous girlfriend I had. She used to live in Amsterdam and moved to Rotterdam about a year ago for a change of scene. She hasn't got family here and is only just starting to make friends. She likes to come with me to our café, but ignores us when we start talking IT. She orders coffee and starts reading a book. She likes art galleries, museums and the theatre, and I'm finding I like those things too. She's thinking of enrolling in an arts course."

"She'll love Lyon, then. There's so much cultural stuff here."

"My dear! Please don't call it stuff in her presence!"

Saskia giggled. "That terrible former girlfriend you had is just so ignorant about the finer things in life."

"Just as well she had other attributes."

They bantered some more, then said their farewells, Saskia feeling much less thunderous. She slipped under the doona on her bed, but stayed sitting up, frowning as she considered what Hans had said about Antoine Aubert. Knowing sleep would elude her until she'd done something to slake her curiosity, she reached for the laptop and settled it over her crossed legs.

First, she searched for Antoine Aubert's social media accounts. He seemed only to use LinkedIn. Using a pseudonym to hide her own identity, she trawled through his infrequent use of the account and whom he linked with.

Nothing out of the ordinary presented itself in that investigation.

Next, and with only a little struggle with her conscience, Saskia hacked into M. Aubert's email account – tut-tutting that it was relatively easy to hack – and found he used two accounts. One was his work account, which seemed to contain nothing more than what a person in his position would be dealing with. She paused her scan of the emails to read the lengthy one about the recent malware incursion, the corners of her mouth turning down the more she read. He had downplayed the incursion's significance and implied her actions had been an exercise in grandstanding. She was particularly disappointed that Ferdinand Fourvier had apparently corroborated M. Aubert's assumption that the bank's IT system was sufficiently robust to detect the virus before it caused harm.

Saskia clicked out of the email with a huff of disgust and continued to peruse messages but found nothing more of interest – or at least nothing unexpected.

The second email account caused her eyebrows to rise with intrigue. All messages were encrypted. She investigated the recipients' addresses. They were all one-time accounts.

"Well, so what!" she muttered. "I know others who do that. But it does seem strange."

*THE BANK*

She then trawled through the bank's archives and personnel files and managed to piece together a profile for Antoine Aubert: aged 45; French father and New Caledonian mother, born in Morocco. He studied for his MBA at EM Lyon Business School, joined the administration in the Moroccan army for some years, and then joined a bank in Morocco. He joined FSB three years ago to establish the Lyon branch; had led the branch to post credible profits despite stiff competition from other banks; was well regarded by his superiors; owned a home at a good address in Lyon; had a wife who was a medical practitioner and two children who attended a Montessori school in the city.

"Doesn't say arsehole anywhere," she murmured.

Saskia closed her computer. "Drop it, Saskia. Get over it. Forget it happened. Maybe he really believes you blew up the whole business."

As she settled for the night, however, she found herself wondering about the seemingly opaque nature of FSB's dealing with scams. Perhaps, as her Rotterdam friends had noted, this muddiness also applied to its measures regarding anti money laundering and countering the financing of terrorism?

# 7
## AT THE MARKET

Saskia liked to visit the St Antoine Market at least once on a weekend and shop for her week's groceries. It was a lively place, especially on weekends. Situated on the banks of the Saône River between Pont Bonapart and Pont Maréchal Juin, the market had been there for more than a hundred years, which only added to its charm. She wheeled her bike between the stalls and their busy and cheerful stallholders, stopping at her favourite ones to make purchases, the basket on her bike filling up with small parcels of foodstuffs. She was settling a baguette in the basket when an outraged shriek caused her to look up. A large woman was shoving people roughly aside, her glare directed at Saskia.

Before Saskia had time to react, the woman's broad hand slapped hard against her cheek, sending Saskia sprawling to the ground and her bike crashing on its side, basket contents spraying out.

"Murderer! Meuritière! Qatil!" the woman howled, throwing herself on to Saskia, fists pummelling her face.

Then the woman's weight was gone, leaving Saskia winded and staring uncomprehendingly up at the bulky, green-clad figure screaming and struggling against three men grappling to keep her from hurling herself down again.

"Tu vas bien?"

Saskia's eyes flickered. A woman with a kindly face, her grey hair held back by a checkered scarf, was kneeling next to her, fingers reaching toward Saskia's cheek. She became aware of pain blossoming in her head.

A piercing cry distracted both the kindly face and Saskia. It distracted the demented woman too, because she stopped screaming and struggling against the men and stood still, though shivering violently, tears flooding from dark eyes that continued to stare venomously at Saskia.

A thin young girl wearing a hijab, skinny jeans and a tee shirt appeared, her black, horror-filled eyes looking up at Saskia's attacker. A little boy threw his arms around the woman's legs and buried his face into the fabric of her embroidered green kaftan.

"Are you alright?" This time, a man's voice asked the question.

"W – wha – ?" Saskia hauled breath past her compressed diaphragm. An arm slipped behind her back and eased her up. Saskia put a hand to her stinging lips. She tasted blood, but her attention stayed rivetted on the woman.

Both the boy and girl now had their heads buried in her kaftan. The men had released her, and she was sobbing loudly into the hollow of another robed woman's shoulder. Both were wearing hijabs. The second woman cradled the first, but glared accusingly at Saskia.

Saskia had only understood the first two words the woman had screamed: "Murderer!" But it made no sense.

The man kneeling next to her asked her again if she was alright.

"I – I think so," she managed.

"Perhaps you would like this?" Saskia accepted the tissue offered to her by the woman with the scarf. She pressed it carefully against her lip.

"Here is a chair for you. Perhaps you would care to sit." With gentle pressure on her upper arm, the man levered her on to a chair.

A large group had now gathered around. Several people were picking up her scattered groceries and replacing them in the basket of her righted bike.

"I – I'm not sure what happened," she said weakly, closing her eyes as her surroundings swayed.

The man kept hold of her arm. "Steady," he said. "Put your head between your legs for a minute."

She did as he bid till the dizziness passed. She sat upright. "Here, sip a little water." The kindly woman held a bottle of water to her lips. Saskia made a greater effort to gather her wits as she sipped from the bottle, confused gaze once more fixed on the two robed women. The one who had assaulted her was still shaking with sobs but was now down on her knees and hugging the children. Her friend was rocking a pram, the sound of a mewling infant coming from within. Noting Saskia's attention, her assailant flung another round of hysterical words at her.

The man at Saskia's side said, "She says you murdered her husband, and Allah will punish you for what you have done."

"I – I murdered her husband?" Saskia stared wide-eyed at him.

"That is what she said." The man's voice and brown eyes were gentle. He studied her. "Is she mistaken?"

"Wh – what? I – I haven't murdered any – anyone! Why would she say that? Who is she?" Her surroundings swayed again. She closed her eyes. She heard the man and her assailant exchange words in the throaty sounds of a Semitic language. His tone was reasonable; hers continued to border on hysteria.

Saskia forced her eyes to open.

"She says you may not have pulled the trigger, but you were the cause of his death –and more its cause than the bullet that killed him."

Saskia shook her head slowly. "I have no idea what she's talking about."

"Shall we call the police?" the woman who held the water bottle asked.

"Non!" The exclamation drew everyone's attention back to the robed women. The assailant's friend spoke rapidly, tugging at her friend's arm and manoeuvring the pram around.

"Pardon! It mistake!" The friend's broken French was difficult to understand, but her panic was unmistakable. "She sad. No police help. Is mistake! Is mistake!"

"Shall we detain them?" asked the man, his head tipping to one side as he watched the two women struggling to push their way through the crowd.

"Umm – I have no idea what's going on," Saskia said. "I didn't m– murder anyone, and I don't want to cause trouble."

"It would appear they are causing you trouble. Are you sure you do not want to involve the police?"

Saskia drew in a deep breath, shaking her head. "Yes. It – umm – I think I'll just go home."

"Are you sure?"

The crowd hemmed the women in. The women turned frantic faces to Saskia, talking over one another in their apologies and pleas. The children wailed. "It mistake! Pardon. Pardon. No hurt! No want hurt!" The assailant's companion tore open the bag slung over her shoulder, and dug inside as she stumbled out her words. "Money fix hurt! Not you murder. Mistake. Pardon. Pardon." She drew out a wallet.

"Please let them go," Saskia said. "I don't want money."

"I will ask them why they thought you murdered her husband." The man left her side and approached the distressed women. There was much headshaking and weeping. Finally, he nodded and asked the crowd to let the women through. With fearful glances back at Saskia, the women and children hurried away.

"They say they mistook you for another small person whom they were told was responsible for the husband's death," the man said to Saskia. He leant over, hands on his knees so that his face was opposite hers. "They don't know the details of his death. They were just told a small person was responsible for causing the death. They now don't think it was you. They wanted to pay for your injuries. I told them you didn't want that." He straightened and looked to where the women were practically running across the street, their long robes swishing around their legs. "It is not too late for me to detain them. Or at least to get their names in case you want to press charges."

"No." Various parts of Saskia's face had morphed from acute pain to throbbing ache. Her lip was still bleeding. "It must be a mistake. They're so upset. Thank you for your help." She bunched the bloody tissues into a pocket of her trousers, and slipped forward off the chair to set her feet on the ground. "Thank you – thank you all for your help. I'll just go home."

"May I help you to your home?" the man said.

"I have a van that will accommodate your bike," the woman offered, passing Saskia a fresh tissue.

"Thank you. Thank you. I'm alright. It was – er – a – a shock. I'm alright. I'm not far from home."

There were a few more offers of help, which Saskia politely refused. She took hold of the handlebars of her bike. Onlookers parted to make way for her. She pushed her bike out of the marketplace, into Rue Grenette, over Pont Lafayette, then through back streets to her home.

# 8

## LAW ENFORCEMENT

Two days later, when Saskia entered the back gate of her lodgings, a woman in a tight black skirt and white shirt, and a man wearing the blue uniform of a police officer, rose from their seats at the garden table. Alongside them, Mme Claire stayed seated, her hand restraining Rufus by the collar. Three mugs sat on the tabletop, indicating the three had been in each other's company for some time.

Saskia grimaced and immediately regretted doing so. Her battered face still did not appreciate movement.

She had barely made it home after the beating at the market, her bravado dissolving within minutes of pushing against the bike pedals to propel her forward. One eye had almost closed shut by the time she reached the garden gate, and blood kept dribbling from her cut lip no matter how often she dabbed at it with a tissue. Thankfully, neither Rufus nor Mme Claire had been in the garden to witness her homecoming. She'd left the bike and its basket of groceries propped against the garden shed wall, hauled herself up the flight of stairs to her apartment and confronted the wreckage of her face in the bathroom mirror.

A shower and painkillers had dulled the physical aches but done nothing to dull her bewilderment. Why had the woman seemed so certain she had killed – murdered – her husband? Who might her husband have been?

After a night of fitful sleep, she'd spent the better part of Sunday in front of her laptop looking for news on murders in Lyon, wondering how anyone could link her to any.

Her face still a painful mess; she'd debated whether to call in sick, but M. Aubert's rebuke about the leave she'd taken a few weeks before still gnawed at her, so she set sunglasses over her eyes, skipped her usual stop for a breakfast croissant at her favourite bakery and spent most of the day hidden in her office.

"Our pardon, Dr van Essen. We have some questions for you," the black-skirted woman said.

"Does this have something to do with what happened at the market the other day?"

Mme Claire's eyebrows rose at her words. Saskia could almost feel Mme Claire's eyes inspecting Saskia's swollen lips and the bruise on her cheek.

Saskia pushed her sunglasses more firmly up her nose, hoping at least to hide the sore eye from examination.

"Yes and no," replied the woman. She introduced herself as Louise Granger, juge d'instruction (investigating magistrate), and the uniformed officer introduced himself as Gabriel Clément.

Mme Claire rose. "Come, Rufus," she said. "We will leave these people in peace. Though, perhaps I could bring you a cup of tea or coffee, Saskia?"

"Thank you, no," Saskia said. "Do you mind if I put my bike away?" she asked the law enforcement officers.

"Please," the magistrate agreed.

Bike parked, Saskia returned to sit on the chair Mme Claire had vacated, dropping her backpack to the ground beside her. "I still have no idea what all of that was about," Saskia said.

"It would appear that you sustained quite a beating," the magistrate said.

Saskia shrugged. "Superficial, but looks a bit awful."

"Can you tell us what happened?"

"Umm – I was doing some shopping at the St Antoine Market when – well, umm – this woman started yelling at me. She knocked me over and hit me. I couldn't understand what she was saying. She spoke – perhaps it was Arabic. I don't know. Some people pulled her away, and a man told me she was accusing me of murdering her husband. When someone suggested the police should be called, the woman's friend said it was a mistake and apologised."

"So, you think they did not want to involve the police? Or do you think this friend believed it was a mistake?" the magistrate asked.

Saskia shrugged. "I admit I wasn't thinking very straight, and I still can't work out why I was accused of murder or why someone should even mistake me for someone else. I was – umm – I guess I was embarrassed to be the centre of – er – attention."

Gabriel Clément, who had pulled a notebook out of his breast pocket and opened it, paused. "You do not like to be the centre of attention?"

It was on the tip of her tongue to say, "A failing of mine," but she said, "No."

"Did you?" Officer Clément asked.

"Did I what?"

"Did you murder her husband?"

Saskia drew back in horror. "Of course not!"

"Have you ever murdered anyone?" the magistrate asked.

Saskia's glance flicked from Officer Clément to the magistrate, who looked expectant, and then back to Officer Clément. "What?" Saskia squeaked.

"It is a simple question, Dr van Essen. Have you ever murdered anyone?" Clément asked.

Indignation flared. Saskia scrambled to stand on the seat of her chair, placed her hands on the table and leaned forward towards the police officer. "Monsieur, not only have I never murdered anyone. I have never even thought of murdering anyone. Even when provoked, I have never thought of murdering anyone!"

"Bon." Clément sat back, a small smile twitching his lips.

Was he smirking?

"Dr van Essen, could you describe these women to us?" the magistrate asked.

Saskia swivelled her attention to Louise Granger. "Yes. The woman who attacked me was heavy-set, perhaps a metre and a half tall, probably middle-aged. Her brows were black, and her eyes dark. She wore a green kaftan and a matching hijab. Her companion was similarly dressed, though she wore heavy makeup – false eyelashes, brows darkened and shaped. She – the companion – understood and spoke some French. I don't think the woman who attacked me – and yes!" she glared at Clément, "it *was* an unprovoked attack!"

Saskia drew breath to calm her irritation at the police officer, and brought her focus back to Mme Granger, who responded with the merest twitch of an eyebrow. "I don't think that first woman understood or spoke any French," Saskia continued. "There were two children with them. A boy of perhaps four or five. Grey shorts, reddish shirt. Dark, short hair. The girl was about ten. Thin. She wore a hijab that hid her hair and skinny denims with a loose brown tee shirt. The children looked neatly turned out. I didn't note their footwear. The women wore slip-on sandals. There was also a baby in a covered pram. I did not see the baby. Is this the information you want?"

The magistrate smiled, nodding slightly. "Merci. Oui." She turned to the police officer, who had been scribbling furiously in a notebook. "You have all that?" To Saskia, she said, "You have good recall, given the trauma of the situation."

"It's what I'm good at, Madame. I notice and remember details." Saskia settled back on to her chair, annoyingly aware that her feet did not reach the ground and that her small stature must have made her standing-on-the-chair outburst look ridiculous.

"That is good news for us, Dr van Essen – "

"Oh, stop calling me Dr van Essen. It's pretentious politeness. And tell me what's going on here. Why are you here? More to the point, why are you, a juge d'instruction, involved in a disturbance at the market? How come the police are involved at all? Has there been a murder at all? And how come I'm being accused?"

Under French law, since Napoleon's days, a magistrate appointed to be juge d'instruction in a case had almost unlimited control of the investigation. The appointment of such a person meant the case being investigated was serious or complex.

The magistrate gave a single, slight nod. "How would you like us to call you? And please call me Louise."

"Saskia will do."

"You are right to guess, Doctor – uh – Saskia, that we are here to investigate more than your assault at the market. However, before I answer your questions, please tell us more about the incident at St Antoine. You say there was a man who understood what your assailant said. Can you tell us exactly what he said the woman accused you of?"

Saskia frowned, fumbling for the memory. "Exact words? Er – well – at first, he just told me that she said I'd murdered her husband. I said I had not. Then he had a conversation with her and he said – ummm – he said that she told him I may not have pulled the trigger but I was the cause of his death and was more to blame for her husband's death than the bullet that killed him."

"Do you have any idea what she meant?" Louise asked.

"Have I not already made clear that I don't?"

"What is your work, Saskia?"

"I work at the FSB. It's a bank. I work in the risk division."

"What does that entail?"

"My job is to research whether the bank is keeping up with the latest European regulations and following them, as well as incorporating organisational structures that encourage responsible behaviour from staff."

"And is the bank keeping up with regulations?"

"I've only been at the bank for a few months, so I haven't done much more than getting to know how the bank operates. I've made a few suggestions for improvements, and I am not at liberty to discuss bank details with you without clearance."

"Do you have people working for you?"

"No."

Clément looked up from his notebook, his busy pencil pausing. "You have nothing to do with the bank personnel?"

"I don't know what you mean by that. I am part of the bank personnel. I report directly to the head of the bank's risk management team, Madame Le Fèvre."

Louise reached into the bag hanging from her shoulder, removed a folder and extracted a photograph. She placed it on the table in front of Saskia.

Saskia picked up the photo. It showed the head and shoulders of a man with a neatly trimmed greying moustache and beard, and grey curly hair cropped close to his head. His eyebrows were black and thick, and his eyes were closed. Foreboding cramped her breathing as she studied the image. Judging by the pallor of his skin, the photo had been taken of a dead man. She took a deep breath as she looked up to meet Louise's gaze. "Umm – I think he was one of the people who attended a recent talk I gave at the bank about avoiding scam emails."

"So," Clément said, sitting forward. "You do have something to do with other people at the bank."

Louise put a hand on his arm, and he sat back.

"Do you remember his name?" asked Louise.

Saskia shook her head. "No. It was an open invitation session, and there were about fifteen people there. A few people introduced themselves to me after the talk. This man didn't."

"Could you find his name?"

Saskia frowned. "You should go to the bank's personnel department for this information."

Clément straightened, this time ignoring the hand that Louise again placed on his arm. "Before we give you further information that might persuade you to help us, tell us about the man who translated for you – at the market. You said that a man was able to understand what the woman said."

"What do you want me to tell you about him? I'd never seen him before. He was kind and helpful."

"It didn't seem strange that a person who understood the lady happened to be on hand to translate?"

"No. Not at all. Lyon is full of people from many nations."

"Can you describe him?"

"I didn't pay much attention to him." Saskia closed her eyes, replaying the scene. "He was dressed in a suit – a fawn-coloured suit. He had a matching scarf, I think. He was old – I mean, like fifty or sixty. He spoke good French, but with a slight accent. I think he wore glasses. There was a woman with a checkered scarf. A stallholder. I remember seeing her before."

"Yes," Louise said. "She described the incident to us. She did not know either the gentleman who helped you or the two women. But she said she had seen you before. She also knew your name. You paid her for her produce with a credit card loaded on your phone, which is how we have been able to find you."

"Are you going to tell me what this is about?"

"I think that's fair," Louise said. "This man," she put her finger on the photo, "was found dead on the banks of the Rhône beyond the Confluence two weeks ago. He had no identification on himself, and we have been at a loss to identify him. Quite by chance, we heard about the disturbance at St Antoine Market and, given there was an accusation of murder involved, we decided to follow up."

"Jezus!" Saskia breathed. "Do you know how he died?"

"A bullet to the side of the head. He was also severely tortured."

Saskia glanced at the photo again.

"We have touched up the photo to hide the damage to his temple," Louise said. "We wondered whether there might be a connection with the murder accusation at the market."

"If there is one, I don't know about it."

"Again, we ask, can you tell us who he is? It would be most beneficial to our investigations if we could at least identify him," Louise said.

Saskia thought for a while. She had already hacked into the personnel files of the bank once when looking for information about Antoine Aubert. Would it be right to do it again? She was tempted to ask if she was a suspect, but instead she reached for her backpack, took out her laptop and set it on the table. Within minutes, she had worked her way into the personnel files of the bank and was scanning names. When she came to a name that sounded male and Middle Eastern, she clicked into the file to peruse the photo. Finally, she turned her laptop screen around for the magistrate and police officer to see.

Clément began to scribble in his notebook.

Saskia said, "What's your mobile number? I'll send you a screenshot of this page."

Louise provided a number. Saskia made the transfer and then closed her laptop. "Madame, Monsieur, I have provided this information to you, but it was way beyond my comfort zone."

"Understood," Louise said. "Thank you."

"Do you think you could find any further information about this – " Clément glanced at his notebook, "Amin Aziz?"

"The information I provided to you says he works in the accounts department. I don't personally know anyone there."

Louise stood. "Thank you for your help, Saskia. We'll make further enquiries. Now that we have these details, we should be able to find his family. Thank you again, Saskia." She reached into her shoulder bag and drew out a card. "Should you think or hear of any further information, please contact me."

Saskia accepted the card and walked the officers into the house and up the hallway to the front door. She turned back into the hallway, having shut the door behind the visitors. Mme Claire stood in the hallway; one eyebrow raised and her head tipped slightly to one side.

Saskia grimaced. "I'd hoped to forget about all of this, but it seems I've been plunged into something I've got nothing to do with," Saskia said to the silent enquiry.

"May I know?"

"Yes. Yes. Of course."

# 9

## GOSSIP

Saskia tapped the keyboard, causing the screens of the two monitors on her desk to display parts of spreadsheets, graphs and diagrams.

She enjoyed working with spreadsheets. She'd been only 11 or 12 when she opened her first Excel spreadsheet on a school computer, but it wasn't until Nicolaas became her teacher that she started to explore the power of spreadsheets. Once she became part of his group of geeky friends in Rotterdam, she began to appreciate how revolutionary the invention of a spreadsheet was. Before spreadsheets, each time a person changed a number in a calculation, all the other numbers needed to be changed too – a laborious process. With the spreadsheet, change one number, and all the other numbers changed too: magic! Her newfound friends had happily debated terms like VLOOKUP and XLOOKUP and helped her dive ever deeper into how to use Excel's built-in formulas and data visualisation tools to organise and query data.

Saskia could spend hours – days even – totally absorbed in sorting and understanding data, forgetting all else, including time and fretful things like assaults and murder investigations.

Throughout her doctoral and post-doctoral years, Saskia had tinkered with Excel's code and then back-ended and front-ended databases and mapping software to the application with more self-created code. With her created application, she could turn data into linked coloured boxes and circles that turned numbers, words, phrases, observations and photos into complex systems maps. With this tool, she could view information from many angles with just a few keystrokes.

Her university supervisors and sponsors had laughed at the app she'd created, telling her the programming and operation were so complex it would never sell, and it would need someone with her bent for understanding patterns to operate it. They didn't need to mention that, should her tool ever be made public, she would probably also run into problems for tampering with proprietary code.

But Saskia had not created the application, nor continued to tinker with it, in order to sell it. She'd created it for her own use and to enhance her special talent for pattern recognition.

Just now, what her tool showed her made her frown, partly in puzzlement and partly in concern.

Mme Le Fèvre had found Phillip Quayle's report on scam notifications and the management meeting notes discussing the report. M. Quayle had recommended that management consider a more proactive stance to reduce the funnelling of scam funds through FSB. He had listed figures on scam notifications and categories of actions taken. Saskia inserted those into the spreadsheet. She suspected they underrepresented the actual figures. She found the concluding remarks troubling: 'The situation will be further monitored. No action needed at this time.'

Saskia clicked into information about FSB's trading involvement in the European Carbon Credit Scheme. The scheme, which had been put in place to encourage companies to progressively lower their carbon emissions, provided carbon-emitting companies with a certain number of credits that allowed them to emit a defined amount of carbon. If they emitted less than allowed, they could sell unused credits on the market to companies that needed more credits. Each year, the number of credits available reduced, making credits increasingly valuable. The aim was to encourage carbon-emitting organisations to innovate to reduce their emissions.

What piqued Saskia's interest was the steep rise in carbon credits making their way through the bank's books. Even more interesting, or perhaps concerning, was that most of the credits came from a new client, TG Securities. Saskia searched for the initial communication with TG Securities. She still felt sufficiently outraged by Ferdinand Fourvier's lack of backbone to have foregone telling him that she had started reaching into the bank's data storage systems to gather information. After all, Mme Le Fèvre was one of the most senior people in FSB Lyon, and she had given Saskia permission to seek out whatever information she needed.

Well, maybe Mme Le Fèvre hadn't quite meant that Saskia should peek into so many corners of the bank's storage vaults. *But*, Saskia told herself, *I only go to places I need to go.*

After days of working her way through emails and stored files, she finally found the communication she was looking for. TG Securities' initial estimate of carbon credits was a third of what they now sold to the bank.

That finding led her to wonder about TG Securities. It appeared that FSB's traders hadn't done much to investigate TG Securities. At least, not so they recorded it. She looked for public and not-so-public information about the company but didn't find much. Their website was well made, and they listed working with several Eastern European companies, some of which were large and well-established.

Saskia typed her observations into a concise report on the morning of her weekly meeting with Mme Le Fèvre. At the appointed time, she left her office, report in hand and detoured to the tearoom to refill her coffee mug. Two men and a woman sat on lounges in the room, leaning towards one another in conversation. They glanced up, nodded politely in greeting and returned to their interaction.

Saskia recognised them as members of the accounts department.

"His phone just rings out," the woman said.

"No one's been able to contact him? Not even Benjamin?" one of the men asked.

Saskia stiffened.

"What did you tell the police?" the other man said.

"Just that I don't know much about him. I mean, he was a good worker, but he never mixed much with us," the woman said.

"They're going to interview everyone at the bank."

Saskia left the room, forgetting to take her coffee with her.

Mme Le Fèvre left her desk when Saskia appeared in her doorway. She indicated the meeting table. "Bonjour, Saskia. How are you?"

"Good. Fine," Saskia said, hoping that her jumpy heart didn't sound in her voice.

Mme Le Fèvre closed the office door behind Saskia. "I see you have something for me. I never know whether to feel uneasy when I see what you turn up, or relieved that you do turn something up."

"Oh?"

Mme Le Fèvre chuckled. "Don't look so concerned. Sit. What have you for me today?"

"A couple of things." Saskia set the report before her superior as they took seats across from one another at the four-seater round table. "I think it may be an idea for FSB to consider a better scam prevention, detection and response strategy than is currently in place. And I think it might be wise for the bank traders to ask TG Securities why there's a spike in carbon credits. I mean, why they are trading more than they anticipated they'd be trading. There's – er... They might say that's a good thing because the bank gets a good commission, but given there's a lot of talk about how the credit market's being scammed, it might be good to enquire."

"These are significant thoughts," Mme Le Fèvre murmured, her gaze dropping to the pages before her.

"My – er – calculations don't add up. I don't think the companies TG Securities works with could be producing so many unused credits."

"Your calculations?" One of Mme Le Fèvre's eyebrows arched higher. Saskia grinned, remembering Mme Le Fèvre's glazed look when Saskia had previously demonstrated her systems maps. Mme Le Fèvre had thrown up her hands. "Mon dieu! Please just give me the report."

But Saskia quickly aborted her grin because it tore at her still-fragile lip.

Her wince did not escape Mme Le Fèvre's notice. She regarded her over the top of her moon-shaped reading glasses. "You have told me about the incident in the market. Do you still not know why the woman attacked you?"

"No." Saskia retrieved a tissue from a pocket of her trousers and gently dabbed at her lip.

"Do you think she was she deranged?"

"I – er – didn't get that impression. After she calmed down a bit, she said she mistook me for someone else."

"Mmm," Mme Le Fèvre sounded doubtful, but returned her attention to Saskia's report and spent several silent minutes reading. Finally, she nodded. "I see how you've arrived at your recommendations. This will require some consideration. To begin with, I will ask our traders to make enquiries." She folded her hands over the report. "But now. On another matter. I had heard there had been a possible malware attack at the bank two weeks ago. What surprised me was to only learn today in a phone conversation with Clint Bailey that you had a hand in halting the attack. He called you for help and you provided it immediately, efficiently and effectively. This detail was left out of the report Monsieur Aubert circulated to senior management. I find that fact curious enough but Mister Bailey further informed me that Monsieur Aubert was unhappy about your actions."

Saskia sighed. "Yes. I'm trying to put this incident behind me."

Mme Le Fèvre's lips rolled between her teeth as she studied Saskia over her glasses for some seconds, then said, "I have spoken to Monsieur Aubert about the matter. He believes the bank's computer system would have picked up the malware and naturally stopped it. He said that you caused a power outage and, therefore, a significant disruption to bank operations."

Saskia nodded. "Yes. He made that clear to me."

"Do you believe our computer system – " she made a slight gesture with her hand, indicating she did not have in-depth knowledge about the bank's computer system, "would have stopped the malware?"

"No."

Both Mme Le Fèvre's expressive eyebrows rose. "That's an emphatic response. Mister Bailey tells me he contacted you rather than the IT people because he was confident you spoke good English, and he was afraid that if he contacted someone else they wouldn't understand him."

Saskia nodded.

"He knew about you because you gave a staff talk on cyber security."

Saskia nodded again, wondering why Mme Le Fèvre was dragging out this issue. It was done and Saskia had indicated she wanted to set it behind her.

"Ah!" Mme Le Fèvre sighed. "In hindsight, perhaps we should have asked Monsieur Fourvier to give that talk."

Having someone give such a staff briefing had been one of the ideas she had worked through with Mme Le Fèvre to increase staff risk awareness.

"I asked him, and he said he didn't like talking in public, and that I should do it."

Saskia had long ago lost her nervousness about making public presentations. She even ensured she brought a collapsible footstool that would raise her to a level for looking over lecterns. Setting up the footstool allowed her to settle people with a quip such as, "This is so I can see you and check whether you're falling asleep".

"Oui," Mme Le Fèvre sighed. "I now recall that you did ask. But Monsieur Aubert tells me Monsieur Fourvier disagreed with the actions you took."

Saskia grimaced. "Not at the time, and he neither agreed nor disagreed when Monsieur Aubert challenged us."

"I see. It would seem that Monsieur Fourvier is reticent about more than public speaking. But you believe you did the right thing?"

"I know I did."

Mme Le Fèvre studied Saskia for a while longer, then gave a single nod. "A pity this has occurred. Let us hope there will be no further fallout from this affair. But would you like me to take it up with him?"

"No. Thank you. I don't think it will achieve anything."

Mme Le Févre nodded slowly. "Very well, Saskia. I am convinced Monsieur Aubert has not treated you fairly. That makes me unhappy. I resent that he disciplined you without first coming to me. If something like this happens again, please tell me. In the meantime, I will suggest that IT develop a procedure so that everyone knows how to deal with such situations." She straightened in her seat, indicating with a flick of her groomed fingers that she had finished with the matter. "Now, what else should we discuss?"

Despite her resolve to put a considerable distance between the Amin Aziz affair and herself, Saskia said, "Umm – Everyone seems to be talking about – umm – Amin Aziz. Do you know what that's about?"

Mme Le Fèvre removed her reading glasses. Her face puckered into a grimace of distaste. "A most unfortunate affair. The poor man was found washed up on the banks of the Rhône beyond the Confluence. The police have opened a murder inquiry and spoken to me and, of course, Monsieur Aubert. Also, they have spoken to all colleagues of Monsieur Aziz. They have not interviewed you?"

"Er –" Saskia groped for a non-revelatory response. "No one has called me at the office for an interview."

"Perhaps they will not. You did not know the man?"

"No. I don't – er – didn't."

"Poor man."

"Do you know if he had – umm – family?"

"A wife and three children, I believe. The bank is reaching out to them." Mme Le Fèvre frowned, eyes searching Saskia's face. "You are upset?"

"I – er – it must be awful for the family. It must be awful."

"Yes." Mme Le Fèvre pushed her chair back from the table, picking up Saskia's report as she did so. "Monsieur Aubert tells me both FSB Personnel and the police are having difficulties contacting the family."

Saskia left the office in a state of alarm.

Could the woman have been Amin Aziz's wife? If so, why the murder accusation?

*Saskia! How did you get yourself involved in this*!

## 10

## A NEW NEIGHBOUR

It started to rain on her way home from the office, but Saskia hardly noticed; she was deep in disquieting thoughts about scams, carbon credits and, especially, Amin Aziz.

By the time Saskia put away her bike, she was soaked through and shivering with cold. She removed her shoes and socks and squeezed water out of her trousers before unlocking the back door.

A bell tinkled as she pushed open the door. Mme Claire had installed it to inform her of the comings and goings of her lodger or others who might be visiting her home.

"Saskia?"

Saskia halted halfway up the stairs and turned at Mme Claire's voice.

"Oh, dear!" Mme Claire said, taking in Saskia's sodden state. "Do you always get so wet when it rains?"

"No. I have wet weather gear in my backpack," Saskia laughed. "I was just too preoccupied to stop and put it on."

"I see. Perhaps you should dry off, and then I would like to talk with you if you have time."

Half an hour later, showered, warmer and in dry clothes, Saskia knocked on the entrance to Mme Claire's downstairs area. Rufus gave a single bark and whined, crowding up to Saskia when Mme Claire opened the door.

"That dog adores you," Mme Claire smiled.

Saskia bent to hug Rufus and let the dog give her a quick lick. "I'm pretty fond of him myself. But doesn't he adore everyone? He's so friendly and loveable."

"He was not very friendly towards the police when they came!"

"Well, Rufus," Saskia said to the dog, "you and I share our suspicions."

"Come inside, Saskia. Can I make you a coffee?"

"No. Thank you. I think I've had my fill of coffees for the day."

"Then perhaps a hot chocolate?"

Saskia hesitated. She was looking forward to simply settling into her own space for the night. But did Mme Claire want company or was there something else? Perhaps something to do with the police that Mme Claire wanted to discuss? Saskia hoped not.

"That would be lovely. Thank you."

Saskia sat at the worn wooden table in the comfortable old-fashioned kitchen as Mme Claire prepared two hot chocolates.

"I am considering taking in another lodger," Mme Claire said, setting a mug in front of Saskia and sitting opposite her. "But I wanted to make sure you were alright with that."

"Madame Claire, that's very nice of you to think of me, but I don't feel I should have a say. This is your house."

Mme Claire smiled. "And you live in it also. You are an easy and undemanding person to have in the house, and I would not like to disturb our peace. The arrangement when you took on the apartment is that you would be the only lodger in this house until my nephew returned."

"No. Really! You mustn't concern yourself about that. It is your decision."

"Then I must tell you that the mademoiselle I am considering is called Isabelle García Gonzales Cruz."

"That sounds Spanish or Portuguese."

"She is Spanish. When I met her, I had not thought of inviting another lodger, but I came to like her, and I learnt she is looking for short-term accommodation. So, I offered. She recently began volunteering at the Rome Museum, as I do a couple of days each week. She came this morning with her uncle. He owns a small gift shop located in one of the traboules."

"May I ask? Why is she in Lyon?"

"Her father was French. She can speak French but it is quite mixed. She decided to come live with her uncle – grand uncle, I think – in Lyon to improve her French. She tells me she wants to further her studies. She is about your age – late twenties, I think. She is also very beautiful."

Mme Claire's bright blue eyes seemed to twinkle. "Even though I invited her to have a look at the accommodation I might offer, I confess I still hesitated. It is easy in this house with just the two of us. You are undemanding, as I said, but Rufus was most impressed by her."

At the sound of his name, Rufus lifted his head, ears pricking forward. "No," Mme Clair said, dropping a hand on to his dark head to fondle his ears, "you have already had your dinner and exercise for the day. That is not what we are talking about." Then, to Saskia, "Should she accept, perhaps it would be nice if we dined together to get to know one another a little better. Perhaps on the Saturday? Would that suit you?"

## 11

## AYAT BENKIRANE

"We are making a nuisance of ourselves, I think," Mme Le Fèvre said, appearing in the doorway to Saskia's office. "The big boss is visiting from his Belgian office and has asked to see us to discuss our report."

"Which report?"

Mme Le Fèvre pointed to a folder on Saskia's desk. It contained a document Mme Le Fèvre had prepared for a senior management meeting. She'd given it to Saskia after the meeting with the words, "I fear it will not be taken seriously".

"This one?"

"Yes."

"I thought it was just for senior management in Lyon."

"It was for that meeting."

"But you say that someone from the Belgian office is here?"

Mme Le Fèvre's smile was coy. "He must have seen the report."

Saskia considered for some seconds. "I'm suspecting," she said slowly, "that you are not surprised the report did not stay in Lyon."

"Do you?" The coy smile broadened.

Saskia rolled her eyes. *This is why I'm a backroom person*, she thought. Mme Le Fèvre must have known the Lyon branch meeting notes might make their way up the chain of command. Then she narrowed her eyes. "You just said that the big boss wants to see us. Does that mean I am included?"

"Indeed. I think the boss especially wants to see you."

"Why?"

"Well. Let us find out. We are called to Monsieur Aubert's office to meet the esteemed Monsieur Benkirane." Mme Le Fèvre's elegant hands folded into a prayer position. "The big boss from Belgium."

Groaning internally, Saskia closed the computer files she had been working on and shut down the devices, locking access.

She accompanied Mme Le Fèvre to Antoine Aubert's sumptuous eighth floor office with its view of the Saône.

Mme Le Fèvre knocked lightly on the office door, pushing it open at the sound of "Entréz".

"Ah!" M. Aubert said from his laid-back position in one of the armchairs arrayed before a picture window that afforded a magnificent view of the river and city beyond. He wore pressed charcoal trousers, a thin-striped pale blue shirt and dark blue silk tie. His shoes were the sort with lots of little holes in the leather; Saskia supposed they were fashionable. They looked expensive. Antoine Aubert looked expensive, complete with gold watch. His goatee beard, which Saskia thought ridiculous, was trimmed to perfection, and not a hair on his full head of oiled black hair was out of place. "Here is Madame Le Fèvre. Come in. Join us."

Saskia had heard of Ayat Benkirane, of course. She was well aware of FSB's organisational structure, which was carefully detailed in her database. But she had never met the head of the European arm of the bank, though the grey-haired man who turned in his seat and stood as they approached seemed familiar. Perhaps from his photo on the organisational chart?

He extended his hand in greeting. "Madame Le Fèvre. How nice to meet you again. And with you is?" M. Benkirane's smile grew, crinkling the skin around his eyes.

"Saskia van Essen," M. Aubert said. He'd shifted forward in his seat and balanced there, looking awkward in the face of his superior's courtesy.

"Doctor van Essen," Ayat Benkirane said, seeming not to hear M. Aubert's dismissive tone. "We have met before, but I see you are grappling with your memory. I see also that your injuries have almost healed?"

"Oh!" Saskia placed her hand into a soft but firm grip, now recalling M. Benkirane was the person who helped her at the market. "Er – yes! This is unexpected."

"Understandably," M. Benkirane chuckled. He released her hand. "I am delighted we meet again." He turned to Mme Le Fèvre and M. Aubert. "Dr van Essen and I met at the market by the river after her rather – " he paused when Saskia winced. "Forgive me Saskia, perhaps you would like to tell us what happened?"

"Er." Saskia felt colour creeping into her cheeks. "Er. I had an – umm – a disagreement with another person, and Monsieur Benkirane – umm – helped me."

"Just so," the European bank chief said, not bothering to hide his faint amusement at her choice of words. "I asked you at the time whether you would like to go to the police with the matter, but you said no. Did you report the incident after all?"

"No. No, I thought just to leave it be. The women were so upset. I – er – didn't want to make things worse for them."

M. Benkirane smiled. "I see."

"You were with Saskia when she was attacked at the market?" Mme Le Fèvre asked.

"I was. But let us say no more about it. I am delighted to meet you in other circumstances, Dr van Essen. Please, take a seat and let us attend to the matter at hand." He resumed his seat and leaned forward, gesturing at the coffee pot on a low table before them. "May I pour you coffee, Madame Le Fèvre? And you, Dr van Essen?"

*Wow! This man takes command!* Saskia was acutely aware that M. Aubert did not seem as sure of himself as when she and Mme Le Fèvre had first entered the room. The gold watch moved in and out of his shirt sleeve each time he fidgeted his hands over the arms of his seat. His hair looked like it had risen in surprise on his head.

M. Benkirane could only be described as distinguished. The precisely trimmed beard was greying, almost the colour of his suit. His coat was unbuttoned, revealing a plain white linen shirt fronted by a gold tie bearing the FSB logo. His clothes fit precisely to his lean figure, adjusting without effort to his every move. His shoes were plain black leather, lightly buffed. Apart from a wedding ring, he wore no other ornamentation.

*Monsieur Benkirane and Mme Le Fèvre would make a good couple*, Saskia thought, then pulled herself back sharply. *Focus!*

"I have read your report, Madame," M. Benkirane was saying. "It makes for very interesting reading and certainly highlights important issues FSB should be aware of." He handed Mme Le Fèvre a cup and saucer, indicating the sugar and milk on a small tray. To Saskia, he said, "Dr van Essen, if I am not mistaken, much of this report is the outcome of work you have undertaken?"

Saskia disliked sitting in armchairs at formal meetings. They swallowed her small frame and made things like reaching for a cup and saucer – and the milk and sugar on the table – an undignified struggle. But, in this case, M. Benkirane anticipated her by half standing to put the crockery in her hands, then holding the tray of milk and sugar out for her. All the while, he continued to talk as if his courtesy required no thought.

"As I have indicated, I have read your report, but I would appreciate it very much if we could start by you summarising for me, Dr van Essen, how you have arrived at your conclusions and then, Madame, if you could explain your recommendations." He looked towards M. Aubert. "Is this an agreeable way for us to proceed?"

"Naturally," M. Aubert said. "Though, as I have indicated, we have already addressed or are in the process of addressing many of the issues."

"Of course. But Madame's initiative in exploring Dr van Essen's method of enhancing our –" M. Benkirane paused to reach for a folder on the table next to the coffee pot, and leafed through its contents till he found the page he was looking for, "– enhancing our social licence to operate," he quoted. "Madame, you are taking us beyond the bank's *raison d'etre* to make a profit for our shareholders. Of course, it is what is expected nowadays. Gone are the days when we could only think about the profit motive, but it remains a difficult balancing act, don't you agree, Dr van Essen?"

Saskia wished he would stop calling her Dr van Essen. It was alright to thrust her title at people like Aubert, who tried to trivialise her, but once done, she'd much rather the conversation moved on as one among equals.

*Though – Interestingly –* It occurred to Saskia that she had no problem thinking of people like Mme Claire and Mme Le Fèvre with titles. *So why did –*

"Umm!" Saskia murmured, irritated by how her thoughts meandered when she was uncertain. She focused on M. Benkirane's question. "Yes. It's a balancing act. But it depends whether an organisation is looking into the long- or the short-term."

"This is the crux of the social licence argument?"

Saskia nodded.

"So, summarise for me how FSB is straying from its social licence."

"I have only looked at the operation of FSB in Lyon."

"Understood. Summarise for me how you have arrived at your conclusions."

"Well. It's sort of simple. I looked at what various French and European Union regulations require of banks. I added information about court cases involving banks and the judgements made, as well as media editorials and news, and relevant academic articles. Then I looked at whether FSB Lyon had safeguards in place to ensure conformance."

"And, if I understand correctly, the bank does on paper but not in its –" Once again, M. Benkirane consulted papers. "Its systems – or at least some of its systems – enable regulations to be bypassed. This is what you find? How does that work?"

It was on the tip of Saskia's tongue to start her explanation with,

"It's simple," again, but she stopped herself in time. "Umm – mostly, regulators can only discover if regulations are being followed through reporting mechanisms or through audits. Organisations can truncate their reports and hide required information from regulators."

"And this is what FSB Lyon is doing?"

"Not at all!" M. Aubert interjected.

"I agree that this report does not accuse FSB Lyon of this. But it would be interesting to understand the full picture. Do you mind if we move to the meeting table, Antoine? I would be most interested to go through this report in detail."

"Of course," M. Aubert said, though his tight shoulders indicated he minded a lot.

Saskia glanced at Mme Le Fèvre. Although M. Benkirane had focused on Saskia, it was Mme Le Fèvre who had taken Saskia's briefs and crafted the report, diplomatically wording it to gloss over the bank's shortcomings and concentrating on recommendations for enhancing the bank's operations and reputation. Saskia suspected that Ayat Benkirane had read between the lines very well, and that Antoine Aubert believed it reflected poorly on his management.

# 12

## ISABELLE

Isabelle García Gonzales Cruz might well have walked straight in off the catwalk. The side-swept fringe of her raven black pixie-bob just skirted black eyebrows and darkly outlined brown eyes in a pale face with high cheek bones. Pink, thin but shapely lips smiled frequently to expose perfect white teeth. A body-hugging emerald dress followed the contours of her slim figure all the way to her knees, and her slender, stockinged legs finished in pointy green and black striped high heels.

Isabelle spoke French very fast, tripping over pronunciation and frequently reverting to Spanish or a grab-bag of other languages when she could not find the right French. The effect was comical, and she seemed to delight in the comedy.

"Tchah!" she exclaimed after tangling words in a bid to appropriately respond to Mme Claire's introduction to Saskia. "Why not everyone speak one way? Molto bene we might do better communications. My mother – she now dead – when she live – she never leave my born – how you say – farm." Isabelle put the tip of her forefinger and thumb together to form a circle. "No understand no people talking, say she. They stupid not talk." With a grin, she raised the glass of wine Mme Claire had given her. "I more – how you say? Cosmopolitan?

That English word but you understand. No? Yes. You speak English? Yes? Ayiee! I will careful not use English word. Some word I know naughty."

On and on the river of words flowed. Within an hour, Mme Claire and Saskia, to frequent bursts of laughter, had learnt about Isabelle's first few years on a farm in the Spanish mountains and her introduction to city life after her father died in a farming accident. She had been sent to Sevilla to stay with her aunt and uncle because, "My mother she say I muy malo bad looking much at boys. She say not good for to keep good figure." Isabelle slid her hand down her slender waist and over her hip. "But only uno boy in close village and he not nice." This said with a pout of the pink lips, followed by a brighter explanation of how there were many more boys in the city. Elbows on the table, leaning forward a little towards Mme Claire and Saskia, a wicked gleam in her eyes, she told one story after another of her risqué adventures. "Descubre," (discover) she finished, again following the curve of her body with her hand. "Still nice little.' Again a pout, "My uncle he say I have need bigger brain." In a quiet voice, as if sharing a secret, she said, "He afraid my brain only in my pants." Then more indignantly. "No true! Pero! I fail exam then exam. Ooof! So boring study history."

"Now I here," she said with a laugh. "Is good here. I Lyon like. I start job with George. He nice old man." She winked at Mme Claire. "I promise I good girl now." She tapped the side of her head. "My brain up here now and you lady I am good with. Now you."

Saskia noted that, somehow, Isabelle had managed to drink wine, eat food and talk almost non-stop without fading the colour of her lipstick. Not even Mme Le Fèvre could do that. In fact, the need to reapply lipstick seemed to be a requirement for those who chose to colour their lips. Saskia had applied lipstick once but, as with making choices about different types of clothes to wear, it seemed like an unnecessary complication when there were more interesting things to do.

*Eh?* Saskia narrowed her eyes as Isabelle's last words ("Now secret yours.") pierced her distracted thoughts.

Isabelle was smiling at Mme Claire and, yes, she was expecting something from Mme Claire.

"Excuse me?" Mme Claire said.

"Mais oui, Madame. I no more secrets. Is good for women to share secrets. No?" Isabelle waved her hand to indicate the room. "Is boring to sneak in each our room in house. No? Amigas – how you say – friends – we share but not in – how say – live in pockets – bolsillos."

Mme Claire laughed. "You are certainly going to be a different type of lodger." She winked at Saskia. "I'm afraid I may have inadvertently unleashed a disturbance in our quiet lives."

"No disturb!" Isabelle protested. "Only nice amigas. I not in your pocket."

"We shall see." Mme Claire chuckled. "But, Isabelle, I don't have any secrets. I grew up in this home. I fell in love with a Scottish man and lived in Scotland with him for seventeen years, then he died and I moved back here. I've been here ever since."

"Much pain!" Isabelle exclaimed. "Non! Non! Tell funny life things. You have children." Isabelle pointed to framed photos of children on the dresser and hanging on the walls.

Mme Claire turned to the photos. "I have two daughters, a son and a nephew who became part of my family. I also now have three grandchildren."

Isabelle pushed her chair back from the dining table and padded – Saskia saw that she had abandoned her shoes – to a photo, drawing Mme Claire and Saskia in her wake. The three proceeded to visit every photo and, step by step, Isabelle drew from Mme Claire many stories of her life. She told of her days in Scotland with her young family, amusing incidents while learning English, family holidays, the dogs, ducks and guinea pigs the family owned, and the delight of times with her grandchildren.

When the round of photos was done, Isabelle clapped her hands, her face alight. "You have interest such much life," she declared. "And you?" She slid back on to her chair at the dining table and leaned across the table towards Saskia. "You in France for little time? You go back to Países Bajos?"

"Holland?"

"Si – yes – that place."

"I don't think so."

"Is family not nice or place or – " Isabelle drew in a sharp breath. "Your amor – lover – he is violence and you hide from him."

Saskia laughed. "No. Nothing like that."

"You never have boyfriend?" Isabelle looked stricken.

"I did. I lived for three years with my boyfriend. We were lovers and thought of marriage but I left to pursue further studies."

"Boyfriend triste?"

"We are good friends, and he has met another girl. They will visit me in Lyon soon."

"Your have family not nice?"

And, Saskia decided after she had entertained Isabelle and Mme Claire with stories about the insular nature of her warm, loving, caring extended family, among whom she felt suffocated, that she had never met anyone quite like Isabelle García Gonzales Cruz before. How was it possible for such an apparently frivolous person to be so clever at making others talk about themselves?

As she climbed the stairs with Isabelle towards their respective apartments, her new neighbour said, "We have maybe give each other phone numbers? And maybe we are friends, okay?"

Saskia sent her contact details to Isabelle's phone, then bid her goodnight.

As she closed the door behind her, she puzzled about Isabelle's language stumbles. Mostly, people who communicated in other than their mother tongue made mistakes related to the grammar and syntax of their first language. Isabelle's mistakes, however, seemed random.

She probably makes mistakes for effect, thought Saskia with a chuckle. I think Isabelle is much smarter than she'd like us to think.

# 13

## JOB OFFER

"We are very impressed with your work, Dr van Essen," Ayat Benkirane began. He sat opposite Saskia at a corner table in a cosy bistro in the old city of Lyon. "I have asked you to meet me here because I perceive that you and Monsieur Aubert are not the best of friends, so an office meeting might be somewhat awkward."

"Please call me Saskia. And, yes, I have offended Monsieur Aubert."

"Do you know the nature of your offence?"

"I shut down the bank's power supply once when I believed there was a ransomware attack. He thinks I overstepped the mark."

"Ah! Is that the incident that caused the rift. I remember reading an email memo about it."

A waiter appeared at their table. Saskia ordered a homemade beer and soup. M. Benkirane ordered wine and a chicken baguette. The waiter wrote their orders on a note pad, but continued to stand uncertainly at the table. He cleared his throat.

Saskia reached into her pocket and showed him her ID to verify her age. "Merci, Mademoiselle," he murmured, "pardon."

M. Benkirane watched the waiter walk away. "Does that happen often?"

70

## THE BANK

"Quite often," Saskia grinned. "I'm looking forward to the day when I am so old and wrinkled they can't mistake me for a child."

"I see. That is a perspective on ageing I haven't encountered before. But we were talking about the ransomware attack. When reading the memo, I recall also thinking that Monsieur Aubert may have misread the gravity of the situation."

Saskia shrugged. "Well, it's in the past, and I don't have much to do with Monsieur Aubert, so we get by."

"This is an interesting feature I am learning about you, I think. You do not dwell on unpleasant events. For instance, am I correct to believe that you have also not thought further about the unpleasantness in the market?"

"I especially try to put that behind me." Saskia paused before continuing, "Though, I have been thinking it's a huge coincidence that you, of all people, were there and that you were able to talk to the women. I didn't ever ask. What language did they speak?"

"Darija."

"Where is it spoken?"

"It is one of the de jure languages of Morocco. Also known as standard Moroccan Berber. And, before you need to ask me, yes, I am originally from Morocco. It is a remarkable coincidence, as you note. I have good friends living in Lyon and my wife and I visit often. We like to go to the St Antoine market. My wife was with me on the fateful day."

"I still have no idea why a strange woman should attack me."

"Do you know the name Amin Aziz?"

Saskia jerked in alarm. Was M. Benkirane associating the women with the murdered man as she had? *Oh dear.* "Amin Aziz?" she repeated unhappily. "Unfortunately, I do. His murder is the talk of the bank. Madame Le Fèvre tells me Monsieur Aziz had a wife and three children, and it did occur to me that the woman at the market may have been Madame Aziz. But, if so, I am no closer to figuring out why she would accuse me of murdering her husband."

"I believe the police have interviewed everyone at the bank. Did they also interview you?"

Saskia did not want M. Benkirane to know she had hacked into FSB's files to provide the police with the means to identify Amin Aziz, so she said, "No, I think the police only interviewed senior management and accounts staff at the bank."

"You don't feel inclined to contact them about the incident at the market?"

"If she is the wife of Monsieur Aziz, then I feel sorry for her loss. The last thing I want is to cause her more grief."

"But if the police contacted you, would you tell them about the incident?"

"Of course." Saskia frowned. *Why are you so interested in this matter?*

The waiter returned to the table and set their drinks before them, and, thankfully, M. Benkirane moved away from the topic of Amin Aziz. "I have a job offer for you. You may not have heard, but we have offered Madame Le Fèvre a position at FSB's European headquarters in Brussels. She has agreed. We are in the process of restructuring her department at the Lyon FSB. For the time being, her staff will report directly to Monsieur Aubert. However, rather than place you in an awkward position, I am hoping you will consider taking on a task that will have you reporting directly to me."

"Oh!" Saskia's shoulders slumped a little. She liked living in Lyon, working with Mme Le Fèvre and her job.

"I understand your reaction. I know she was instrumental in bringing you to FSB Lyon and you've been working closely with her. As I noted at the outset, we are most impressed by your work. You have demonstrated an impressive ability to uncover weaknesses in the bank's organisational structure. Madame Le Fèvre is loath to lose your skills, as indeed am I. She has asked that we offer you a similar position in Brussels to the one you have here."

Inwardly, Saskia groaned. She didn't want to move to Brussels.

M. Benkirane smiled, lifting his wine glass to his lips. "Do I detect a grimace of distaste?"

"Umm – sorry. I'm not very keen on the idea of leaving Lyon. I'm not long here."

"Then, I have another proposal for you. As I said, I have read your reports and recommendations. Indeed, the reason why we have asked Madame Le Fèvre to join us in Brussels is to enable us to utilise headquarters' greater reach into the organisation to examine improvements we can make as a result of your recommendations. My proposal is twofold. In the first instance, I – we – would like you to action your recommendations for setting up a seminar series for all branches of FSB on topics you have already flagged for improvement, especially the security of customer and bank information. Madame Le Fèvre informs me that the feedback she received from the two such sessions you have already given is most positive. For setting up such a seminar series, we would provide you with the resources of our education unit in Brussels, but, if you prefer, you can continue to operate from your current office here. When the round of seminars is complete, I would appreciate it if you would, at least temporarily, base yourself in Brussels and become my personal research assistant, looking into the issue of the future of banking, especially with regard to the impact of technology. I believe this is your special area of interest."

Saskia's thoughts scrambled to take in the proposal. The waiter provided a welcome distraction by bringing their meals.

"Naturally, you will want to think about this," M. Benkirane said, cutting into his baguette. "Naturally, also, there will be a rise in your wages." He smiled. "As a third 'naturally', we should discuss further what I have just offered."

# 14

## WINE AND CHEESE

Saskia returned to her apartment feeling dispirited by the events of the past few weeks in ways she couldn't quite explain to herself. The meeting with M. Benkirane and his job offer had particularly unsettled her. Her mind also kept cycling back to why Amin Aziz's wife would think her a murderer – assuming the woman in the market was Amin Aziz's wife.

She prepared herself a basic meal of rice, vegetables and cheese, then sat in front of her laptop in the hope of steadying her thoughts by checking the feed from her favourite online chat groups.

Her phone rang.

Hans.

"Hi, Saskia. We arrive tomorrow afternoon and will be in Lyon for two nights, so we have the whole of Saturday with you and Sunday morning. We go on to Geneva on Sunday. Will you have time to spend with us?"

"Of course! But I didn't expect you till next weekend."

"We changed our plans because there's a festival in Geneva that Melanie wants to go to. So, we will go first to Lyon rather than otherwise. Is it okay with you?"

"Of course. Where are you now?"

*THE BANK*

"We've stopped for the night in Reims. Sorry not to call you earlier. We've only just decided that's what we're going to do. And we have found somewhere to stay in Lyon. So don't worry about that. I know your apartment is too small for us."

"Okay, then. I look forward to seeing you."

*Ah well! That's my weekend sorted*, thought Saskia, returning her attention to her meal and laptop screen.

The phone rang again.

Her mother.

Well, thought Saskia with a wry smile, I might as well drown in the latest family dramas rather than chat groups.

"Saskia. Your computer not working!" her mother complained in her high-pitched voice. "You talk with father, but first, you talk me on you."

Saskia provided a sanitised version of the days since her last conversation with her mother: she'd been to another eating place with a dish she thought her mother would be interested in; Rufus had dug up one of Mme Claire's gardens and been roundly scolded; the weather had been very warm; last Sunday she had spent the day with friends in nearby mountains cycling through villages. Yes! They were quite different from Dutch villages. Saskia then extended a further invitation for her parents to visit.

"We have no time," her mother said. Saskia smiled upon hearing her mother's usual excuse. Sophia van Essen's first love was her café and clients. She was not attracted to travel beyond her neighbourhood. Saskia asked about friends and family and received a download of the latest gossip, which she did her best to commit to memory in case she was quizzed about it in a future conversation. Then it was Saskia's father's turn to commandeer the phone, complaining that the "computer is playing up!"

Neither of her parents understood more than the most basic operation of the computer system Saskia had set up for them in the café. Her brother understood it a little better, but all three expected Saskia to be on call if a problem arose. While chatting with her mother, she had already remotely accessed the café's computer system and located the issue troubling her parents. It was an application neither her parents nor Jan seemed to understand how to work properly. Saskia inserted a temporary fix, and then, having bid her parents goodbye, set about coding a more permanent workaround.

A soft knock on her apartment door startled her.

Saskia expected to see Mme Claire, but it was Isabelle standing in the doorway. She lifted a bottle of wine in one hand and a bottle of beer in the other. "Is inappropriate I visit?" she asked.

"Of course not!" Saskia stood aside.

"You am busy?" Isabelle asked, her attention on the open laptop with its nearby accompaniment of crockery and cutlery.

Saskia grinned. "Not really. Please make yourself comfortable. I was just trying to work out how to make a system I set up for my parents in their café easier to use." She closed the laptop and moved her dinner plate and cutlery to the sink, then climbed on to a small stepladder to remove two glasses from an overhead cabinet and set the glasses on a low table in the lounge area. All furniture and fittings had come with the apartment. It had been one of the attractions of the apartment – that, the location and the bike shed. Saskia had added a few stepstools and, with Mme Claire's permission, better internet access. Her family and friends would have commented on the lack of personal touches, but Isabelle merely asked whether she preferred wine or beer.

"Wine would be lovely. I've got some nice cheeses we can have with it if you like cheese," Saskia said.

"I like cheese. Where to buy cheese in Lyon. But I intrude, no?"

"I buy cheese in the market. It's my indulgence. I'm glad to share it."

"You like Lyon, yes?"

"I do. What do you think so far?"

Though Isabelle was still gorgeously made up, she had dressed in plain jeans and a shirt, her feet enclosed in low-heeled sandals. She poured the wine. "Is strange for me not with friends." She winced. "But you maybe not think too good for me here?"

*THE BANK*

Saskia waved the hesitation aside. "I know how it feels. This is my third move to a totally different place."

"Madame Claire good lady, no?"

"Very nice."

"You not spending time much with her?"

Saskia hesitated, unsure how to answer the question. "I guess I don't. I live here, but I don't think she rented out this part of her house for companionship."

"Money only," Isabelle nodded as if that made perfect sense. "Is good I know. I afraiding I making mistake with her." She indicated the laptop on the kitchen table. "I asking more question, okay?"

"Sure."

"You clever with all computer?"

"I'm cleverer than most people, but not as clever as my friends."

"Maybe one day I can learn from you? Now not. Now I learn English. Ooooh. Much difficult! My uncle he say I learning is good. My French also not good, no?"

Saskia grinned. "It's charming."

Isabelle pulled a face. "When shop people come, they stare me and some say, 'what you say?' When English people come I – how you say – I want say *entro en pánico.*"

"I panic," Saskia translated.

"You understand Spanish?"

"A little."

"Hablas todos los idiomas?"

Saskia laughed. "No. I don't speak all languages. Only a little Spanish. Maybe you can teach me to speak it better."

Isabelle looked delighted. She lifted her glass. "Para beneficio mutuo."

"To mutual benefit," Saskia echoed in French, then wondered what she was promising. She had few friends beyond her bike friends in Lyon. They had been enough, and even then she had often been content to opt out of invitations to join them in favour of her own company.

As if reading her thoughts, Isabelle said, still speaking Spanish, "We will only be to mutual benefit when and if it suits you. I think you are a person who is happy with her own company." She leaned across the table and said in a quieter voice, mischief in her eyes. "So am I, even if I behave as if I go to parties all the time."

"Are those stories you told Madame Claire and me not true?" Now it was Saskia's turn to struggle to find vocabulary and grammar to express herself in a language she did not often use.

Isabelle smiled in delight. She pinched together thumb and forefinger, meticulously shaped, pink-lacquered nails touching. "Maybe a little exaggerated. But it is true that my youth was wild, and I am now turning a new leaf. Or, at least, trying to."

"By working in a shop?"

"It is a start, no?" Isabelle sat back. "Not many people come to the shop, and it gives me time to study."

"English and French?'

"Also, I am very interested in ancient Roman history. I want to become an archaeologist, but I first must pass exams, so I study a lot. That is why Lyon is so fascinating for me. There is much Roman history here and there is more and more being found. I like to read everything at the Lugdunum museum at Fourvière and I like volunteering at the museum."

Saskia decided that Isabelle was indeed an intriguing person.

# 15

## MELANIE

Saskia secured her bike and helmet to a rack near Place Bellecour and hurried to the entrance of the metro. Ten minutes later, she saw Hans climbing up the stairs, holding hands with a pleasant-looking woman dressed in a simple pink cotton dress with short sleeves.

*Melanie.*

Upon seeing Saskia, Hans released Melanie's hand and ran the last few steps. He picked her up, giving her a hug and a kiss. "Hey, Saskia. It's so good to see you!"

Saskia returned the affection and then wriggled to be set down.

"He's the only person allowed to do that," Saskia laughed, turning to Melanie and holding out her hand. "Hello, Melanie. Hans never stops talking about you. I'm so pleased to meet you."

Melanie took Saskia's hand in her warm one. "Well, I've heard a lot about you, too," she said. She smiled, but her eyes flicked uncertainly as she looked between the two friends.

Hans snaked an arm around Melanie's waist, dropping a kiss on her cheek. "I can't help my exuberance," he said. "I am only an imperfect male in thrall by beautiful women."

"Who needs his eyes tested," Saskia said.

Melanie giggled.

"In the eye of the beholder," Hans retorted. He kept his arm around Melanie's waist and took Saskia's hand in his free one. "What have you planned for us today?

"Well, I thought we could cross the river from here and go into the old city. We could start by taking the funiculaire to Fourviére. Then we could go to the Basilique Notre-Dame de Fourviére, wander over to explore the Roman ruins, and maybe visit the museum. It depends on how much history you want to see and how much you want to walk."

Hans looked at Melanie. "My sweet. What do you think?"

"That sounds like a great little tour."

It was impossible to visit the grand Basilique without gasping at its grandeur, architecture and rich décor. From its four-towered white exterior to its elaborately coloured vaulted ceilings and intricate decorations, there was much to admire. Melanie's eyes grew wider as she wandered around the exterior, and upon entering the building, she clasped her hands before her. Tears starred her eyes. "Oh!" she whispered. "It's beautiful. Do you mind if I spend some time here?"

"Of course not," Saskia said. "I've been here a few times, and I still love visiting. There's always something new to discover."

A couple of hours later, having fortified themselves with baguettes and coffee, Saskia led Hans and Melanie to wander around some of the remains of Lugdunum, once an important Roman city.

"Would you believe," Saskia said as the three stood on the wooden platform at the base of the larger of two amphitheatres set into the hillside, "these Roman theatres are the oldest in France. They were built in the first century CE and used to seat about fifteen thousand people. After four centuries, they were covered by a landslide and forgotten for over a thousand years."

"How could that be?" Melanie exclaimed.

"Apparently, a mathematician bought land on this hill in the eighteen hundreds and tried to grow grape vines, but the ground was too stony. People told him it was because of old Roman walls. He started investigating, uncovered a few walls and traced out a curve. He posited that he'd found the historical Lugdunum theatres. Fifty years later, archaeologists took him seriously and these theatres were unearthed."

They walked up the steps of the larger of the two theatres, taking in the view of the modern city of Lyon, and then went down to the steps of the smaller theatre, stopping to read explanatory signs along the way.

"Shall we go now to the museum?" Saskia suggested, pointing to two enormous glass windows set into the hillside. "You'll get a good idea of what this place and Lugdunum must have been like in Roman times."

They were walking down the museum's gently sloping display hallway when Isabelle appeared, pushing a cart of drink bottles before her. Saskia introduced her friends.

"You like all here?" Isabelle asked, waving an arm to encompass the museum displays.

Hans spoke Spanish, but Melanie did not, so Saskia translated, and added. "I'd intended to show them more of Lyon, but we've sort of got stuck on this hill."

Hans drew Melanie in with a one-armed hug. "This little lady is practically jumping out of her skin with excitement at seeing it all. She loves looking at this history and art."

Saskia translated the Dutch into Spanish for Isabelle, who beamed and said she knew exactly how Melanie felt. She went on to list displays they must absolutely not miss in their museum tour.

"Do you work here?" Hans asked.

"I volunteer only. I am happy to be here. It's great meeting happy people. I do a little work cleaning and doing this," Isabelle pointed to the cart. "I'm off to give drinks to important people who are working on cleaning some new artifacts. I'm finishing in an hour or so."

"Join us, if you like?" Saskia invited. Then she glanced at Hans and Melanie, switching to Dutch. "Do you mind if my friend joins us for dinner?"

"Of course not," Hans and Melanie said in unison.

Isabelle accepted the invitation eagerly. "Take your time," she said. "I'll wait for you at the entrance. The museum closes at six, so you'll have enough time to enjoy it." She glanced around quickly, snagged three drink bottles from the cart and handed them out. "Fortify yourselves," she said.

It was still warm as the four of them took the funicular off Place de Fourvière down to the old city. Saskia suggested they walk past Cathèderal St-Jean and then along the waterfront past the Palais de Justice. They stopped at a cream statue of a man carrying another man who could be his twin slumped in his arms.

"The weight of oneself," Saskia explained.

Melanie stared, moved almost to tears. "It's so evocative," she breathed.

They crossed Pont La Feuillée over the Saône to Place des Terreaux.

"This is one of my favourite squares in Lyon," Saskia said.

"You've said that a hundred times today. You have so many favourite places in Lyon, I'm surprised you can remember them all," Hans chuckled. "But I hope this favourite place has somewhere to sit and eat. My feet are sore. And a baguette and coffee for lunch, plus a stolen bottle of water, is not enough to keep this body and soul together."

A waiter showed them to an outdoor table with a good view of the large square and its impressive Fontaine Bartholdi.

"The fountain," Isabelle explained in Spanish, "depicts France as a female seated on a chariot controlling France's four great rivers. They are the four horses she has the reins of."

Hans translated for Melanie.

"I know of this fountain," Melanie said. "It was supposed to be built in Bordeaux, but it was sold to Lyon. The same person who designed it actually designed the Statue of Liberty for America!"

Hans covered one of Melanie's hands and squeezed it. "Hey, love. You're having the time of your life, aren't you?"

Saskia felt a spurt of happiness to see Hans's affection for Melanie. She liked Melanie, too – she was older than Hans and herself, and there was a sadness about her, but she was unpretentious and seemed to drink in her surroundings with real pleasure.

A waiter took their orders. The dinner-time crowd became noisy.

Children played around the fountain and waterspouts in the middle of the square. Isabelle helped the conversation to flow along, asking about Rotterdam and the Netherlands in general – Saskia and, sometimes, Hans, providing ongoing translations. They ordered a second bottle of wine. The three women shared a laugh when reviewing how they had escaped their birth homes to spread their wings and forge new lives. Melanie began to tell of her dissatisfaction with schooling as a teenager, then made a swiping motion with her hand over her shoulder to dismiss the subject.

"I've put it behind me," she said. "Saskia, I'm interested to know more about your run-in with your boss." Melanie glanced at Hans, uncertainty jerking her bottom lip sideways. "Maybe I shouldn't have asked?"

Hans patted her hand reassuringly, saying to Saskia, "I told Melanie about your problem at the office. Did anything come of it?"

Saskia glanced at Isabelle. "I – er – had an altercation with my boss and – um – got quite irritated."

Isabelle nodded, a mischievous smile tugging the corners of her lips. "And what did you do?"

"Umm –well – I wanted to know more about my boss so I scanned his social media accounts. When I didn't find anything, I hacked into the bank's personnel files."

"That's my girl!" Hans chuckled, murmuring the translation into Melanie's ear. "I love it that you don't always let your principles get in the way. The man sounds odious enough to deserve a hack. But anything of interest?" he continued in Dutch.

"No. Disappointingly. I didn't find anything nasty about him that would make me feel vindicated. The only thing I got out of it was that I learned the route to get into personnel files."

"Eh? This sounds interesting. Tell us more," Hans said, leaning towards Saskia across the table.

Saskia shifted uncomfortably, clearing her throat again. "Well – umm – I'm not sure I should talk about it at all." She had not told any of her friends about how she had helped the police identify a murdered man and her suspicion that the woman at the market was his wife and she felt uncomfortable about revealing this even to Hans, especially with Melanie listening eagerly. Instead, she told them about the incident at the market.

"You were attacked by a random woman, and she accused you of murder!" Hans burst out when she finished her tale.

"Er – that sort of sums it up."

Since most of this last exchange had been carried out in Dutch, Hans turned to Isabelle and said in Spanish, his grin wide, "Saskia's been accused of murdering a man."

Isabelle raised her dark eyebrows, impressed. "Did you?"

"Of course not!" Saskia said. "Anyway. I don't want to talk about it anymore. Here's another bit of news, though. The head of FSB from headquarters in Brussels wants to transfer my supervisor to headquarters, and he noticed that Monsieur Aubert and I don't get on very well, so he's offered me a new job."

"Doing what?" Hans asked.

"Setting up a seminar series on bank security and customer service."

Hans sat back, lips pursed. "That doesn't sound like something you'd want to do."

Saskia shrugged. "I'm thinking of taking it."

"But the thought of it doesn't make you happy?"

Saskia shook her head. "No. I feel I am doing something worthwhile here."

"What do you mean?" Melanie asked.

"Uncovering issues concerning the bank's structure and procedures that could make the bank vulnerable to abuse by criminals."

"Used by criminals?" Melanie's eyes widened. "Like how?"

"Money laundering, abuse of the trading licence, enabling scam funds to flow through the system."

"Isabelle, you have no idea what this woman can do," Hans said, switching from Dutch to Spanish to include her. "She's got a brain the size of a planet and she's now sniffing out wicked bank dealings like money laundering and trading licence abuses."

Saskia shifted uncomfortably under Isabelle's studied gaze. "Hans is blowing it out of proportion. I use a mind map system and put a whole lot of factors into it, then look at what comes out."

"A mind map!" Hans chuckled. "Saskia should add she's developed the mind map. If you ever want to trace how things fit together and what you need to focus on to fix a problem, employ her." More seriously, he said to Saskia. "Am I being overly suspicious that what this big boss really wants is for you to stop digging for problems at the bank?"

Saskia shrugged. "That had crossed my mind."

## 16

### SIMON

Saskia met Hans and Melanie the next day for a late breakfast then for a tour of a few of the more than 200 famous Lyon traboules. These enclosed corridors, winding haphazardly through apartment buildings and providing access between streets, were intricately bound in Lyon's history. They had provided ancient silk makers with dry passage when carrying their bolts of cloth ready for shipments and been used by locals in every age since the ruin of the original Roman city to evade capture by would-be city conquerors or law enforcement authorities. Some traboules were simply arched hallways. Some had courtyards, with doorways into the courtyards and stairs leading down to basements or up to apartments. Some were combinations of styles. A special sign on a door facing a street indicated it was an entrance to a traboule, but only a few were open to the public.

Their tour guide was a font of information and Melanie was eager to continue exploring more traboules even after the tour finished, but Hans drew her to himself in a hug and told her laughingly that it was time to leave Lyon and embark on the next part of their journey.

Saskia said her goodbyes to the couple and returned home.

She had barely entered her apartment when her phone rang.

It was an unknown number. She considered rejecting it but pressed the answer icon instead.

"Hallo?"

"Mademoiselle, this is Louise Granger. You may remember we met some weeks ago?"

Saskia's shoulders slumped. She would rather not have heard from the juge d'instruction again. "Oui. I remember."

"I would be most grateful if you could meet me at the police station."

"What? Now?"

"Am I interrupting something?"

"What? Well – um – I've just got home."

"Shall I send a car to pick you up? It is imperative I speak with you."

Saskia's shoulders slumped a little more. She looked around her apartment. She'd had a vague idea of doing laundry and housework, hardly a good excuse for avoiding a meeting that Louise seemed determined to have.

*Well, at least I can get a bike ride out of it!* "Er – no. Where should I go?"

Louise gave her the address of the police station.

Forty minutes later, Saskia secured her bike and helmet to a stand, drew in a deep breath and entered the police station to find Officer Gabriel Clément waiting for her .

"This way," he said and led her along a long corridor. He knocked at a door and pushed it open, indicating that Saskia should precede him. Louise Granger and a man dressed in a three-piece suit who looked like he belonged in the executive suite of a very wealthy finance institution, stood up from a small table as she entered.

Louise introduced the man as Simon. "Enchanté," he said, extending his hand and keeping it low for her to reach. Saskia liked that he preferred to do that rather than bend down. The hand she clasped was large and felt strong but didn't squeeze uncomfortably. She looked up into friendly brown eyes and a welcoming smile that suited the clean-shaven, square chin. She thought him very handsome with his dark brows and short-cropped hair. He was maybe her age. Maybe a little older …

*Focus, Saskia!*

"I believe you prefer to be called Saskia," he said. His voice was deep.

"Um – er – yes. Thank you."

"Please, take a seat," Louise said, gesturing to a chair on the opposite side of the table to her seat. Officer Clément sat next to Louise. Simon manoeuvred a fourth chair away from the table and sat back, crossing his legs and folding his arms as if his role was only to observe.

"Our apologies for calling on you to make this visit," Louise began, surprising Saskia by not offering a further explanation about Simon's presence.

Saskia nodded.

"There are further developments concerning the murder of Amin Aziz. We hoped you might be able to help us again." Louise opened a folder, extracted a photo and slid it across the table. "Is this the child you saw at the market?"

Saskia studied the photo. The child's eyes were closed. The face looked distorted. With a frown of disquiet, Saskia realised she was looking at the face of yet another dead person, and probably one that had been dead for a while. She glanced up at Louise.

"Do you recognise her?" Louise asked.

"I can't be sure. It could be the girl I saw at the market. I didn't pay much attention to the children."

"Saskia, we have ascertained that the woman who confronted you at the market was Amin Aziz's wife. We have also located the community Amin and his family lived in. The family has disappeared and no one seems to know or be willing to tell us where the family has gone. They all seem to have disappeared soon after you were confronted at the market."

"There was another woman with them."

"We think that person may have been Amin's wife's sister. She has disappeared also."

"People don't just..." Saskia's voice trailed away. She was going to say "disappear", but she knew people did. She inspected the picture again. "And this photo?"

"A few days ago, a hiker's dog found the body of this girl. We've conducted an extensive search of the area and found nothing more. We know the family originally came from Morocco." Louise gestured toward Simon, "Interpol and Europol have become interested in this matter, as it appears to have a bearing on one of their investigations. We will take this photo to the school the child attended, and hopefully the teachers can help us further. But we wanted to get your input first."

"I can't be sure. Do you know how the child died?"

"We can only guess. She may have been hiding. She was tucked into a hollow and covered over with branches; possibly she'd pulled them over herself. There were no marks to show she had been abused." Louise replaced the photo in the folder. "There is another piece of information we'd like to share with you. We believe Amin Aziz was the person who released the malware into the FSB computer system."

Saskia froze, staring at the juge. After a second of blankness, her mind clicked pieces together. She pressed her hands to her cheeks. "My God! I stopped the malware. You think he may have been murdered because the ransomware attack didn't succeed?"

"Perhaps."

"How do you know it was he who released the malware?"

Louise turned to Simon.

He gave a single nod, uncrossed his legs and leaned forward towards Saskia, elbows on his knees. "Hash CaseIt Ten gave us sufficient information to be able to locate the site Aziz sent the emails from. It was a café popular with users who want good internet connection. One of the waiters remembered seeing him on the day of the malware attack."

"You – you know hash CaseIt Ten?"

Simon gave another single nod. "Saskia, we asked you to meet us here partly because of the further developments to the Aziz case, but mainly because we want your help." Simon paused, his gaze steady and compelling. "You have inadvertently become a focus in a number of our enquiries."

"Oh! I don't think that makes me feel good," Saskia murmured. *He's from the south of France,* she thought. *I think his accent is from the south of France.* She glanced at the door. It was still as shut as when she last glanced at it.

Simon smiled slightly. "I'm sorry if this makes you feel disconcerted. Allow me to explain." He shifted his chair closer to the table. "We believe that Aziz was involved in trying to help unaccompanied minors from Morocco and Algeria find homes that would care for them," Simon continued. "As Louise said, Aziz's community profess to know nothing about him and his family, but several non-government organisations who attempt to care for these minors have told us that he regularly brought children to their attention for treatment. We suspect that he fell afoul of one of the criminal gangs that use such children as drug mules and to distribute drugs."

Saskia stared at Simon, then at Louise and Gabriel.

"Er – um – I don't know anything about – er – criminal gangs."

"No. But you have been busy at your bank uncovering the probable avenues these gangs use to move their finances around. What's more, you have given us an 'in' into another problem we've been chasing for some time. That is, the trade in carbon credits."

"My – my work at the bank?'

"Indeed."

"Has – I mean – how do the police know about that?"

"Let me back up a little. You are well versed in the abuses of the carbon credit scheme and have flagged it as a potential problem for the bank?"

"Did someone at the bank tell you this? I mean, my reports aren't – er – public."

Simon turned to the police officers. "Are you aware of the issue?"

"A little," Louise said.

"Only by comments. Not really," Gabriel said.

"Do you mind if I explain, Saskia?" Simon asked.

"Of course not."

# THE BANK

Simon sat forward, forearms on the table, hands loosely clasped as he told how the carbon trading scheme was meant to encourage companies to implement methods that would reduce their carbon emissions.

"There was a problem because too many credits were issued, wasn't there?" Louis asked.

Simon nodded. "Initially, that was the case."

"So the scheme didn't stop companies emitting?" Gabriel observed. "And what has this to do with criminals?" Gabriel asked.

"It has to do with Value Added Tax. The VAT," Simon said.

"The VAT? We're often chasing VAT problems but what's that got to do with carbon trading?" Gabriel paused, frowning, and slumped back into his chair with a groan. "Don't tell me there's VAT attached to carbon credit trading."

One of Simon's eyebrows rose as if faintly amused by the officer's reaction. "Indeed there is," he said. "And the VAT on carbon credits is particularly vulnerable for a number of reasons." He held up three fingers, curling down a finger as he listed the reasons. "They are intangible and easily transferred. Different VAT rules across EU countries and real-time trading makes them hard to track. With carbon credits, no physical goods need to cross borders." Apparently not happy with his explanation, Simon rolled his lips between his teeth, considered, then said, "Let me give you an example. Have you got a notebook?"

Gabriel passed Simon a notebook and pen.

Simon leaned forward, shifting the notebook towards the centre of the table. Louise and Gabriel hunched over the table, eyes attentive. Saskia didn't move, vaguely hoping they would forget she was in the room. She glanced at the door. Perhaps this conversation would lead the three law enforcement personnel to believe she was superfluous to their requirements.

"Let's say that a company called SustainabilityTrade buys ten thousand carbon credits for fifteen euros each from the UK market without VAT. SustainabilityTrade sells these credits to GreenLeaves in France for fifteen euros fifteen cents. That gives it a base price of one hundred and fifty-five thousand euros. The VAT in France is nineteen point six per cent." Simon wrote numbers and formulas on a blank notebook page as he spoke. "GreenLeaves quickly sells the credits to a legitimate French company for sixteen euros. That's a base price of one hundred and sixty euros plus a VAT of thirty-one thousand three hundred and sixty euros." He glanced at Louise and Gabriel. "Okay so far?"

They nodded without taking their eyes off the page.

"The French Government is obliged to pay the legitimate French company the VAT but the two companies SustainabilityTrade and GreenLeaves never pay the VAT to the government. Instead, they disappear." Simon drew lines through the names of the companies, "They were sham companies set up by fraudsters. The criminals can run the same credits through multiple times in a carousel, thus making the VAT theft much bigger than the value of the underlying credits."

Simon turned to Saskia. "Would you care to explain what the scammers need to do with the money they pocket?"

Saskia blinked, feeling the same adrenalin spurt she used to get when a professor unexpectedly singled her out in a lecture theatre to answer a question – or to check if she was attending to the lecture.

"Um – well." Saskia pulled her legs up to kneel on the chair so she could lean over the table like the other three. "The criminals pocket the VAT they stole and move it through shell companies and trusts and into overseas accounts, making it virtually impossible for authorities to trace the identities of the thieves, let alone claw back the funds. Er – they often use banks with – umm – lax protocols in France to transfer funds to banks in Israel, Panama, China, Dubai and the like where French authorities have no jurisdiction at all."

Simon tapped the notepad with the end of the pencil. "Saskia's put her finger on the issue. The scammers make it almost impossible for us – that is, the authorities – to track the beneficiaries."

"You're saying we know what the problem is with the VAT fraud but we can't fix it?" Gabriel asked, a frown causing a deep furrow between his brows.

Simon said, "We know how the scam works in France, but the French authorities are currently loath to change the trading scheme because the current trade is making the government's scheme look good in the eyes of the EU, which is keen to make the carbon credit scheme work." He tapped the notebook again.

"That's rubbish!" Louise huffed, sitting back in her chair. "Any idea how much this is costing the French taxpayer?"

"Billions," Simon said. "Things are changing. Authorities are currently working on implementing a reverse charge mechanism where the buyer, rather than the seller, becomes liable for paying VAT and strengthening verifications requirements."

"Well, that's something at least." Gabriel grunted, sitting back. "I wouldn't mind a wages increase instead of paying billions of euros to criminals. But what has this to do with the abuse of minors?"

Simon also sat back in his chair.

Saskia, feeling silly that she was still on her knees and feeling even sillier that she had scrambled up on the chair to increase her reach, shifted one leg from under her to drop it over the edge of the chair and was trying to think of how to get purchase to drop the other leg out from under her without toppling off the chair or grabbing the table when Simon turned to her.

"We believe the VAT fraudsters are also heavily involved in the European drug trade and the exploitation of children, which is our primary interest. We believe that the criminals are using the lessons they learnt and the connections they made when dealing with the VAT fraud. We believe they are exploiting weaknesses in banks such as FSB."

Saskia held on to the table to drop her other leg over the side of the chair and settled herself firmly on the seat of the chair. "I see," she said, giving up on the idea Simon had possibly made a mistake targeting her.

As if neither Louise nor Gabriel were in the room, Simon focused entirely on Saskia. "The children being particularly exploited are often recruited in their home countries by affiliates to the European gangs. They arrive in Europe, often through the Brussels train hub, without language and work skills. There are no systems in place in Europe to stop them from falling prey to criminal elements. These vulnerable children are conscripted, told to sell a set quota of drugs or risk punishment, such as being beaten or gang raped. If a child is caught by the police, he or she is beaten by gang members as soon as they are released by the police. Some children are converted into child soldiers to hunt down those who are not living up to the gang's expectations."

Saskia grimaced at the mental image Simon drew. He was taking her into a murky world she knew little about and would prefer not to know anything about.

Simon scraped back his chair so that he could swing himself around and lean towards her, elbows on his knees. His intense, brown-eyed gaze holding hers, he said, "My team is attempting to target the criminal organisations exploiting children and importing illicit drugs into Europe. One of the ways we do this is to follow the money and identify who the beneficiaries are."

Simon paused, then continued, "Our interest has landed on you because of your demonstrated capacity to trace money and your embeddedness in one of the banks of great interest to us. We hope you can help us."

Saskia stared at him for a full minute before her brain defrosted, her eyelids blinked and she realised her mouth was open. "You – umm – are you saying want me to use my – er – access to the bank's system to trace illicit funds?"

Simon nodded.

"Why not ask the bank? Haven't you got the authority to ask the bank?"

Simon shook his head. "Sadly, not. We've tried. We've had meetings with European bank managers and managers of overseas banks, but they claim client confidentiality. We've tried to capture information from reports of dodgy transactions that banks are, by EU law, supposed to report to financial authorities, but we believe there are significant gaps in the information."

Saskia shifted uneasily. She had indeed already flagged such shortcomings to FSB managers. It was a publicly known shortcoming. She had published articles and given lectures on her views that the largely unregulated global financial system was a recipe for undermining a well-functioning capitalist system.

She glanced at Louise and Gabriel. Both sat in their chairs as if they were observers in a theatrical production.

"There's another reason why we'd prefer to work with an undercover person in FSB," Simon continued. "We suspect that the criminal organisations have embedded people in FSB."

"Under – cover!" Saskia fought to keep her head from swivelling around to look for a way out of the room. She took a deep breath, struggling for a more mature, less alarmed response. "Do you know who in FSB is – er – embedded?"

"No. But it must be someone senior enough to impact their decision-making structures."

*Undercover! For heaven's sake! I'm just an ordinary nobody minding my own business! How did I get caught up in murder investigations? And now this!* "Look! I don't think I'm the person you should be trying to recruit. I don't know anything about investigating criminal stuff or being – being undercover – or whatever!"

"On the contrary, Saskia." Simon's voice was very calm and sure. "You are exactly the type of person we should be trying to recruit. We know a lot about you, your background, your interests and, especially, your skills. We also know, as I've indicated, that you have started to uncover details about FSB that are uncomfortable for the bank and that, recently, you have been asked to perform another function for the bank – a training function."

"How do you know all this – I mean, how do you know about my work at the bank? Have you got someone you're already talking to at the bank?"

Simon shook his head. "No. We have other ways of finding such information. We are particularly interested in the possibilities that your new position at the bank will provide. You will be visiting bank branches throughout Europe and will be able to observe their operations." Simon sat back in his chair, hands loosely together in his lap as he regarded her. "Saskia, we have approached you for this work after a great deal of thought. We have already begun implementing processes in the event you should agree. Asking you to come to the police station on the pretext of more questions regarding the incident at the market is just one of the processes we have in place. Others are heightened surveillance of where you live and the main company you keep in Lyon." Simon leaned forward slightly, gaze intent. "Our surveillance has turned up something that should be of interest to you whether or not you agree to help us. You are under surveillance by another party. You are often followed, and your conversations are often being recorded."

"I – I'm being followed and – and?" The words practically squeaked out. Her head swivelled of its own accord to look over her shoulder. "By whom?"

"We don't know. But it's clear to us that you are a person of interest to someone, and we suspect it is because you are skirting too close to information at the bank that might not reflect well on the bank. Know also that there have been two attempts by unknown parties to enter your home. The first was thwarted by Madame Claire's dog, Rufus. The second attempt was thwarted by our people, who posed as Madame Claire's home security service. We have no doubt there will be further attempts."

"On Madame Claire's home? But what for? Is Madame Claire in danger?"

Simon lifted a shoulder. "We think the target is you, not Madame Claire."

"But I haven't done anything?"

"Oh, but you probably are a threat. As I've outlined, you have revealed uncomfortable issues to bank management. You have stopped a ransomware attack, which we suspect is somehow tied to a criminal organisation. And it may be that others guess you are not as ignorant as you make out to be about the identity of the people in the market incident."

Saskia clutched the sides of her chair. "I – I'm only a backroom person!" She squeezed her eyes shut. *What a stupid, stupid thing to say!* She felt heat coursing up her neck and opened her eyes.

Simon sat quietly, studying her.

"Listen! I mean – look!" Saskia swallowed hard, now wrestling not only to control her flight reflexes but also her swirling thoughts. "I could just leave the bank. Go back to a university job or something. Something else, and then there's no reason for anyone to have an interest in me. I could just tell the bank that I don't want the new job. It's a perfect excuse to get out of the bank, and that'll be the end of the matter. They've got no reason to suspect me of anything. And what's this to do with Madame Claire? I should move out of the house." The thought that either Madame Claire or Rufus might be in danger was even worse than thinking she might be in danger herself.

Simon nodded slowly. "These are options. I doubt it would entirely stop interest in you. And we would be disappointed. Perhaps you could give our conversation today some thought." He reached into the top pocket of his coat and pulled out a small burner phone. He stood and handed it to her. "Should you want to talk further about our request or, even better, agree to help us, please use this phone. It will only dial one number. Only call if you are fairly sure you want to help. Mention my name to the person who answers and take it from there. If you choose not to help us, please forget this conversation ever happened and discard the phone. Either way, please remember not to mention this conversation or me to even your closest friends. Thank you for your patience and your attention."

He bowed slightly to Louise and Gabriel. "Thank you for your assistance. I'll see myself out."

## 17

## THE HANDLER

"Oui?" A woman's voice.

Saskia took a deep breath. *This is it!* Either ring off or say something!

Five days of restless sleep. Five days of jumping at shadows, looking over her shoulder to see if someone was following her, afraid that every phone call might announce that something bad had happened to Mme Clarie, Rufus or Isabelle. Two days of racing home after work afraid she would find it a crime scene – work that was becoming increasingly non-sensical because no one was interested in what she was doing, and she had not yet said 'yes' to Ayat Benkirane.

Most of all, five days of wondering whether she should or would be capable of helping law enforcement authorities.

"Er – Simon said to call this number."

"Bien. Je te trouverai." (I'll find you.)

The burner phone died.

Saskia stared at the screen. *That's it?*

She groaned out loud, then yelped when her own phone buzzed.

"Get a grip, girl!" she hissed as she retrieved her phone from her back pocket.

"Hey, Saskia, we're going to ride to Saint-Didier-au-Mont-d'Or. Do you want to come?"

That might settle her nerves. "When?"

"We're getting ready now. We can pick you up and throw your bike in with ours. Half-an-hour?"

"I'll be ready."

Jean-Paul, Charlotte and Pierre were fun to ride with. Unlike some other bike club members, they were not much interested in challenging mountain biking trails. Instead, they liked well-paved routes that led them through villages where they could explore markets, cafés and historic sites.

The four friends climbed up Lyon's northern hills, stopping often to enjoy the early autumn colours spreading over the countryside. The sun shone and a small breeze blew, carrying with it a slight chill from the nearby Alps. People hiking through the countryside or sitting in parks or the outdoor spaces of cafés kept their coats zipped up. Saskia took in her surroundings as if seeing them for the first time, especially when the group decided to lunch and explore Saint-Cyr-au-Mont-d'Or with its Roman ruins, neo-Gothic style church and castle. Her stomach roiled when she learned that Saint-Cyr-au-Mont-d'Or housed a branch of the École Nationale Supérieure de la Police, where chiefs of police received further training. *What am I doing, getting involved in that sort of stuff?* She glanced around and then over her shoulder. No criminals lurking. Just people going about their day. Some were smiling and chatting, others intent on tasks.

Inwardly, she moaned. *I'm so far from being a vigilante it's laughable.* Many people treated her as if she was a child. So what if she knew her way around digital domains? And could she really perform work that might undermine the organisation that paid her salary?

"Ma chérie, you are quiet today," Charlotte said, placing a hand on Saskia's. "Usually you ride as if you have wings. Today, your face is closed and your head is bowed."

Saskia scrunched up her nose, pushed hair back off her forehead and retied her ponytail. "I've been offered a new job, and I don't know if I want it."

Telling her three friends about the training position she'd been offered felt like a lie, because, if she accepted it, she was de facto accepting a job with Simon.

"Oof!" Jean-Paul said, "Danny Prendergast at the cycle club will not be happy if you are gone from Lyon a lot. Who will he rely on to give free bike-trick lessons for his young patrons?"

Saskia shook her head impatiently. "If I stew about my job much longer, I may apply to him for a new job. Come on, let's go."

At the finish of the day's bike riding, Saskia declined an invitation to join the three for an evening meal and headed home. As she climbed the steps to her apartment, she met Isabelle making her way down, looking fresh and dressed as gorgeously as ever.

"You today a hard day having?" she asked, her dark eyes flicking up and down to take in Saskia's grimy appearance. "Is good day?"

"Yes. Good ride. Are you going out to a theatre? You're all dressed up."

"Non." Isabelle regarded Saskia for a second, then seemed to come to a decision, her eyebrows rising, right hand held out, palm up in invitation. "You not have eaten? Maybe we dinner together, no? I think restaurant two maybe near? Maybe we stay not long because you are tired?"

Saskia opened her mouth to say no, but ... *oh, why not?* The restaurant served good pasta, and the promise of a quick meal was attractive.

"Yes. Alright. In maybe half an hour so I can shower and tidy up?"

"I will patient wait. Knock on door mine when ready you are."

The waiter had barely placed their pasta dishes before them and glasses of wine each when Isabelle said, "So, you are considering Simon's proposal to work with us?"

Saskia practically dropped the fork she had just stabbed into her plate of ravioli. Isabelle had spoken in perfect French without a trace of accent. She stared at the woman, her jaw slack with shock.

Isabelle calmly twirled spaghetti onto her fork. "I apologise that I have practised subterfuge with you these past few weeks, but it will be necessary for me to continue to do so except when I judge we are very certain we cannot be observed or overheard."

Again, perfect French.

"Have you decided to work with us, or are you still considering and want to ask me questions? Either way, now that I have revealed myself, know that I will continue to be around to help keep you safe till we judge the matter you have inadvertently become embroiled in is resolved. And I would appreciate it if you will help me to continue practising my deceit." Then, with a smile glimmering in her eyes, Isabelle said, "I hope you don't mind me pointing out that with your mouth open in that way, you look silly."

Saskia snapped her jaw shut, then forked ravioli into her mouth to give it something to do while she continued to stare at the beautiful woman who was suddenly someone else.

"Alright. Alright. Alright," she said eventually, trying to gather her scattered thoughts. "Umm – er – this is – umm – I think I badly need some answers," she said.

"Of course. I'll do my best to answer them. I will revert to speaking Spanish. French is my preferred language, but there is a gentleman – please do not turn to look over your shoulder! There is a gentleman at a table near the door who is showing some interest in us. I do not know whether he is a casual observer of attractive young women or someone with a more nefarious interest. Nevertheless, it would be better if I continue in my cover role as a Spanish speaker. If he is a good observer, he will be able to tell from looking at my lips and movements which language I speak. Your Spanish is good enough to understand me, but you may respond in French if that language is more comfortable for you to communicate in."

Saskia badly wanted to turn around and look at the man Isabelle so casually referred to. She hunched her shoulders. It was like someone had a hand close to the back of her neck.

"Er – umm – who is Hash CaseIt Ten?"

"Hmm. An interesting place to start your interrogation. A friend of Simon's to whom he mentioned FSB as an institution of interest. Hash CaseIt Ten told Simon about your intervention in the ransomware attack. He then began to investigate you."

"How did Hash CaseIt Ten know it was me? I used my handle – oh! Wait! I gave them my details for the invoice."

"Just so," Isabelle smiled.

Saskia groaned. "You see! I'm not up for undercover work! Why are you people even considering it?"

Isabelle's smile stretched a little wider. "You have other questions?"

"What? Er – um – yes. How do the police – Simon – know about my work – my new job at FSB?"

"I told Simon. You discussed it with Hans, Melanie and me when we dined a couple of weeks ago."

"So – so everything I said to Hans and Melanie you've passed on to Simon?"

"Yes. Also, what you may have discussed in Dutch and didn't fully translate for me. I don't speak that language, but I do speak German, and the two languages are similar enough that I could understand the substance of your discussion. I have also passed on other details about you that I've gleaned since moving into my apartment."

"Really! This is too much!" She stuffed more ravioli into her mouth, followed by a swig of wine. *Careful with the wine! You're too small for an adult size glass. Shit on that! What's that got to do with anything!* "Are you part of this project Simon's talking about?"

"Indeed. That and the extra surveillance on Madame Claire's house."

"How did you even get that apartment?"

"Ah. In that case, it was truly fortune who smiled. We worked out there was a second apartment in Madame Claire's house and that the resident nephew is away for some months. I befriended Madame Claire at the museum and let her know I was looking for somewhere to live in Lyon for a few months."

"So, you don't know anything about Roman civilisation? It's all an act?"

Isabelle grinned. "I have done a crash course in Roman civilisation and know quite a lot as an interested amateur."

"What if she hadn't offered the apartment?"

"We would have had to devise perhaps a more complicated plan to stay close to you."

"Look! Is the best thing to do – to keep Madame Claire safe and me out of this ridiculous situation – for me to just leave FSB? Cut my ties. Maybe even leave Lyon. Tell them this new job is not really what I want to do?"

"That is, of course, your choice."

"You agree, don't you? That there's no way I can help you."

"On the contrary, I think you would be very good at helping us. You have the skills we need to get the information we require."

"How would that work?" *No! No! Don't even contemplate this. What are you asking?*

"We will become very good friends, you and I, and spend more time together. You will come to the shop in the traboule where I work. You will pass on information to me. We will teach you how to stay safe and drive a car."

"S-stay safe! Drive a car?" Saskia realised her voice was squeaking again.

"Si. Drive a car. Sometimes we might need to travel together. It is a good idea to learn to drive a car."

"What's wrong with just meeting in our apartments? And, anyway, I can't reach the pedals in a car."

"Not a problem. Extensions to pedals are all we need, and a booster seat. As for meeting in the apartment, there may be listening devices."

"Simon said no one's managed to get into the apartment."

"There are other ways of listening."

Saskia shook her head. She wanted to groan but put another ravioli into her mouth instead and thought about her situation.

"You will notice," Isabelle leaned forward, "that I have seated us at a corner table where I have a good view of the room. Perhaps you have also noticed that when I speak, I usually obstruct the movement of my lips with the rise of my hand, or with a lift of my wine glass, or some such. Should someone come within hearing, I will immediately switch to a mundane topic."

"I knew there was something odd about your way of speaking

French. A Spanish speaker would not make the sort of mistakes you make. The pattern's wrong," Saskia muttered.

Isabelle regarded her intently for a couple of very long minutes. Saskia felt colour creeping up her neck and blossoming over her cheeks. "Sorry," she murmured. "That was rude."

"On the contrary." Isabelle sat back in her chair. "That is astute and excellent. I will certainly work on that very significant flaw. Thank you for pointing it out." She lifted her wine glass in a toast. "You are good. You are very good and will be a very great asset to this investigation."

# 18

## TRABOULES

Isabelle worked as a sales assistant in a gift shop located inside one of the traboules open to the public. A sign with the shop's name and hours of operation hung near the elaborately carved and open wooden doors at both ends of the traboule.

Saskia entered the darkened corridor, thinking that without the inviting sign, many people would not bother to go into the uninviting, arched and somewhat musty-smelling space. Yellow light shone from sconces embedded in the white-washed walls, but did not dispel the gloominess. Fifteen metres in, however, the corridor curved and opened to a sunny, circular courtyard. Saskia stopped to look around. Stone stairs hugged a wall to a balcony that gave access to several apartments. A long table flanked by benches stood in the centre of the courtyard, and beyond the table was an imposing double door painted a deep red, made beautiful by the highly polished and intricately worked brass bracing on hinges and door handles. Next to the door, water from a wall fountain spouted into a stone basin surrounded by large pots of colourful flowers. The traboule continued through another corridor a few metres from the double door.

Saskia barely had time to take in the sight when Isabelle appeared from under the stairs, her face bright with a smile. "It is very pretty, non?" she said, speaking French.

"It is."

"But you have been here before?"

"No. I know of the shop but haven't been into this traboule."

"It is a good little shop. Come."

Isabelle led the way back under the stairs, where stands holding gift cards flanked open glass doors. The shop was brightly lit, with shelves full of many types of dolls and ornaments, cabinets with jewellery displays, and clothes racks.

Isabelle indicated the shop's offerings with a wave of a hand. "We have almost everything here a tourist might want, from the cheap to, as the English would say, 'the eye-wateringly expensive'." She touched a patchwork jacket displayed on a mannequin. "This is made of the finest silk, and if you are a millionaire, you can afford it," she said.

Saskia looked for cameras in the corners of the ceiling. "How did you know I had come?"

Isabelle glanced down at her, amusement on her lips and in her eyes. "You are straight to business."

"I am troubled."

Isabelle tipped her head inquiringly, then nodded. "Let me show you." She walked to the far end of the shop to a large, old-looking desk, which was bare except for a large monitor, a laptop, a card reader and a book on English grammar. "From here, I can see all that goes on in this traboule," she said, sitting on one of the two office chairs behind the desk. She patted the seat of the second chair. "Please sit with me." The monitor showed four images: the two entrances to the traboule, and two views of the courtyard. With a touch on the laptop keyboard, the courtyard images changed to reveal views of the streets beyond the traboule entrances. With another touch of the keyboard, the view changed to show the courtyard, stairs and walkway. "When there is movement in any of these areas, except the streets, my watch vibrates, and the monitor shows me what causes the movement." She smiled and winked. "It is clever, yes? That is how I knew you were here."

Saskia cast her eyes around the room. "This isn't just a shop, is it?"

## THE BANK

"Well, yes, it is a shop, but it is also a secure place that we can use for discussions and work with people like yourself. No one can hear or see us unless they walk into the courtyard. Those who live in the three apartments overlooking this courtyard are, shall I say, our people. This includes my uncle." She stood. "But, before we work, I will make us a coffee or a tea, or perhaps you prefer another drink? And I have some very delicious, sweet things."

"Tea. Thank you."

Isabelle disappeared through a narrow doorway behind the desk and reappeared some minutes later with a tray holding a teapot, two cups and saucers and a plate of small cakes. She set the tray on the desk, pushing back the laptop to make room. "It has been a slow morning," she said. "Only two customers. Milk? Sugar?"

"A little milk."

Isabelle handed a filled cup on its saucer to Saskia. "What troubles you?"

"I am afraid for Madame Claire and Rufus. I don't trust they are safe if I – and you – live in the house. Would it be better if I moved away to live somewhere else?"

Isabelle leaned back in her chair, cradling a saucer in the palm of her left hand and lifting the cup to her lips. She took a cautious sip, and nodded. "Yes. This issue has also troubled me." She pursed her lips, eyes thoughtful. She took another sip of tea. "You may be correct. Let us discuss this with Simon now."

"What? Now?"

"Indeed." Isabelle set the cup and saucer back on the tray. "He will be ready to speak with us. But first, let us set up our devices. You have your laptop in your backpack?"

"Yes."

Isabelle pulled out a slim drawer. "Your laptop will fit in this drawer. Should a customer arrive, you will close the laptop and slide the drawer back, so your device is invisible. While you do that, I will choose entertainment to amuse us." She leaned towards the laptop on the desk. "Let me see. I have uploaded a comedy opera. I think you will like it." Her fingers tapped until an image of a large, white-pillared house surrounded by a formal garden replaced the traboule and street images. "I will fast-forward this movie – hmmm – maybe ten minutes in. The story is of a wealthy couple who have been married for seven years and have decided to divorce. They are preparing to celebrate their divorce with many friends. It is a quirky but enjoyable movie. One day, you should watch all of it."

The scene fast-forwarded through views of luscious rooms, flower arrangements, scurrying kitchen hands, a marquee being set up in the garden and people who appeared to be singing to one another. "That's far enough, I think." Click, click. The scene on the monitor reverted to images of the traboule and courtyard. "Bon. Your laptop is snug in the drawer? Push the drawer in for now. Come closer so Simon can see both of us. Should anyone come into the traboule, the movie will immediately play. Our conversation with Simon will disappear and we will become just two friends enjoying tea and sweets and watching a movie together." She quirked an eyebrow at Saskia. "Yes?"

"I understand."

"Don't let your tea get cold. And please enjoy the sweets."

Simon's face appeared on the screen.

"Bonjour, Saskia. Thank you for continuing to consider working with us."

"Er – bonjour."

"Simon," Isabelle said. "Both Saskia and I are concerned for the safety of Madame Claire. The safeguards we have in place may not be enough."

"Saskia, tell me why you are concerned."

"Umm – mostly it's the behaviour of Rufus. He's usually a calm and friendly dog. Lately, he seems to have become very protective of the property. Whenever someone walks past the back fence, he growls and barks at them."

"Can you see who walks past?"

"No. The fence is high. Even from my bedroom, I can't see who is passing by."

"Is it always the same time of day?"

"I can't answer that since I am – " Saskia's words stumbled to a stop as the screen blanked. She glanced at the monitor. It briefly showed a man and a woman in the traboule corridor, then began to show the movie Isabelle had prepared earlier. Isabelle picked up her teacup and a cake and attended to the movie, her face alight with interest. Saskia sipped tea, doing her best not to look flustered by the sudden change. "I love this part," Isabelle said in Spanish with a giggle. "Jolene doesn't like agapanthus, and every vase has them."

*What are agapanthus?* Saskia thought, then realised it must be the large-headed purple and white flowers the two women on the screen were gesticulating and singing about.

The man and woman caught on the surveillance camera walked into the shop, pausing at the entrance to look around.

Isabelle paused the movie and pushed back her chair.

"Bonjour, Madam, Monsieur. Bienvenue dans notre boutique. Y a-t-il quelque chose que je peux vous aider ou aimeriez-vous simplement regarder autour de vous. Vous êtes invités à le faire."

*Wow!* Saskia thought. Isabelle's speech had reverted to being heavily accented, though it had lost many elaborate, awkward mistakes.

"Do you speak English?" the woman asked.

"A leetle bit," Isabelle replied brightly, approaching the couple. "You look for something, yes?"

"We want to get something for our grandchild. Something very French. She's only five."

"I have just things like so for you. I show you." Isabelle led the way to a shelf of dolls and toys. From the corner of her eye, Saskia saw the monitor screen flash a view of a man striding down the traboule corridor before reverting to the frozen view of the two women in dramatic poses at a vase of large flowers.

A minute later, the man appeared at the shop doorway. His gaze fell on Saskia, still seated behind the desk with teacup and cake in hand, and then his gaze swept around the shop. Isabelle diverted her attention briefly from the couple to greet him and tell him she would attend to him soon.

The man stepped to the desk. "I want to buy something cheap," he said in heavily accented French. *Middle Eastern,* Saskia thought. He was in his thirties, dressed casually in a polo shirt and jeans, loafers on his feet, thick black hair neatly combed to the side, dark eyes and swarthy skin tone.

"Er – I'm sorry, Monsieur. I'm just a visitor to the store. My friend can help you." Saskia indicated Isabelle. "She's just helping someone else. I'm sorry."

"I look around," he said, looking at the frozen laptop screen. "What that?" he asked, chin indicating the monitor.

"Um – you mean the picture? It – we're watching a movie."

The man gave a single nod and began to prowl the shop, eyes darting frequently up to the ceiling. He picked up a snow globe and brought it back to the desk. "I get this."

Saskia was about to explain again that she could not help him when Isabelle glided up and asked pleasantly if she could assist. He swept his eyes over her lovely form. "You beautiful lady."

"Merci, Monsieur," she smiled. "You buy this for someone? I gift wrap for you, yes?"

"My daughter," he said. "Gift wrap yourself, too. I take you both. How much you cost?"

Isabelle laughed, bending to a roll of wrapping paper. "You funny, Monsieur. This pretty snowball. Your daughter, she will love."

The couple came to the desk, the woman holding a puppet. "We'll take this one," she said.

Isabelle deftly wrapped both gifts, congratulating the purchasers on their selections and used the laptop and card reader for payment. The man with the snow globe looked at the parcel Isabelle handed him and stuffed it in his pocket as he walked out, head moving this way and that as if searching for something.

"An unpleasant man," remarked the woman, carefully placing her wrapped gift in a shopping bag. "Are you safe in here by yourself?"

Isabelle grinned. "He is only talk, Madame. Merci, your concern. More people nice like you come here."

"Well," Saskia said when the shop was again empty of customers.

"I confess to not feeling safe with him. He made me feel very uncomfortable."

Isabelle merely looked amused. She tapped keys on the laptop, and Simon reappeared. "What do you think, Simon? Was our friend happy with his purchase?"

Simon shook his head, seeming to share Isabelle's amusement. "I think he was unhappy about paying the money."

"Did you see all that?" Saskia asked.

"Yes."

Isabelle turned to Saskia, mischief dancing in her eyes. She put a finger to her lips. "We must not tell our secrets here. Simon will hear all. This shop is always monitored." Then to Simon. "Have you seen him before?"

"He is a person of interest. It's good you've seen him, Saskia. If you come across him again, do your best to steer clear of him." Saskia nodded slowly. "Now before dealing with other matters." Simon's face grew a little larger on the monitor as he leaned forward. "Back to the issue with Madame Claire. We've been looking into her background. She lived in Scotland till her husband died. While there, she gained a degree in social work. Then she worked in social security. She worked in an equivalent position in Lyon before retiring. Reports are that she was an exemplary employee and not afraid to front up to management if she thought they were not caring for clients appropriately. I believe she is the type of person I could explain our position to and ask what she would like us to do."

"Oooh!" Isabelle said, her tone teasing. "You mean you will consult your victim and corner them to do as you wish with your charm."

Simon smiled, but his attention was on Saskia. "What do you think, Saskia? You know her best. Do you think that's a good idea?"

"I respect Madame Claire."

"He will have a clandestine chat with her," Isabelle said. "He is good at that."

"Do you agree, Saskia?" Simon asked again.

"I suppose I do. I'm at sea with all of this."

"This is the next item I wish to discuss with you. Isabelle has a smartwatch and a phone to replace yours. They have extra applications that will enable you to contact us. Isabelle will show you how they operate. She will also add an application to your laptop. In addition, it will be necessary for you to undergo basic safety training with us. Ask Monsieur Benkirane if you can have two weeks leave before starting your new position with the bank. Make it known you are going on a road trip with Isabelle. The sooner, the better."

# 19

## VIENNA

Saskia paused at the exit of the baggage collection area and scanned the crowd until she saw a man in a black suit and shiny shoes holding up a sign with her name on it. His gaze passed over her and continued to scrutinise the crowd.

"You're looking for me," she said, standing before him.

He glanced down at her, seeming not to understand her. He stepped back as if to let her pass, and continued to scan. She reached into her trousers pocket and held up her ID card. He jerked back, his expression changing rapidly from the beginning of annoyance to confusion to embarrassment. "Wie bitte!" he blurted, lowering the sign. "Wilkommen."

"Danke," she smiled.

He lifted her wheeled suitcase. "Please follow me. My name is Alex. My car is not far. I will take you to your hotel." His German was heavily accented. Saskia guessed he might be from Slovakia. She expected to meet many more people from Eastern Europe during her week-long stay in Vienna, which had earned a reputation as a gateway to Eastern Europe. It was one of the main reasons FSB had decided to locate a branch in Vienna.

"Your first time in Vienna?" Alex asked as he opened the back door of a shiny, black Mercedes. He didn't wait for her answer but reached for her backpack. "Shall I take your rucksack?"

"No. Thank you." Saskia slipped the straps off her shoulders as she climbed into the car, settling the heavy pack containing two laptops at her feet.

"It is beautiful city," Alex said as he manoeuvred the car out of the airport.

Saskia nodded. She'd attended and presented at a cybersecurity and finance conference in Vienna two years ago and explored parts of it then. The city was culturally rich with museums and concert halls; its famous buildings were a feast for the eyes, as were the riverside parks, and it vibrated with its endeavours to internationalise the commercial sector. Most of all, Saskia loved Vienna's cafés and restaurants. She reflected that it would be easy to become obese in Vienna.

Alex pointed out landmarks and imparted history with a sprinkling of gossip, as if he were her personal tourist guide. Maybe he was. The last time she'd been in Vienna, she'd negotiated the public transport system and relied on information downloaded on her phone to find her way around. She'd also stayed in a relatively cheap hotel and loved its cosy atmosphere. Not so this time. the FSB travel agent who had made her travel and accommodation arrangements had told Saskia that M. Benkirane's instructions were to provide her with the very best. Saskia found it unusual to be treated to business class seats on the plane and a chauffeur-driven limousine. She wondered why he seemed so focused on her wellbeing.

Her hotel room was luxurious, with an enormous bed strewn with too many cushions and pillows, a sumptuous bathroom and a floor-to-ceiling window that provided a view of Belvedere Palace and the trees – their leaves showing a blush of autumn gold – lining avenues and adorning parklands.

She thanked the concierge for bringing her to the room and showing her its amenities, then stood for some time staring at the view. Eventually, she began a slow wander around the room, phone in hand as if she were texting. In fact, she had opened the 'bug finder' app on her phone, designed to locate hidden cameras and listening devices. She found three in the main room and two in the bathroom.

With an inward and disgruntled sigh, she sat on the bed. Clearly, there was no privacy in this room.

It was late afternoon. She lay back on the bed and called her parents for an extended gossip session. Duty done, she extracted the FSB-issued laptop and relocated to the floor. She sat in front of the picture window and spent an hour reviewing notes for the workshops she would facilitate during the coming week.

As the sun set, she packed the FSB laptop into the hotel's safe, shrugged on a warm coat and slipped the backpack holding her personal laptop over her shoulders. She descended in the lift to the hotel's foyer, then out to the street. She wandered the streets till she found a restaurant that attracted her. From a corner seat, she ordered a meal and a beer, then opened her laptop. She reported into Isabelle over a secure line before amusing herself with more standard pursuits on her laptop. Protocol now demanded that, regardless of her location, at least once every twenty-four hours she needed to contact Isabelle. If all was well, she would use the phrase, 'all is good here' in English and in exactly that way. Forget the phrase or say it differently, and Simon's team – "there'll always be someone nearby," he had assured her – would be there to check on her safety.

Learning this protocol, as well as basic self-defence, handling guns and knives, awareness of surroundings and training in the use of security devices, had been the substance of the two-week training session Simon had organised for her.

The training did not end with the fortnight's intensive session. Whenever Saskia visited the shop, supposedly to watch a movie with her friend, she was 'subjected' (as she grumbled) to more training, provided in the well-equipped gym behind a hidden door in the small kitchen area annexed to the shop. Monsieur Silva de Luz, whom Isabelle called uncle, was her instructor in those sessions. Whenever she walked with Isabelle, she was rarely allowed to relax. While seemingly conversing about nothing in particular, Isabelle would say things such as, "Why do you think that person is standing in the doorway?"

"Have you seen the person on the other side of the street who seems to be keeping pace with us?" "What is causing that person's jacket to bulge?" "Are there places here to run to or hide?" and "Where are you sitting in the restaurant?"

After dinner and back in her hotel room, Saskia did her best to ignore the cameras. She was glad they pointed away from the toilet and that she was not body shy as she showered and pulled on pyjamas. Once in bed, she read a novel on her phone for an hour before turning off the light to sleep.

Next morning, she packed FSB and private laptops into her backpack, called a taxi to a café she had fallen in love with the last time she'd been in Vienna, and had breakfast while she checked her private emails and scanned the chat groups and news channels she stayed up to date with.

At eight-thirty, she presented herself to the security guard at the FSB branch to meet with a member of the IT team to set up the workshop room. Saskia already had access to the bank's integrated network. She needed access to the Vienna branch's internal network, which the IT technician freely gave her. She thanked him for helping her and assured him she could manage if any technology issues arose. Privately, she wondered if, or hoped, he would be less accommodating after attending her cybersecurity and risk management workshop.

Saskia turned her attention to the keyboard, accessed the internal network of the Vienna branch and deposited a code packet that would disappear in 30 minutes. In that time, the cyber team working with her on the case would take what they wanted from the branch's computer system.

## 20

## BAD NEWS

Saskia stepped out of the uber ride into the chill air of Lyon winter. The porch light flickered on as she climbed the steps to the front door. Rufus greeted her with a happy wag of his tail and the usual thrust of his head at her midriff as she stepped through the doorway.

She placed her palm print on the device just inside the door. It blinked green in recognition, and she bent to give Rufus the fuss he demanded. He was a calmer dog nowadays, though more alert. Madame Claire had been adamant that she wanted Saskia and Isabelle to remain as her lodgers. In return, she had the insight to request training for Rufus and extra security instalments around the house.

Saskia dumped her suitcase on the floor of her bedroom, her backpack next to it, and slumped on to her bed, too exhausted to do more than peel off her coat, toe off her shoes and pull a cover over herself before falling asleep.

"It's a bad idea to go to bed fully clothed," she grumbled as sleep slowly lost its grip on her in the morning. Trousers were fine when she was moving around, but tight around her waist and buttocks when asleep. And her shirt had twisted uncomfortably around her shoulders.

She rolled out of bed, padded to the bathroom, shed her clothes and showered, visualising washing away the grime of a fifth week of workshops over the past three months, which included subtle digging for data from participants and late-night probes into computer systems. It was 'grime' because she was still not entirely comfortable with her role as a spy, even though, she reflected grudgingly as she worked shampoo through her hair, she enjoyed the task of sifting and ordering her findings.

The conclusions, however, were increasingly disturbing, especially when she presented them to the team, who married them to their data.

Saskia heard her phone ring as she stepped out of the shower. She let it ring out, not rushing to dry herself. The phone rang twice more, each time ringing out. On the fourth attempt, she abandoned combing out her long, tight curls and retrieved her phone from the back pocket of her discarded trousers.

It was Hans. And the phone battery was almost dead.

"Hoi, Hans. Is er iets mis? I was having a shower."

"Saskia, has Melanie contacted you?"

"Melanie? No. Just let me put you on speaker and check messages." As she spoke and fiddled with her phone, Saskia walked to the kitchen bench where she kept a phone charger cable. She plugged it in. "No. Nothing from Melanie. Is something wrong?"

"I haven't heard from her for a week, and she hasn't turned up to her workplace."

Saskia frowned. In her last few conversations with Hans, he had indicated that all was not well in his relationship with Melanie. Saskia felt sad about that.

"Saskia, something is up with her. She's stopped studying. She said she wanted to take a holiday from her studies. I told you before – I think she's ill, but she says she is not, and that she had a problem she needed to solve. She promised to tell me what that was, but she wasn't ready to do it yet." There was an edge of panic in Hans's voice. "I'm really worried about her."

"That's – that's – I am sorry to hear that. But why would you think she'd contact me?"

"Just lately, she asks about you a lot. She wants to know everything about you and about conversations I have with you. I think she is jealous. I told her that you and I are friends, but I don't think she believes me. We had a fight. She said that I keep secrets about you from her. She's not returning my calls. I don't think she looks well, Saskia." His voice caught. "I love her, Saskia. I'm scared for her. It's like she's disappeared."

"Have you called the police? Do they know about this?"

"Yes. Yes. I've talked to them. They've put her on a missing person's list, but I don't think they're taking it seriously. I've also been trying to contact her family, but she didn't ever tell me much about them, and the police say they can't trace the family if I can't give them more information."

"What about her place of work or the school? Did she give them information about her family?"

"No." Hans's voice hitched again. "I'm really scared for her."

"Oh, Hans! That's terrible. I don't – don't know what I can do."

"Just if she contacts you. Let me know. Okay? Let me know straight away."

"Of course."

She clicked off the call and stood staring at the phone in her hand, her brow furrowed.

A knock came at the door.

Saskia set the phone down on the bench and hurried into her bedroom, calling, "Un moment!" She wrapped a dressing gown around herself and hurried back to the door, flicking the deadlock to open it.

Isabelle stood in the hallway, looking as groomed, beautiful and fresh as ever. "Bonjour, Saskia. Can I invite you to lunch with me?"

"Lunch? What's the time?"

"It is past mid-day. You have only just woken?" Isabelle's mischievous smile took in Saskia's dishevelled appearance.

"I am attempting to have a shower – or at least finish dressing. Come in. Yes, I'll have lunch with you. Why aren't you at work?"

"Mon dieu! You are grumpy. My uncle has given me the day free, and I heard you moving about in your room, so I thought – "

"I'll just get dressed." *Maybe Simon and Isabelle can help with finding Melanie. Would it be alright to ask? Why not?*

Ten minutes later, Saskia – damp hair stuffed into a beanie – and Isabelle strolled down the street, rugged up against a biting wind, towards Café Deux, which Saskia now knew was one of the places used by Simon and Isabelle's people for debriefs.

Monsieur Baron, the proprietor, hustled the women inside out of the cold. Grabbing a cushion, he led them to their preferred corner seat and set the cushion on a chair for Saskia. "Today, I have a special risotto," he said, taking their coats. "Shrimp and mandarin. A special Sicilian dish. Perhaps a glass of red wine to warm you up?"

"Maravilloso, Georges," Isabelle said. As always, when in the café, she reverted to Spanish.

"I'll have the risotto, Monsieur. But please, coffee instead of wine for me."

M. Baron looked unhappy. "Coffee with risotto?"

"Umm. Well. Coffee first and – er – perhaps with your lovely warm bread rolls? Then I'll have the risotto."

Their host's face brightened. "Bon! That I can do. And you will also have a fresh salad." He hurried away.

Leaning slightly across the table, Isabelle said, "Tell me about the incident with the taxi that caused you to miss your flight last night."

As protocol demanded, Saskia had sent Isabelle a message to tell her she was involved in an incident and would likely need to catch a later flight to Lyon. "The taxi was on a dual-lane highway. A child ran across the road. My taxi braked to avoid her. The car in the lane next to the taxi did also. Both cars spun and swiped each other. The driver's side door of my taxi was torn off, and the taxi driver sustained injuries to his shoulder and arm. No one else was hurt. By the time the police had sorted out the mess and I managed to get another taxi to the airport, I'd missed my flight. I only just managed to get another, later one."

"You are well?"

Saskia nodded. She reached behind her head and threaded her hair through a band to create a ponytail. "To tell the truth, the crash was all over before I had time to panic. I was in the back seat and couldn't see out the front of the car."

Saskia had come to admire Isabelle. The woman's professionalism was awe-inspiring. To most people, she was the somewhat frivolous young woman from Spain who worked in a shop and volunteered at the Lugdunum museum. When in a safe zone, she became a professional handler focused on Saskia's safety.

"Do you think there was anything suspicious about the accident?" Isabelle asked.

"I doubt it. The child and father were both very distraught," Saskia said.

Isabelle nodded. "Nevertheless, I will ask Simon to look into the incident."

M. Baron arrived with coffee, a basket of small warm rolls and butter for Saskia, and a glass of wine for Isabelle.

Saskia took a grateful sip of coffee. "I think it would be better if I didn't need a caffeine hit first thing each day."

"You are tired."

"I must admit, I'll be glad to have a break for a couple of weeks."

Isabelle leaned forward, "We have a problem, Saskia."

"I assume you are not referring to my caffeine problem?"

Isabelle allowed herself a small smile. "No." She became serious again. "Our problem is Melanie."

"Melanie! You mean Hans's fiancée?"

Isabelle nodded.

"Did you hear me talking to Hans? I was talking to him just before you knocked?"

"No. I did not hear that. What did he call about?"

Saskia related the substance of the call.

"Mmm. Poor Hans. You could not know, but she came looking for you the day before yesterday. Madame Claire answered the door to her and told her you were away for a few days."

"But Melanie has my phone number. Why didn't she call me?" Saskia reached into her back pocket for her phone. "I'll call her now."

Isabelle extended a restraining hand. "Hear me out. Melanie said she would look you up again when you returned. But Saskia, I regret to tell you that Melanie is in deep trouble. We have been looking into her background. Does Hans know she is an addict?"

Saskia's set down her coffee mug with a thump. That Isabelle had looked into Melanie's background did not surprise her. It seemed that everyone she came into contact with had their backgrounds checked. "He's never mentioned it to me."

"I suspect he doesn't know. Let me briefly tell you her history. She entered rehab in Limburg two years ago, then moved to Rotterdam, cutting ties with family and friends. Six weeks ago, she was admitted to a hospital in Rotterdam with an overdose. Since then, she has been back to using again."

Saskia sank her face into her hands. "Oooh! That's awful for Hans and for her."

"Yes. But the problem is even worse, Saskia. Her supplier is a person of interest to us. We believe that her presence here in Lyon is no accident. As you know by the constant surveillance in hotel rooms you stay in for your workshops, suspicion continues to follow you. Though, I must say that your behaviour has been so innocent to all observers that they must be truly beginning to wonder whether you deserve suspicion." Isabelle sat back in her chair. "Please continue drinking your coffee before it gets cold. I will butter you a bread roll or Georges will be unhappy."

Saskia sipped coffee and munched bread, though her enthusiasm for both was gone. "What should I do?"

"Of course, continue your excellent work. When she contacts you, do your best to uncover her real reason for her interest in meeting with you."

M. Baron arrived with two plates of risotto and a tossed green salad. He set them down without a word and hurried away to greet a group who entered the café, seating them at the table furthest away from Saskia and Isabelle.

Isabelle glanced at the newcomers, then concentrated on Saskia again. "Did you have plans for today?"

Saskia rubbed her forehead. Anxiety made her diaphragm feel tight. "I think I'll go to the Lyon Bike Centre and work out on my bike for a while. I need the exercise."

"Do you mind if I accompany you?"

## 21

## LYON BIKE CENTRE

"Hey! I see you've brought your BMX. Tell us you've got time to help us this afternoon," Danny Prendergast said as Saskia wheeled her bike into the vast indoor space of the Lyon Bike Centre. One end of the space featured an elaborate skate park; the other end was flat, with ridges on the sides. All areas were busy with children and adults practising their skills.

"Only if you also give me pointers," Saskia said.

"But of course! And who have you brought with you?" Danny's eyes widened as he turned his attention to Isabelle.

"Umm – this is Isabelle. She's my housemate, and she was – er – at a loose end, and wanted to come along."

"You are very welcome. Are you also a world-class cyclist like Saskia?"

Isabelle pulled a face. "Non! Non! I no ride in the bike. I am better in position of sitting or in dancing."

Saskia cleared her throat to stop a burst of laughter. She had seen Isabelle in action in the gymnasium and knew her to be a human weapon. It would not surprise her if Isabelle rode with the skill of an expert. Hastily, she said, "Umm – Isabelle is from Spain. Her – er – French is improving."

"It's wonderful!" Danny said, glancing at Isabelle's stilettos. "I can't boast to speak French like a native yet, and I've been here for a decade."

"I trying best," Isabelle said. She indicated the stands overlooking the practice area where spectators sat. "I think I sit there, sí?"

"Sure. If you want to get a good view of the whole area, sit up there. The best spot is where that group of parents are."

"Bon. I do that," Isabelle said and left them.

"Nice," Danny said in English, watching Isabelle negotiate her way up to a seat.

"I never understand why people don't ogle me like that," sighed Saskia with mock confusion, also speaking English, which she knew Danny was more comfortable conversing in.

He chuckled. "You get enough ogling when you start on the park. Go on. Put on your gear and do your stuff before I set the kids loose on you."

It had been a while since Saskia had had time to enjoy the skate park. Within minutes, she forgot Isabelle, Melanie and the strain of working undercover. Barely an hour into her time in the park, she'd naturally morphed into working with others practising their skills, sometimes tutoring, sometimes perfecting her own style. A few hours later, she stopped to quench her thirst, glanced up at the stands and practically dropped her water bottle when she saw Melanie sitting beside Isabelle.

She inserted the wheel of her bike into a stand and vaulted up the steps to the women. "Melanie! What a surprise! What are you doing here? When did you arrive?"

Melanie bent down to hug Saskia. "Your landlady said you would be here, so I caught a taxi. I've been here for about an hour. We were watching you. Oh my God! How don't you kill yourself doing all those things on your bike?"

"How lovely to see you! Hans rang me this morning asking after you."

Melanie flinched. "How did Hans know I was here?"

"He didn't. He's been looking for you. He's very worried about you."

"I guess I should contact him. I haven't because – because I haven't been able to get up the courage to tell him we can't marry." Tears gathered in Melanie's eyes. She blinked rapidly to clear them. She looked thinner. And twitchy.

"We have been watching you," Isabelle said in Spanish. "We did not want to disturb you. We enjoyed exclaiming and cringing at what you do but I am afraid I am unable to talk with your friend. I am sorry for my deficiency."

"What? Oh! Melanie, Isabelle just said she's sorry she doesn't speak Dutch."

"No. It's alright. I was – you know – enjoying being here. I recognised her sitting in the stands when I came and sort of forced myself on her."

"Should we move from here?" Isabelle asked. "Perhaps you could take a break from your labours for some refreshments?"

Saskia relayed the suggestion to Melanie, and the three women made their way to the bike centre's refectory, ordered snacks and drinks and were about to sit at a table when Isabelle said, "Perhaps you would like to speak alone with Melanie?"

Saskia translated this for Melanie, who hesitated. "I don't mind if she stays. It's just that I don't – can't – speak French or Spanish."

When Saskia translated this for Isabelle's benefit, she nodded. She took her phone from her purse and turned in her chair to sit side-on to the table. "I will read my book or maybe text some of my friends while you speak."

Turning her full attention to Melanie, Saskia said, "Tell me what's happened, Melanie. I thought you and Hans were happy together. I was so happy for both of you."

Melanie looked miserable. "I think he thinks I'm jealous of you, but it isn't that. I – " Melanie hesitated for so long and shifted so uncomfortably in her seat that Saskia wondered if she would continue, and then, with her eyes fixed on the glass of orange juice gripped in her hands, she said, "It's just that, well, you know, I needed to re-think things, and I thought, well, you are so happy and certain of what you are doing, I want to spend time with you. Be more of a – you know – friend to you. Learn things from you."

Saskia frowned. There were so many levels at which this made no sense that she was uncertain how to respond. "Do you want to move to Lyon?"

"I've found a place to stay. I won't be any trouble. Just, maybe we could meet sometimes, and you can tell me – tell me about – about your work."

"My work? I don't understand. Why would that interest you?"

"I... Well. I can't – I don't want to be a check-out girl all my life. I thought I could find out more whether the sorts of things you do might be interesting."

"I thought you were interested in culture and – er – an arts degree?"

Melanie jerked her head up and glared at Saskia. "Look! Can't we just be friends? I haven't made friends in Rotterdam except for Hans, and I'd like to have a girlfriend." Just as quickly, she dropped her gaze back to her juice.

"Of course!" Saskia said cautiously. She sat back in her seat and rubbed her forehead. "Do you know that I travel a lot, and sometimes I'm away from Lyon for a while?"

"I could join you in things like Isabelle does. And you're going to be in Lyon for a while now." Desperation underscored Melanie's tone. One of her legs began to jitter, causing the table to shake. "Maybe I could even come with you when you travel. I wouldn't be any trouble. I just want to know what you're doing. Hans wouldn't ever tell me. What do you tell him?"

*How do you know I'll be in Lyon for a while?* "Tell Hans? I talk to him about the workshops and the places I visit. We just chat. He tells me about his work and fills me in with what our friends are doing. Is he reluctant to tell you about our conversations?"

"It's not that. He doesn't tell me what you're finding out. What you're looking for when you go to all these places."

"Looking for? What would I be looking for? I'm teaching people about risk and security."

"But you get a whole lot of data from the places you go to."

"I do? Oh – er – do you mean the research I do before I go to any place to run workshops? Are you interested in that sort of stuff?" Saskia tipped her head to the side, her frown deepening. "Melanie, what is this about?"

Melanie stood suddenly, almost knocking her chair back with the motion. "I've got to go." She seemed ready to burst into tears. "I'm really making a mess of this! I'm sorry!"

"Wait!" Saskia jumped from her chair and grabbed Melanie's arm, causing the woman to stumble in her haste to flee. "Melanie, what's wrong? What can I help you with? Where are you going? Where are you staying?"

"I've just got to go." Melanie wrenched her arm free and rushed from the room, leaving Saskia staring after her. Other patrons, Isabelle included, looked curiously from Saskia to the doorway through which Melanie had disappeared.

"Your friend has left?" Isabelle asked, as if she had not understood any of the conversation. "She seems distressed."

"Mon dieu!" Saskia breathed. "What was that about?"

"Is there a problem?" Danny asked, appearing next to Saskia.

"Eh? Oh! Er – I'm not sure. My friend's upset."

"She sure left in a hurry. The kids are asking if you're coming back."

Saskia hitched up on to her chair. "I think I'm finished," she said wearily.

"We're having a party for Jessamine tonight. It's her birthday. I'm sure she'd love you to come."

"Thank you, Danny. I'm going to miss it. I've had a hectic week; I think it's caught up with me."

Danny placed his hands on the table looking down at her, his brow furrowed in worry. "Hey, are you alright? You've been acting stressed lately. Are you working too hard?"

"Yes, I am working too hard."

"Leave your job. Come work for me. I promise I'll give you computer work as well as bike work."

That made Saskia smile. "You know what? There may come a time when I take you up on that. But not now. Thanks."

## 22

### DIAGRAM STUDY

"May I come in?" Saskia swivelled her office chair around to see who had asked the question. With a start, she moved to slide forward to stand.

M. Benkirane waved her down. "Please. Stay seated. I apologise if I startled you. I knocked, but I think you were engrossed."

"I beg your pardon. I didn't hear the knock."

"May I come in?"

"Yes. Yes. Of course."

M. Benkirane closed the door behind him. "I thought I might come to see how you are managing with your new duties since I am in Lyon. I have just spoken with Antoine. He tells me he has had no reports from you."

"Er – was I meant to give him – "

"No. No. He is no longer your direct superior. However, to alleviate friction, it may be diplomatic to include him on the regular reports you send me, since you are using the Lyon office as your base."

"Certainly. I didn't realise – didn't think it was – "

M. Benkirane shook his head slightly, urbane smile in place. "Don't worry. Just do it in future." He indicated the complex, colourful

*THE BANK*

diagram of rectangles, circles, triangles, lines and words on the screen of Saskia's laptop. "May I ask what that is?"

"Er – it's stuff I've researched and use for workshops."

"How?"

"I gather data, map it out to get the context of the bank I'm going to visit, and adjust the workshops to try to ensure I'm properly hitting the mark for things they might be missing out on."

"And how does that help you to prepare for the workshops? Do you not provide the same workshop at each venue?"

"Sort of, but I change examples and emphasise different issues depending on the context."

M. Benkirane studied the diagram in silence for some time. "You draw up a very elaborate context," he said finally. He pointed to a rectangle outlined in green with the words 'staff turnover 18.2%'. "How do you use this information?"

Saskia shifted the laptop closer to herself with one hand and pushed away the keyboard and mouse she had been working on with the other. Using the laptop's trackpad to move the cursor on to the rectangle, she clicked. The screen blanked for a millisecond and then displayed a different colourful arrangement of rectangles, circles, triangles, words and lines. "I break it down into various known causes of turnover."

The bank's chief studied the new diagram and asked, again. "How do you use this information?"

"I don't know if it's relevant at all. I collect this data and look at it from time to time, but it's just data at this point. Mostly, I work with data that I think might be more relevant."

"Which is?"

Saskia touched several keys on the laptop keyboard to bring up a diagram in the form of circles within circles. "I start with the bank's strategy, then move to statements about risk appetite, then KPIs and the like, and then I layer actual outcomes." As she spoke, Saskia pointed to icons on the screen.

M. Benkirane frowned. "So, if I understand you properly. Each of these is linked to the diagrams you just showed me, in, as you say, layers?"

"Yes."

"This is very comprehensive," he said slowly. "What is this software you are using?"

"Er – it's something I've designed myself."

"Hmm. Madame Le Fèvre mentioned that you had a complicated way of working. I didn't realise it was this complicated. Can you download all of this and send it to me?"

"All of it?"

"Indeed. Or perhaps the – " he indicated the laptop with a wave of his hand. "Give me access so I can see how you layer the data for myself."

"Umm. No. I regret I can't do that. I keep the application of how I produce these maps on my laptop. It's sort of a mishmash of several software packages and code that I've written. It's something I've developed as part of my academic studies. I would be breaching copyright rules if I provided access to the hybrid application. I developed it for personal research purposes; however, I can certainly send you all the map layers."

"I see. Am I to understand that you are developing these maps on your personal equipment, not the bank's equipment?"

"Yes."

M. Benkirane frowned. "It is a condition of your employment that bank work must not be stored or completed on personal devices."

"It isn't. I mean. For me, these maps are equivalent to doodling on scraps of paper." Saskia pushed her laptop away, replacing it with the keyboard she had been working on. "The information in those maps is public information from annual reports, press releases, newspaper articles and the like." She pointed to the document open on the desktop monitor. "So, this is my working document on the FSB computer. It is the one that contains proprietary bank information and the background document I use for the workshops I'm currently preparing for the FSB branch in Zurich. In preparing the workshop's documents, I look at my doodles – that is, the public information sorted by using my application – and I get a feel for whether there might be specific issues I need to look out for. Then, I go digging for further information in the bank system and put that into these documents."

"And I have access to that document?" He pointed to the screen.

"They are on the bank system. I have them password protected, of course, but if you want access, I can give it to you."

"Who gives you permission to dig for proprietary bank information?"

Saskia felt as if she were under interrogation and determined she would not allow herself to feel intimidated. "As part of my preparatory work for training, I discuss my needs with the bank I'm going to workshop with. Umm – you cleared that with them. I asked you to do that to make it easier for me to gather preparatory information."

"Yes. I did," M. Benkirane murmured. "When you worked with Madame Le Fèvre, did you also work like this?"

Saskia shook her head. "No. She wanted me to use the application I developed, so I used my private laptop."

"I see." M. Benkirane sat on a spare chair, drew the keyboard and mouse close and scrolled through the document on the monitor, then he pushed the keyboard and mouse away and pulled Saskia's laptop towards himself. "So, all you do is click on words to get another layer?"

"Er – yes." Saskia strained to hide her flare of anger; her personal laptop was sacred territory.

"And how do I return to the topmost layer?"

"Click on the small cross at the top of the screen."

Saskia watched as her superior worked his way up and down the layers of maps, studying each one for several minutes. After fifteen minutes of watching, Saskia asked if he would mind if she continued her work on the document she had been busy with. For the first time in her interactions with him, she thought she saw a flash of displeasure in his dark eyes. But he said, "Of course. I beg your indulgence. I am finding this fascinating. Don't let me hold you up." He returned his attention to the laptop.

It took M. Benkirane over an hour to work through the maps. "This is not just what is on the public record," he said. "You are using other information to make connections."

Saskia left off her document. "I am." She tapped the side of her head. "I use my studies, that is, my familiarity with the finance sector to help me make the connections."

"This is powerful work."

Saskia shrugged. "In reality, all I've done is make pictures of what journalists write about and investors bet on."

M. Benkirane indicated the document showing on the desktop monitor. "Why don't you use such diagrams in your workshop preparations?"

"Oh! I do." With a few strokes on the keyboard, Saskia revealed a diagram showing IT failures in the Zurich branch. "I take the broad observations of my doodles on the laptop, and plug in bank-proprietary information to arrive at these sorts of patterns – er – diagrams."

"Is this also using this application you use on your laptop?"

"No. This is mapping software I've asked the bank's IT section to get a licence for."

"And you say I can access this application?'

"It's a bank licence, so anyone from FSB who wants to use the software can use it."

M. Benkirane's gaze shifted from the laptop to the monitor. He was clearly disturbed about something. Saskia waited respectfully for him to continue. A soft knock on the office door interrupted his contemplations. "Er – should I – " Saskia began.

"What is it?" the bank chief snapped, facing the door.

"Monsieur, the meeting you called." Saskia recognised the voice of Crystal Benoit, M. Aubert's personal assistant.

Ayat Benkirane glanced at his watch and rose. "I'll be there in a minute," he called back. To Saskia, he said, "You are as clever a lady as Madame Le Fèvre assured us. And you could be dangerous."

Saskia stared at him with what she hoped would pass as wide-eyed confusion. "Dangerous, Monsieur? I don't understand?"

He smiled. "You are a gatherer and user of information." He patted the top of her head.

Of all the insults levelled at her height, this was the one she found hardest to tolerate. M. Benkirane noticed her flinch of rage. He withdrew his hand and balled it into a fist at his side. "My sincerest apologies. That was unforgivable of me and demeaning of you in ways that are totally without foundation. It will not happen again. Know that I hold you in the highest regard. This has been a most instructive time. I will think hard about how FSB can better use your considerable talents. Perhaps we will have time to interact again in the few weeks you are in Lyon."

With that, he left her office, the open doorway showing Saskia that he walked towards the lifts with Crystal Benoit, his head slightly tilted towards her as he politely attended to what she said.

Saskia adjusted her seat and swivelled to face the computers, her back to the doorway. She set to work at the keyboard that was linked the office computer again, noting that her fingers trembled slightly, echoing her elevated pulse. She wasn't sure if the tremble was a reaction to his effrontery at presuming he had permission to touch her laptop or the insulting pat.

Fear that her superior might have found his way into the further layers of information on her laptop, shared only with Simon's team – now called Project Archane – was not the cause of her disquiet. She had worked for weeks with the team's cyber colleagues to modify her program to 'hide' proprietary bank information from exactly the types of investigations that Ayat Benkirane had just conducted.

Project Archane's cyber team were good, but it was her expertise in pattern recognition that was gradually putting together a picture of the criminal networks operating throughout Europe.

There was no doubt that money was being laundered through the bank's systems in eye-watering amounts. The bank accepted deposits and funnelled money to other banks in safe havens around the world. Many of FSG's European branches had inadequate systems in place to monitor and report suspicious transactions. The bank rewarded its senior management with significant bonuses linked to profits, thereby – perhaps inadvertently – motivating them to turn a blind eye to due diligence. Disappointingly, the reports she had written about this and presented to Mme Le Fèvre had apparently done nothing to change the bank's failing. The only indication she'd received that senior management had read them was the one meeting with Ayat Benkirane and Antoine Aubert just before Mme Le Fèvre and herself were reassigned to other tasks. Increasingly, Saskia believed that they had both been moved aside to stop them from uncovering more information on the bank's shortcomings. From Project Archane's viewpoint, however, Saskia's broader access to FSB's European operations was a boon. The map they were developing linking transactions to companies, trust funds and those helping to move money around was impressive. The Project had identified some of the criminal beneficiaries, but frustratingly, not who they believed were the criminal masterminds – the primary beneficiaries of much of the funds-flow.

Finding secure places for Saskia to work with the Project Archane team for more than a couple of hours at a time had been a problem. She could make only so many visits to the traboule's shop before arousing more suspicion among the people watching her. Two months ago, the team hit upon a creative solution. "Two people from The Netherlands have joined the cycle club. You will be delighted to join your fellow countrymen for weekend bike trips. They are particularly enamoured of taking you to remote places," Isabelle had informed her.

She regretted seeing little of the remote places she visited. Her time was spent working with the cyber team while her 'new Dutch friends' spent at least a few hours each day riding, taking photos of where they'd cycled, noting people they saw and putting together a story that Saskia could share with friends and family about her supposed adventure. The friends often returned cold and dishevelled, complaining that winter was not the best time to be adventuring on bikes in the countryside. Saskia considered their complaints as a salve to her regret.

*I think I might be getting good at lying*, thought Saskia. But the more she learned about the criminal networks, the more her disgust at their inhumanity infuriated her. And now, she was particularly furious that they appeared to have involved Melanie.

Hans had been frantic when she'd called him about meeting with Melanie at the bike centre. "I don't know where she is. She just rushed out, Hans," she'd said to him. Of course, Isabelle knew where Melanie was, but since Isabelle had not volunteered the information, Saskia had not asked.

She promised Hans that when she next spoke with Melanie, she would do her utmost to persuade her to return to Rotterdam.

## 23

### THEFT

Saskia opened her apartment door to Mme Claire's knock. "Your friend Melanie is at the door to see you. Should I invite her in?"

"Melanie! Merci, Madame. I will attend to her."

It was late in the evening, and dark and bleak outside. Melanie stood in the hallway below, glancing nervously at Rufus sitting before her. His ears were pricked forward, eyes intent. He was not menacing, but he was not friendly either.

Saskia stepped past the dog and gripped Melanie's gloved hands. "I'm so glad to see you! I've been worried about you!"

"Come, Rufus," Mme Claire commanded. Dog at her heels, she went into her lounge, closing the door to the entrance hall behind her.

"I'm sorry to call on you so late. It's just –" Melanie took a deep breath. "I couldn't stay at the place I was staying at anymore, and I hoped –" Her voice trembled, tears leaking. She looked worn out, afraid, pale and dejected.

"Come up to my rooms." Saskia drew Melanie to the stairs. "Have you eaten? Can I get you something to drink? Tell me what's happening."

Once in the apartment, Saskia coaxed Melanie to relinquish the duffel bag she carried, take off her coat and gloves, and sit in an armchair. "You look cold. Can I get you a warm drink?"

"You're so nice," Melanie said, her tone a lament. "Can I have some hot water? Just some hot water."

"Of course." Saskia flicked on an electric kettle to boil. "Tell me what's happening."

"I was staying in a hotel, but this afternoon they told me they didn't have a room available for me anymore. I tried a few other places, but they're all so expensive. Do you – Saskia, I hate to ask this. Do you mind if I stay here till I sort myself out?"

"Of course, stay here tonight, Melanie. I'll help you find somewhere to stay tomorrow. I can easily help you pay for somewhere. It would be my pleasure."

"You – don't – think it would be alright for me to stay with you?"

Sakia took the woman's cold hands into hers. "I'm sorry, Melanie. I don't own this apartment, and I agreed with Madame Claire that I would be the only occupant. I can fix the couch for you to sleep on tonight and help you find a place tomorrow. I'm sure I can even find a place nearby so we can be together more easily." *And maybe we can work out who is causing you to come after me like this.*

Melanie nodded mutely, and Saskia returned to the boiling kettle. Melanie scratched the backs of her hands absentmindedly as her eyes roved around the apartment. "It's nice here," she said, taking the mug Saskia offered her. "But it's sort of bare. Like a hotel room."

"My fridge and the kitchen cupboards are well stocked, but, it's true, I don't spend much time decorating. I'm not much of a homebody, as Hans may have told you."

At the mention of Hans, Melanie flinched.

"Have you spoken to him yet, Melanie?"

She shook her head, eyes lowered. "I'm too mixed up to talk to him yet."

"Is there something I can help you with?"

Melanie shook her head again, then plastered on a smile. "Lyon's pretty, isn't it? Even in winter. I've gone back to the places we visited when we were – I was last here."

"It is a nice city." Saskia sat on the edge of the couch with her body turned towards Melanie. "Have you eaten? I can fix you something."

"Hans told me you don't like cooking. But he says you know how to cook well."

"As you know, my parents have a café-restaurant. From my earliest days, I had to help in the kitchen. I can wrap pastry around portions of ground meat or vegetables at the speed of light."

"Hans said you left Holland because you didn't want to be trapped into that kind of life."

Saskia tipped her head to the side a little. "Do you and Hans only talk about me?"

"Uh? No. Sorry. I just think about him a lot." Tears dribbled from Melanie's eyes again. "I'm so mixed up."

"What can I do to help?"

Melanie looked around the room again. Her eyes rested briefly on the two laptops sitting on the kitchen table and then continued their restless search, stopping again at the open doorway to the bedroom. "Is that your bedroom?"

"Yes."

"Is your bathroom in there, too?"

"Yes. There's an ensuite attached to the bedroom."

"Do you mind if I use it?"

"Please. Make yourself at home."

Melanie hefted up her duffel bag and walked to the bedroom door, where she paused to look over her shoulder. "Please don't tell Hans I'm here while I'm in the bathroom. He texted me that you told him about the last time we met."

"Alright."

Forty-five minutes later, Melanie reappeared with her hair washed, a clean tracksuit on and altogether looking brighter and more alert. Saskia noted without surprise that her pupils were dilated.

"Thank you so much," Melanie said, dropping her bag at the foot of the couch. "I needed that. I hope you don't mind. I found a clean towel and used it."

"I'm glad you did."

"It's quite late. I guess you were getting ready to go to bed. You've got your pyjamas on."

"Well, yes."

"I'm ready to lie down too. I can make myself comfortable on the couch."

"I'll get you a sheet and a doona."

"Thanks."

"Are you sure I can't get you anything to eat? You look like you need a bit of fattening up."

"I was getting too fat. I'm fine."

Saskia helped Melanie settle on to the couch and told her to help herself to anything in the kitchen and to enter the bedroom if she needed to use the toilet again. She picked up her phone and retired to her room, shutting the bedroom door behind her. Surreptitiously, she switched on the bug-finder app and walked into the bathroom.

It was all she could do not to burst into tears when the app located two bugs in the bathroom, and one imperfectly hidden behind a wall hanging in the bedroom.

She lay on the bed with the lights off but did not sleep. After some hours, she heard Melanie moving around in the living room: the scrape of a chair, cupboard doors opening and closing, the fridge door protesting about being left open too long, something falling and the sound being quickly smothered, Melanie's voice murmuring as if talking to someone.

Suddenly, Rufus began barking loudly. Saskia leapt off the bed and flung open the bedroom door, switching on the living room light. Melanie came rushing in from the hallway, duffel bag over her shoulder. She slammed the door shut and leaned back against it, breathing heavily, her eyes wide with terror.

"Melanie, what are you doing?"

Melanie burst into tears. "That dog gave me such a fright!"

"What were you doing in the hall?"

"I decided not to bother you anymore, and I wanted to leave." She pointed to a piece of paper on the coffee table. "I wrote you a note. But the dog started barking at me when I went downstairs."

"Why do you want to leave? Melanie, I want to help you. I'm sorry about Rufus. He's quite suspicious of strangers."

Melanie slumped on to the lounge, sinking her face into her hands. "I just wanted not to be a bother anymore."

"You aren't a bother. Please stay the night. We'll find you a place to stay tomorrow."

"I can't sleep."

"Then let me fix you something to eat. You look exhausted."

Melanie shook her head. "I just want to sleep," she whimpered.

Saskia sat next to her. "What is wrong, Melanie?"

In a gesture of defeat, Melanie lolled her head over the back of the couch. "I wish I could tell you." Her voice was barely audible. She closed her eyes.

"Rest then." Saskia placed a hand on Melanie's thigh and stroked gently.

After a long silence, Melanie murmured. "You're so nice to me. I hate what I'm doing." Her voice drifted away as she relaxed into sleep, Saskia covered Melanie with the doona and picked up the note.

*Dearest Saskia*

*Thank you very much for your hospitality. I regret that I have not been a good guest.*

*Please forgive me.*

*Melanie*

*PS: When you next talk to Hans, tell him I love him and I'm doing everything I can to deal with a bad situation.*

She set the note on the table again and was about to settle into an armchair when her gaze fell on the kitchen table.

The laptops were gone.

Careful not to wake Melanie, Saskia opened the duffel bag and extracted both laptops. She took them into the bedroom and locked them into a drawer of the bedside table. Disheartened, she donned dressing gown and slippers, returned to the living room and curled into an armchair.

## 24

CONSCRIPTED

The sound of groaning woke Saskia.

Weak winter sun shone through the windows. She glanced at her watch. It was almost eight. She would be late to the office today – or maybe she would not go to the office at all.

Melanie groaned again, her face pulled into a grimace. She lay awkwardly on her side, one leg tucked underneath her, the other dangling to the floor. She twitched and moved as if in pain for some minutes, then her eyes fluttered open. Her gaze roved about the room and landed on Saskia.

She sat up with a jerk and then cried out, hands clutching at her head.

When Saskia reached towards her, she drew back. "Leave me alone," she moaned.

"Do you have a headache? Can I get you something for it?"

"What have you got?"

"Er – some paracetamol."

"As if that's any good," Melanie moaned, curling up over her thighs, head still in her hands. "Haven't you got anything better?"

"Umm – I've got Nurofen. Is that better?"

Melanie lurched to her feet and rushed to the bathroom, where she was noisily sick in the wash basin. Saskia stood at the door, not knowing what to do as Melanie heaved and moaned, alternately clutching at her stomach and her head.

"Should I – should I call an ambulance?"

"Just leave! Just leave me alone!" Melanie shrieked, whirling around in pale-faced fury. She shoved Saskia away and slammed the door shut.

Saskia stood undecided, listening to more moaning and retching, the sound of bottles rattling and water running. She retreated to sit on her bed, aware that a camera was watching her. She tried to look as if she was simply nervously fiddling with her watch. In fact, she was sending a second-order alarm signal that would alert Isabelle that she needed help but was not in immediate danger.

Eventually, Melanie opened the door to the bathroom. She had washed her face and seemed more in control. "I'm so sorry," she said. "I get stir-crazy when I get these headaches."

"Does it happen often?"

Melanie shuddered. "Look! I've got to go. Can you get me past that dog?"

"Melanie – "

"Stop! Just let me out of here. What are you? My jailer or something?"

"I'm sorry. I'm trying to help."

"I know." Melanie made a visible effort to control herself. "But I must go."

Saskia nodded, leading the way out of the bedroom. Melanie stooped to pick up her duffel bag, started lifting it and then grew rigid. She dumped the bag on to the low table, unzipped it and began searching frantically through the contents. She turned to Saskia, face blotched with red and a mask of rage and terror. She held an open flick knife in her hand.

"Where are they?"

Heart feeling that it might break, Saskia shook her head, backing away from the threatening knife. "Melanie," she began, her voice pleading.

Melanie let out a howl and lunged. Saskia startled back. It flashed through her mind that this was a situation in which her self-defence training should be deployed, but her mind was numb with shock, and her reactions echoed her mind. Melanie grabbed her, turned her about and held the knife to her throat.

"Give them to me!" she spat. "I need them! I'll kill you if you don't give them to me! Give them to – "

"Is there a problem here?"

Melanie whirled, crushing Saskia to her body, the knife nicking Saskia's neck.

Isabelle stood in the apartment doorway, one hand holding the ears of two mugs, the other holding the door handle. Her eyes were wide.

"Don't you come anywhere near us. Go away, or I'll kill her."

Isabelle stared. "Melanie! What are you –"

Isabelle stumbled, spilling coffee as Rufus burst past her legs with a menacing growl and leapt, front paws landing on Melanie's shoulders and knocking her back. Saskia fell to the floor and Rufus crouched over her, teeth bared at Melanie.

"Get him away! Get him away!" Melanie shrieked, knife pointing at the dog as she scuttled backwards.

"Stop!" Mme Claire's command rang out urgently. Rufus sank more protectively over Saskia, ears flat back over his head, lips pulled back in a snarl. A growl rumbled deep in his chest.

Melanie stumbled into the bedroom and slammed the door shut behind her.

Mme Claire pulled Rufus off Saskia. Isabelle helped Saskia sit up. "My friend, what problem?" She touched her fingers to Saskia's neck. They came away bloody.

"She went crazy!" Saskia exhaled shakily.

"Is this the woman I let in last night?" Mme Claire asked.

Saskia nodded, pushing herself up, then grabbed Isabelle's arm because her legs refused to hold her up.

"But why?" Isabelle asked. Eyes wide, she appeared bewildered and afraid.

Saskia blinked at her, confused thoughts coalescing on the realisa-

*THE BANK*

tion that, despite the situation, Isabelle was still playing her undercover part. *She's put cameras around these rooms! She's been conscripted by criminals!* Saskia wanted to scream. But she drew in a deep breath. "She wants to steal my laptops."

"Your laptops?"

Mme Claire glared from Saskia to the closed bedroom door. "Did I hear her say she would kill you?" she demanded.

"She's not well," Saskia said.

"Is it we should call police?" Isabelle asked.

Saskia released Isabelle's arm. "I'll try and talk to her. She seems to be alright one minute, then crazy the next."

With Isabelle hovering anxiously next to her, Saskia stepped to the bedroom door. She put a hand on the knob, ready to say something soothing to Melanie. Instead, she froze because she could hear the murmur of Melanie's voice. Saskia pressed her ear to the door.

"... drawer," silence, then, "What do you mean she's listening at the door?"

Saskia pushed open the door. Melanie stood near the bed, a phone pressed to her ear. She whirled around to face Saskia, Isabelle, Mme Claire and Rufus, her expression fierce, the knife held out threateningly. "I know you've put your computers in a drawer," she said. "Give them to me. I need them." Melanie's body gave a violent shudder. She staggered but pulled herself together, knife held out at the ready again when Saskia moved towards her. "Stay back!" she yelled.

"Dois-je appeler la police?"

At the word 'police', Melanie shrieked, her face blanching. Fight seemed to leave her, her shoulders shrinking into one another. The knife dropped from her fingers. "I go! Ik ga!" she sobbed and continued in Dutch, "An auto – a car's waiting for me." Her tearful gaze landed on Rufus. "Keep him back. Please keep him back."

Accepting defeat, Saskia said, "Let her go. She says a car's waiting for her outside."

The three women and Rufus, with Mme Claire's hand on his collar, followed Melanie as she hurried out of Saskia's apartment, duffel bag slung over her shoulder, along the hallway, down the stairs and to the front door. There, she struggled with the lock, managed to slip it open and practically fell down the stairs in her haste to get to the car parked at the kerb. She had not yet closed the car door when it sped away.

Beside Saskia, Isabelle murmured the licence plate number into a phone pressed to her ear.

## 25

## EXTRA SERVICES

Isabelle bent to embrace Saskia, who leaned into her. Tears forced past Saskia's tightly closed eyelids and choked her throat.

"Come into my kitchen," Mme Claire said, closing the front door and locking it. "Let us tend to that cut on your neck. Then we will have coffee and breakfast, and you will tell us what happened."

Simon had told Mme Claire only that Saskia was involved in an ongoing police investigation into dangerous criminals and that there was a chance the criminals might target the household. He had offered to encourage Saskia to rehome, but Mme Claire had been adamant that increasing the security of her home was enough. She did not know that Isabelle was part of the safety package.

Saskia struggled to explain Melanie's behaviour without revealing that the woman had hidden cameras throughout her apartment.

"But why did she want your computers so badly?" Mme Claire puzzled. "Do you think that's why she wanted to stay with you. To steal them?"

Saskia shook her head, fingers worrying the edge of the band-aid on her neck. She could not tell Mme Claire her suspicions. "I don't know." She frowned, staring down into her coffee. An image came to mind of Ayat Benkirane and his intense interest in the diagrams she had created.

"Maybe she selling for to buy drugs?" Isabelle suggested.

Mme Claire pushed freshly baked bread and condiments closer to Saskia and Isabelle. "Please have some breakfast," she said. "Rufus and I had only just returned from the bakery when we heard the commotion upstairs, so the bread is fresh. But, Saskia, has this got something to do with what the police are investigating? Don't you think you should tell them about this incident? The car outside didn't seem to be just a taxi or uber she called."

"You're right," Saskia said. "I'll contact the police. I've got the direct number of the person in charge of the investigation."

"Is good idea," Isabelle said. "But now, maybe we take walking maybe after one hour when you are bathing and dressing. I am ringing my uncle I am not in shop. Yes?"

"Take Rufus with you," Mme Claire advised. She rolled a slice of ham and fed it to the dog, who swallowed it without a bite and looked eagerly for more. She stroked his head. "You are a brave boy," she said with a fond smile. "But don't get your hopes up that you will now always get ham."

Saskia returned to her apartment and called Hans, providing him with a less than full account of her evening with Melanie. Distressed, he wondered whether he should travel to Lyon to find her. "You think she's using drugs. Maybe I could talk to her, persuade her to get help. I don't understand why she is fixated on you."

"I don't know, Hans. Maybe she isn't ready to be found. I mean she left me a note and says she wants you to know she's trying to work things out." Saskia read out the note then held the phone helplessly to her ear, listening to his sobs.

Officer Gabriel Clément arrived at the house within half-an-hour of Saskia contacting him. He took statements from the three women and said he would put an alert out for Melanie, though Saskia was sure he was only going through the proper motions for the benefit of Mme Claire and anyone else who might be observing how the household reacted to Melanie's incursion.

Isabelle confirmed her suspicions on their walk.

Saskia told Isabelle about the cameras and her speculation that Melanie's fixation on the laptop might have something to do with Ayat Benkirane's interest in the same. "You think Melanie's being used by these rotten people, don't you?" she finished bitterly.

"We have carried out several investigations regarding Monsieur Benkirane. Some of the people he associates with are persons of interest, but there is no evidence pointing to him as a criminal. And the fact that he seems to be using you to improve staff knowledge of cybersecurity and regulations also makes us wary about pointing a finger at him."

"I suspect I'm a front for him."

They were passing a bench. Saskia decided to sit. Isabelle looked down at her, one sculpted, questioning eyebrow raised.

"Is that woman trailing us one of theirs, or one of ours?" Saskia asked, one hand partially covering her mouth.

Isabelle grinned. "Oh, very good! She is one of ours. We are using you for training operatives. I will need to report that she failed this test."

"So, I am having many uses. I will need to increase my fees for service."

"Please provide the request in writing and I'll ensure it goes into the inbox of a very busy bureaucrat." Isabelle's grin changed to a look of concern. "But you are tired?"

"I am." Saskia slid off the bench to her feet. They walked in silence for a while, Rufus jerking frequently on his lead to sniff at this or that. Isabelle indulged him by stopping each time, waiting till he had finished his investigation.

"Poor Melanie. Isn't there anything we can do for her?" Saskia asked at last.

"My colleagues followed her car to the Part-Dieu railway station, where she boarded a fast train to Paris. We will continue to look out for her. Come, let us return to the house. I think you would do well to rest a while."

They had just begun their return walk when Saskia's phone buzzed. She pulled it from her back pocket.

"It's Monsieur Benkirane," she said, glancing at the screen. She swiped to answer the call. "Oui? Bonjour, Monsieur."

"Bonjour, Saskia. Have I caught you at an awkward moment?"

"Non, Monsieur. I am walking with my friend."

"You are not in the office?"

"Non. We had a disturbed night at the house and needed to wait for the police to investigate."

"Is everything alright?" He sounded concerned.

"I think so, Monsieur. It was a friend of mine who, sadly, has succumbed to drugs. She tried to steal some of my things, but we caught her doing it."

"Mon dieu! That is distressing."

"Oui, Monsieur. We have notified the police. I will work from home today and return to the office tomorrow. How may I help you?"

"Ah. I have been thinking very greatly about our last interaction. I think it would benefit us if you take up the research position I spoke to you about initially. Could I persuade you to move to Brussels? I will arrange travel and accommodation at the bank's expense."

"A transfer, Monsieur?"

"Non. Perhaps not a permanent transfer. Perhaps secondment is the better word. Only a few months. I think your situation at the bank in Lyon is not very satisfactory for you. You have just an office with an uncomfortable senior. You will work directly with me in Brussels for some months. Please consider this offer. I will not disturb you further now. I'll call you again tomorrow."

"Merci, Monsieur."

Saskia put her phone away.

"He wants me to go to Brussels."

Isabelle's eyes were on the pocket where Saskia had stowed the phone. She tapped her ear.

"No," Saskia said. "The phone can't listen to me. Not only have your people ensured that, I've turned off app permissions to listen to me. I'm pretty sure I'd get an electric shock from your people if they discovered I hadn't taken those precautions."

Isabelle chuckled. "I like the way you refer to us as 'your people'. You are exhibiting all the best qualities of an undercover agent."

"I failed in the self-defence category this morning." Saskia touched the band-aid on her neck.

"True. It is not a strong point of yours. On the plus side, you are most adept at telling the truth while leaving out crucial details."

"Brussels." Saskia sighed. "Do you think I should take up the offer?"

"I'll discuss it with the team. But it might be a good opportunity. The city is a strong hub for the criminal network we are investigating."

"So, I'll leave my apartment after all the trouble Melanie took to instal spy cameras."

"I'm afraid you will need to continue to pretend you don't know about them. The longer you keep showing them your innocent face, the safer you'll be."

"If only it was just my face. I stay in the best hotels all over Europe and I can't even go to the toilet in private."

A single line appeared between Isabelle's flawless eyebrows. "Your reports said that the last two hotels you stayed in had no bugs. Was that incorrect?"

"No. I didn't find any. I hoped that I'd managed to shake suspicion of my activities."

"So had we."

"But now this."

"But now this," Isabelle echoed.

## 26

## BRUSSELS

Brussels is sometimes called the capital of Europe because of its status as the de facto capital of the European Union and international hub for rail, road and air traffic. Simon and Isabelle told Saskia it was also a major route through which drugs entered the European market. Even more disagreeably, it was a significant hub from which the trafficked African minors Simon had told Saskia about were recruited into the drug trade.

"We will continue to be close at hand to help you and keep you safe," Simon promised.

"Is Isabelle going to Brussels with me?"

"I don't think that would be wise."

M. Benkirane's personal driver met Saskia at Brussels Airport and introduced himself as Phillipe. Saskia guessed he was in his early forties; his hair and beard were streaked with grey, and his brown eyes were surrounded by lines. A dark suit moulded perfectly to his slender frame, and his manners were impeccable, though all he said after greeting her was that it would take approximately twenty minutes to arrive at her accommodation.

Nineteen minutes later, he parked the limousine at the entrance to a twelve-storey building with an art nouveau façade.

# THE BANK

"We are not far from the Grote Markt," Phillipe said in French as he opened the car door for her. He pointed to a street sign on the opposite side of the road. "It is that way. As you may know, it is a UNESCO World Heritage Site and attracts millions of visitors every year. However, this street is seldom disturbed by such visitors. Monsieur Benkirane hopes you will find the apartment and its central position more comfortable than a hotel room. The FSB building is in Rue Jules Van Praet. It is only four street blocks from here." Phillipe hurried up the three steps to the entrance of the apartment block to open a large glass door that seemed out of place on the older style building. The foyer looked more like that of a five-star hotel reception area than the entrance to a residential building.

A middle-aged woman dressed in a tight-fitting black uniform rose from behind the reception desk. She had a dark complexion, a substantial waistline and black hair woven into hundreds of tiny plaits. "My name is Annalise," she said in Flemish, which was close enough to Dutch for Saskia to understand. "Welcome, Dr van Essen. I hope your stay with us will be most pleasant."

"Er – thank you."

"Could I trouble you to complete paperwork?" She put a page and pen on top of the reception counter.

Saskia stood on tiptoes and filled in the documentation.

"Many thanks, Dr van Essen." Annalise leaned over the counter to give Saskia a keycard. "This will open the doors both to your apartment and to this building. A concierge and a porter are available at all hours should you require assistance. We lock the front doors between nine at night and seven in the morning. Should you need to call for our assistance at any time, please dial the number on your keycard. We are happy to arrange transport, food deliveries, tours, extra cleaning or whatever other services you require. Please do not hesitate to call. And, please, avail yourself of information about our services on our guest website."

"Thank you."

"Unless you have questions of me, Mario, the porter on duty, will take you to your apartment and ensure you have everything you need."

She indicated a man dressed in a grey, high-collared uniform with red piping who had materialised next to Phillipe, already with her suitcases in hand. He bowed when Saskia turned to him. "May I also extend my welcome," he said, his French mangled by an Italian accent.

"Er – thank you. That's – umm – kind of you."

In situations like this, Saskia had the overwhelming desire to wave her arms about and say, "Boo! You're all being absurd!" But, of course, that would be unfair. They were doing their best. Annalise had widened her eyes in dismay when she saw Saskia struggling for height to reach the counter top. She and Mario – and Phillipe, for that matter – were trying to contort their bodies so they did not tower over her. They were all having problems giving her adult-royalty obeisance while grappling with her child-like size.

Saskia resorted to her usual tactic of honesty to help them with their dilemma: "Er – I'd appreciate it if you just call me Saskia. Somehow, Dr van Essen doesn't fit my stature. And I'd appreciate it if you could arrange for a stepstool to be delivered to my room so I can reach things a little easier. Also," she smiled, "I don't mind if you look down when talking to me. I'm used to looking up."

Relief dropped tension from three sets of shoulders. "We'll organise a stepstool immediately," Annalise said. "And could we arrange something else?"

"No. Thank you."

Phillipe stepped forward. "Monsieur Benkirane would be honoured if you would join him at his family home for dinner this evening."

"That's most kind of him."

"Then, may I pick you up at half past six?"

"That's most kind of you."

Mario led the way to the lift and pressed the button to the fifth floor. He asked her if this was her first time in Brussels. "Yes," she said. "And how long have you been here?"

"Five years. My wife is Belgian. I am from Roma."

"And you like living in Brussels?"

"Bellissimo! I have a son and a daughter. Be careful, or I will start showing you photos of them," he laughed.

*THE BANK*

Left to herself in her apartment, Saskia shrugged off her backpack, glad to be rid of the weight of her laptops. She then set to exploring her new temporary home. It was nice. Two rooms and a bathroom, about the size of her rooms in Mme Claire's house. The entrance room was a study-cum-sitting area. The matching furniture – a large desk with a desk chair, sofa, small table and two chairs – appeared comfortable and had an antique look, upholstered in dark green suede with a faint floral pattern. The wall opposite the couch held a large TV screen. An empty bookshelf stood next to the desk. Tucked into a corner of the room was a small but serviceable kitchenette, well-equipped. The bedroom held a queen-size bed, bedside tables, bed lamps and a wardrobe. A large window showed a view of a street leading to the main square and its impressive buildings. An armchair, matching the sofa in the other room, stood near the window. The red-gold carpet was plush and soft and matched the slightly darker curtains, both contrasting tastefully with the green and gold embroidered bedspread. Even the pictures on the walls looked like someone had taken care with their artistic quality. The bathroom, which she was glad to see featured a shower head that could be lowered, featured marbled white tiles with Delft-blue trim plus a large mirror over the basin with inset lights.

And there were four hidden cameras: two in the study-sitting area, one in the bedroom and one in the bathroom.

Saskia unpacked and shoved her emptied suitcases into a corner, then lay on her bed and called her parents. She dutifully described her surroundings, asked after family members and friends, and listened to gossip. Smiling fondly, she blew kisses into the phone to sign off.

She made herself a cup of tea and had just settled at the desk and opened her laptop when her mother called again.

"Saskia, I forgot nearly to say you. A nice man is in Delft. He coming to café was. He say son of him in Brussels since two weeks. He show me picture of son. His face very handsome."

"Mama!" Saskia groaned. She knew where this was going. Her mother took every opportunity to introduce her to possible suitors, convinced Saskia needed to marry someone.

"I give him your phone number –"

"Mama! Are you joking?"

"No! No! Not joking. The man in café is very, very nice. He say his son is barista. He travel in Europe and stay some time in Brussel. You maybe like him."

"Mama, I'm here to work!"

"Ah! Child of me. You not work all time, all time. He give you call. I tell the father you will happy for him for calling. Bye. Bye. You go out with nice son just one time. Okay?"

"She is impossible!" Saskia grumbled, setting the phone aside, "I don't want a boyfriend!"

## 27

## THE SAFE

Once Saskia had started working for more than subsistence wages at the university in Munich, she'd found a seamstress to make clothes for her. All her adult life, she had only ever worn slacks and blouses (except for bike gear, of course), but even her limited wardrobe requirements had been challenging. She did not have large breasts, but blouses that fit the length of her arms did not fit the breadth of her chest.

Saskia now had a variety of short and long-sleeved blouses and black slacks made from different types of material. For everyday wear, she chose stretch fabric, straight-leg slacks and plain shirts, but when required to dress up for a special occasion, she selected one of her more tailored black slacks and creative blouses.

For dinner tonight with M. Benkirane she decided to wear a blouse with different shades of grey stripes, black collar, cuffs and buttons, and slipped her feet into dress-up soft, black, flat leather shoes. She regarded herself in the mirror (ignoring as best she could that someone else was probably also looking) and frowned. She much preferred preparing for a bike ride than getting dressed up for dinner.

Apart from having her clothes tailor-made, her other indulgence was a regular visit to a beauty therapist. Mostly, it was because she enjoyed being pampered, but there was no doubt that her eyebrows were better behaved now that a therapist had control over them.

It was winter, so her brown skin was lighter than it was in summer. Tight black curls feathered her forehead and temples. Her brown eyes had tiny flecks of black in them. Hans used to tell her they were code for her brain, and he'd try to decode them, making her laugh. The beauty therapist once remarked that she had a sharp chin, which accentuated her graceful neck, though she stopped short of telling her she was beautiful.

Saskia had never let a hairdresser loose on her curls, fearing their efforts at styling would force her to do more than wash and comb her tresses. Occasionally, Saskia snipped off the end of her hair, but she always wore it tied back, changing the band and including ribbons for variety. Tonight, she chose a white ribbon and twisted the ponytail, hoping the curls would align and keep the tail neat.

"Stay!" she told the ponytail as she finished the twist and stepped off the footstool Mario had brought to the room. She pocketed phone and wallet, locked the laptops into the room safe, picked up her puffer jacket and left the room.

Phillipe was already in the foyer, leaning on the reception desk talking with Mario and the night-duty concierge, who introduced himself as Abdullah. He led her to the limousine parked in the small bay at the front doors of the apartment block, and opened the back door.

"Do you mind if I sit in the front seat?"

"But, of course, you may!"

"Have we far to go?" Saskia asked as they set off.

"Monsieur Benkirane lives in the Woluwe-St-Pierre district. It is a little distance from here."

"I don't know Brussels at all. But I presume you know it well?"

"Quite well. I have been Monsieur's family chauffeur for almost six years."

"I think he became head of the bank at that time. Have you always been a chauffeur?"

"No. I was in the French military. My problem is that I love to read

# THE BANK

and this is the perfect job for me. I spend much time idle and have many hours for reading." They stopped at a traffic light and he reached across and opened the glove compartment to reveal a science fiction book by Martha Wells. "This is my current obsession, but my tastes are eclectic."

"A book written in English. So, you speak that language well?"

"I do. I read French and English books. The variety is greater in English."

"Yes. The English language does rather dominate the book market at present."

Phillipe closed the glovebox. "This is La Rue de la Loi," he said, noting Saskia's inspection of the buildings on either side of the street. It is the home of many prominent EU institutions."

"It would appear that each institution is determined to show off its unwillingness to cooperate with the other!"

Phillipe chuckled. "An astute observation. It is indeed an uncoordinated streetscape."

Saskia shook her head at the ad hoc mixture of marble, concrete, pillars, steps, variations in windows and height crammed against one another. She reached for her phone but then put it down. "I like to take photos for my parents," she told Phillipe, "but I'll do it in the daytime. It's too dark now."

"Your parents have not visited Brussels?"

"They rarely venture beyond the confines of the small city they live in. They live vicariously on my travels. If I don't send them regular updates of places I visit, I am accused of neglecting them."

"Brussels is not only buildings," Philipe said. "We now go under Parc du Cinquantenaire. I hope you will find time to visit that park. It was built to mark the anniversary of Belgium's independence and is full of monuments, sculptures and French-style gardens. This tunnel takes us to Avenue de Tervueren. The people of Brussels sometimes call it 'the Champs Élysées of Brussels'. Unfortunately, it is currently the site of controversy with redevelopment plans. Some residents complain that bike riders will likely become more out of control and parking spaces will be lost."

"The car continues to dominate," Saskia sighed. "Us poor bike riders are under-appreciated."

"Indeed," Phillipe chuckled, and Saskia noted that he didn't enquire further about her bike riding. She wondered what else he already knew about her.

The car exited the tunnel on to a broad avenue of six- to seven-storey buildings, again in eclectic styles.

"We will now travel down to the Woluwe-Saint-Pierre municipality. Monsieur Benkirane lives not far from Mellaerts Ponds."

Minutes later, Phillipe turned the car into a long driveway towards a grand house surrounded by formal gardens. M. Benkirane met Saskia at the front door, dressed casually in loose fawn trousers and a zigzag patterned pullover, the collar of his shirt showing at the neckline.

"Welcome. Come in, come in." He introduced Saskia to his wife, Noor. She was a slender woman with dark eyes and greying hair mostly covered by an artfully draped long, white scarf, one end slung over a shoulder. She wore a vibrant, embroidered blue kaftan. "Welcome to our home," she said, her voice and smile warm, though there was a sadness about her dark eyes.

Turning to lead the way, M. Benkirane waved his hand and a woman appeared at Saskia's side. "May I take your coat?" she said. Saskia hurriedly unzipped her coat and let the woman slip it from her shoulders as she continued after her hosts through a marble hallway hung with oriental tapestries and into a wide living space that looked out through floor-to-ceiling glass into a brightly lit formal garden edged by forest.

Saskia stopped, arrested by the scene. "Wow!" she said, then took in the rest of the room. At one end, a table was laid for seven, complete with crystal wine and water glasses, polished cutlery and gold-rimmed crockery. Men dressed in black trousers and white shirts stood at attention against sideboards laden with trays of canapés and drinks.

"Unfortunately, it is still winter," M. Benkirane said. "Our beautiful garden is bare of blooms. But I hope I will gladden your heart by drawing your attention to our other guests." He touched Saskia's shoulder to direct her towards the couple making their way across the room towards her.

"Madame Le Fèvre!" Saskia exclaimed, tipping her face up to accept and return kisses.

"It is indeed a pleasure to see you again, Saskia," Mme Le Fèvre said, "and this is my husband, Armand."

M. Benkirane extended his hand, palm up in invitation. "Please, sit. Please sit, everyone." he said graciously. "I hope I have delighted you, Saskia."

"It's a pleasure to see Madame Le Fèvre again," Saskia agreed, shifting on to the sofa next to her former supervisor.

"Monsieur Benkirane tells me that even in your role as trainer, you continue to uncover anomalies in the bank's systems," Mme Le Fèvre said with a smile. "I did warn him that you would not be able to resist looking for such anomalies."

"Indeed! I'm delighted," M. Benkirane chuckled. "I have found Saskia to be an invaluable asset to FSB. I am hoping to put her to use to make ours the best bank in Europe."

Mme Le Fèvre patted Saskia's knee, eyes crinkling with amusement. "Our esteemed leader tells me he has fallen in love with your maps in the same way I did." She turned to Armand and Noor and proceeded to tell them about Saskia's systems maps and how she had discovered her.

Saskia sampled canapés and sipped at a glass of Dom Perignon. When they moved to the dining table, laden with lamb and chicken tagines, a waiter placed a glass of Châteauneuf-du-Pape before her. She knew little about wines except that some tasted better than others, but Armand assured her it would delight her tongue.

It did. She had just agreed with Armand that his insight into wines was good, and swallowed her disappointment upon learning that Mme Le Fèvre was soon to leave Brussels to take up a secondment at the New York branch of FSB, when her phone vibrated in her pocket.

It was a particular vibration that required immediate attention. She excused herself and left the room. Someone was attempting to access her laptop!

Thoroughly outraged, Saskia dialled the number of the concierge, Abdullah. She introduced herself and demanded to know who was in her room. Flustered, Abdullah promised to investigate immediately. Saskia said she would wait online to hear from him. Seven minutes later, he was back on the phone to tell her he had asked Mario to investigate, and the porter had found the room undisturbed.

"Does Mario have a keycard to my room?" Saskia demanded.

"No, Doctor. I've just given one to him."

"Who has access to the safes in the apartment building?"

"No one, Doctor."

"If someone forgets their safe number, how do you help them?"

"We have to call a locksmith, Doctor."

"No one is in my apartment now?"

"No, Doctor. I double-checked the room with Mario."

Saskia rang off. *Liar!* she thought furiously. It was one thing to be continuously spied upon. It was unforgivable to have anyone tamper with her laptop!

"Is there a problem?"

Saskia looked over her shoulder to see M. Benkirane and Mme Le Fèvre standing in the hallway.

"Someone just tried to access my laptop."

"And you know that?" M. Benkirane asked, his eyes wide with surprise.

"Of course I know that!" Saskia snapped. "I'm not some stupid nerd who doesn't keep tabs on her equipment."

"I see. And whom have you just spoken to?"

"The concierge, who says no one was in my room!"

"But you are certain your laptop was tampered with?"

"I know the information on my laptop was not accessed, but I know someone tried to access it."

"Do you know if someone is still attempting to get into it?"

Saskia pocketed her phone. "Not anymore."

"Why would someone want to access information on your laptop?" Mme Le Févre asked.

"I don't know."

"Do you have an FSB laptop as well?" Mme Le Févre asked.

"Yes. That's with my laptop. But it wasn't opened."

"But you would know if it was?" M Benkirane asked.

"Of course."

"Mon dieu! I think I need you to install that capacity on all our equipment."

## 28

## OLIVIER

A white bulldog lolled in a basket near the entrance to Kaffabar, its black-speckled jowls hanging over the basket's edge. Saskia guessed the dog would be a complete failure as a guard dog. She scanned the terrace. The black umbrellas were all down and tied up, allowing weak sunshine to bathe the grey tiles. Three of the dozen or so tables were occupied, two by couples and one by a man who sat at a table close to the planter box fencing separating the terrace from Doornikstraat, which ran along the side of the café.

The single man stood up and waved to her.

Saskia's shoulders slumped, though she also felt a small spurt of guilt. She had deliberately delayed her arrival, hoping that the man – he'd introduced himself as Olivier when he'd telephoned – would decide it was not worthwhile to meet her.

"I'm a small person with black trousers and an oversized maroon puffer jacket," she'd said when he asked how he would recognise her. She had expressed her reluctance at a forced meeting between them, saying that her present mood was not conducive to small talk with strangers. But Olivier had seemed bemused by his father's conspiracy with her mother and persisted. "Please," he'd said, sounding like he was smiling "let's meet at Kaffabar. Perhaps we can be friends and, if nothing else, we can enjoy a good coffee."

He was a tall man with swept-back dark hair, a clean-shaven face and thin-rimmed owl glasses over blue eyes. He wore a tight jersey that showed off his muscular arms and chest, attire that told Saskia he was untroubled by the cold. Indeed, the large hand that enfolded her cold one was warm, as was his smile.

"I'm pleased you decided to come," he said with a chuckle. "I was beginning to think I'd have to disappoint my father with stories of how I was jilted by a woman of his choosing without even meeting her." He spoke with a pronounced Parisian French accent, though she thought she'd heard his voice before. *You were on the phone to him, Saskia!*

She cleared her throat, pulling her thoughts back from speculation and noting her cheeks had heated with embarrassment about dragging her feet to this meeting. "Um – sorry I'm late."

He waved the apology aside. "We are now in springtime but it's a cool morning. Allow me to try to make our seating more comfortable." With quick steps, he picked up several neatly folded blankets off nearby unoccupied chairs and deposited them on a chair at the table he'd chosen. "That should provide a comfortable padding," he said, holding one blanket aside and handing it to her to arrange over her legs when she settled on the soft, elevated seat.

"Er – thank you. Um – you obviously don't feel the cold."

"Not so much…" He glanced at the doorway into the café. "It's quite busy inside – I think the staff are preoccupied. I'll wander in and order for us. What will it be?"

Saskia watched as Olivier bent to pat the slumbering bulldog and then disappear into the café. Her brow furrowed, mind returning to the puzzle that something about him was familiar. She tucked her hands under the blanket over her thighs and looked around, wondering as she often did when in a public place, whether any of the people sitting or standing around where part of her guard detail or, more worryingly, part of the group spying on her.

"So, what is it about your mother that has induced my father to be so insistent upon this meeting?" Olivier asked upon returning to his seat.

"I could ask the same about your father."

Olivier grinned. He sat back in the chair, crossing his legs. "Since the death of my mother, my father travels. He has a significant interest in history, particularly the background to the Peace of Westphalia. As you probably know, Delft – where my father met your mother – was the site of a significant military engagement during the Eighty Years' War."

"Yes. I know Delft's history, but it is not a topic that would have engaged my mother, who has zero interest in history of any type unless it has to do with food or family." Saskia's tone was short, because something about Olivier was very distracting.

"I believe the conversation between your mother and my father only involved their preoccupation with the unmarried status of their children. Your mother was pleased to learn that I am a keen bike rider and like to keep fit. She told my father that you had the same interests, and an unhealthy interest in computers. She also revealed that you had taken a temporary bank job in Brussels as a bank teller." At this, Saskia's lips pulled into a grin. Olivier smiled and continued, "My father excitedly told your mother that I, his son, had not long ago also decided to visit Brussels. After my father told me about you, I was curious. So, I looked for your name on the internet. I was rewarded with information that indicated your status at the bank – indeed, your status in the scholarly finance and computer science fraternity – is somewhat further up the hierarchy than that of a bank teller."

Saskia's head tipped slightly to the side. "So – o," she said slowly, her eyes narrowing, "you already knew what I looked like and had no need to ask me for that information."

"I needed to make sure." Olivier uncrossed his legs and sat forward.

Saskia blurted, "You're Simon!"

Olivier leaned further across the table. "Not so loud!" he said softly. Then, he wrinkled his nose in disappointment. "Did I do so badly in my disguise?"

Saskia blinked, taking a moment to come to terms with her discovery. "Um – no. It's just that your eyebrows looked familiar."

"My eyebrows?" Simon's eyebrows rose obediently to express his surprise.

"Um – yes. I've got a bit of a thing about eyebrows. I've discovered that people find them hard to control. So, you can sort of read what they're thinking by concentrating on their eyebrows. And everyone's eyebrows are unique."

Olivier sat up straight, fingers tracing his eyebrows. "You are a revelation a minute, Saskia. My admiration of you goes up each time we meet. Should I do something about my eyebrows, or do you think my disguise is otherwise passable?"

"Well – um – you also do that thing of sitting back in your chair and crossing your legs."

Simon's eyes widened in mock horror and his eyebrows rose higher, his forehead wrinkling to make room for them. "I am an abject failure," he moaned, then grinned. "In my defence, I was working hard to give you hints about my identity." He touched his eyebrows again. "Though I did not consider these. And I would very much appreciate it if you would think of me and refer to me as Olivier Lynch."

Coffee arrived at their table, along with pastries.

Olivier thanked the waiter.

"Is Isabelle still in Lyon?" Saskia asked when the two were alone again.

Olivier lifted the coffee cup to his lips. "She will be arriving in Brussels within the next couple of weeks. At present, she is on her way to Spain to spend a little time with her aunt and uncle. She will then accompany them on their yacht for an extended tour of the Mediterranean. That is to say, her uncle and aunt will continue on the tour, but she will slip away to become another person and fly here to Brussels."

"But you haven't abandoned Madame Claire, have you? Are you sure she'll be safe? I mean, given the cameras in my apartment, it seems someone is still suspicious about me."

"With both you and Isabelle gone from the house, Madame Claire has decided it is a good opportunity to take an extended holiday. She has come into a little money and decided to visit family and friends in Scotland. Rufus, of course, is accompanying her. She has engaged a gardener to take care of her lovely garden while she is away. "

"What about Melanie? Are you still keeping an eye on her?"

"Melanie is still in Paris."

"How is she?"

"Not well. It would seem that her ready source of drugs has disappeared."

"So, you think they've stopped trying to get to me through her?"

"That's our hope."

"You're not abandoning her, are you?"

"No, Saskia. That would not be fair to you. We have enlisted the help of a social worker." Olivier kept his coffee cup hovering in front of his lips. "Leave aside the problem of Melanie at this point. We are doing what we can. In terms of arrangements for assistance to you while you are in Brussels, know that I am now your handler. The reports you have previously provided to Isabelle now come to me. I anticipate we will become the best of friends. And I hope you will report to your mother that you have found me surprisingly good company."

"I suppose I will be."

"Excellent." Olivier indicated the pastries. "Please, help yourself to the pastries."

"So, you'd better give me more background. Why are you in Brussels?"

"Me? I have resigned from a very stressful job with a liquidating firm based in Marseille. I retrained as a barista and currently enjoy a much more relaxed life working at Petit Café. I started my job just two days ago after searching for a position these past two weeks."

"What a surprise that Petit Café happens to be close to my apartment."

"Astonishing! But it was the best we could do given your rapid transfer out of Lyon. Now, tell me more about the report you filed concerning the attempted access of your laptop. You also reported you have evidence it was Mario, the porter. As a consequence, we have looked into Mario's background –"

Saskia held up her hand, silencing Olivier. "Let me give you the information I did not provide in my report. I was feeling very annoyed about being spied upon, and then people tampering with my things, on top of being pushed from pillar to post with little say in how I run my own affairs. Just so you understand the depth of my annoyance, people trying to direct my affairs is the situation I chose to leave behind when I left the clutches of my family." Olivier raised his eyebrows and gave a slight nod in mute acknowledgement. "So," Saskia continued, "on the back of my extreme annoyance at the time of the laptop incident, I filed a notice with the police about the invasion of my apartment. They gave me a complaint number – or whatever it's called – but made it clear they would take no further action, suggesting I take it up with the apartment's security detail, which I'd already done. Security looked at the CCTV footage and declared there was no evidence someone had entered my apartment.

"So, I hacked into the CCTV footage. I found someone had attempted to override the relevant footage by inserting other footage in its place, but I managed to resurrect the original recording. I pieced together segments that showed Mario and the concierge, Abdullah, talking at length not long after I left the building. Abdullah passed various items to Mario. About an hour later, Mario entered my room. Abdullah received my call and hurried to tell Mario to leave my room, then returned to tell me that Mario found no one in my room."

Saskia glared at Simon. "I don't need to be told chapter and verse about Mario's background. I know enough. I cornered Mario in his little room when there was no one else around and showed him the footage I'd stitched together. He confessed he'd been offered the equivalent of two years' salary – half to start with and half when he finished the job – to get into my room and download information from my laptop. Abdullah had given him an override code to access the safe, as well as a device to plug into my computer port. He'd been told that, once in the port, the drive would start blinking and do its work, then cease blinking when it finished its work, whereupon Mario was to remove the drive and return my laptop to the safe.

"I believe Mario's motive – and maybe that of Abdullah – was no greater than wanting to secure extra money. When not working as a porter, Mario has a second job delivering UberEats meals. His wife is a hairdresser and pregnant with their third child. They live in a tiny apartment and are saving money to afford something a little larger. He has no idea why someone would be interested in my laptop and begged me to forgive him. He said he really needed to keep his job. I said I would keep quiet, but in return, he would never do something like that again and, further, would let me know if he suspected others might be tampering with anything in my apartment. He asked me why someone might be interested in information on my laptop. I told him I didn't know, but it might be that I was special assistant to the bank's chief executive officer.

"And, before you ask, no, I have not confronted Abdullah. Mario and I decided we would keep my knowledge of the concierge's involvement our secret, but that Mario would tell me if ever Abdullah or anyone approached him again, or if he suspected the apartment's security detail was compromised, which must have occurred with the CCTV footage tampering."

She straightened her back, sitting tall. "So, that's the story. And, no, I didn't wait to get all my instructions from you lot. And, so far, apart from Mario telling me that Abdullah was nervous about their failure and had left the USB drive in an envelope for collection by some unknown person, it would appear the matter has not gone further. And if the drive has any information from my laptop, it would only show my parents' accounts, my academic work and heaps of personal stuff."

Olivier, who had sat unmoving through her long monologue, his gaze never leaving her face, continued to regard her for a time longer. He nodded slowly. "I see," he said, the words uttered without inflection.

Saskia took a bite of a pastry, determined to hold on to her pique. *Surely*, she thought, *I don't have to just allow myself to be some punching bag moved from place to place?!* "What I'm interested in is what sort of application was on that drive that could potentially just zip stuff from the laptop?"

"That is an interesting question," Simon mused, the intensity of his gaze relaxing as he lifted his mug of coffee to his lips. "We have such applications, of course, but they are not readily available. Do you intend to take further action as a result of this incident?"

Saskia paused mid-chew. "Er – what do you mean?"

"It seems you have created the perfect opportunity to find the listening devices installed in your apartment."

"I have?"

"Certainly. If I may, could I suggest you visit a store selling spy cameras? I will tell you which one. You should purchase a top-of-the-line indoor surveillance camera. In the process of installing this camera in your apartment, I suggest you 'stumble upon'," Olivier set down his mug to hold up his fingers in imitation of quote marks, "the spy devices already installed in your apartment. In high dudgeon, which you have just demonstrated you are quite capable of pulling off – you will take these devices to the concierge and the apartment security service and demand an explanation for how these devices came to be in your apartment. I suggest you fail to find at least one listening device, just so you have opportunities to continue to demonstrate your innocence to whomsoever is carrying out the surveillance."

Saskia blinked. "Er – that's actually not a bad idea." She took her time to finish the pastry, her irritation gradually giving way to a mild sense of discouragement. "I wouldn't have thought of that. It increases my belief that I'm not cut out to be much of a devious spy. I'm more the stewing about injustice type. You and Isabelle are better at creating devious, entrapping scenarios."

"You are formidable enough. Please do not change your methods of gathering data. But let us move on. You have now been in your new position for two weeks. How are you finding it?"

Saskia sighed. "Actually, it hasn't been too bad. On day one, Monsieur Benkirane himself took me around to meet the executive team, and they threw a little welcoming drinks thing for me in the afternoon. I feel quite welcomed, and people talk to me."

"A little different from the Lyon office?"

"Quite different. There, I was on the outer and never felt part of the team. I think that was because Antoine Aubert didn't want me there. Once Madame Le Fèvre left, it got worse. Here, I've already made a bit of a name for myself for being good with Excel spreadsheets and other databases, so people are coming to me to assist them. Consequently, I've managed to uncover some interesting bits and pieces. I'll put it all together for you lot, of course."

Olivier's eyes widened slightly. He pushed his owl glasses further up the bridge of his nose. "Phew! Let me reiterate that you are formidable. Care to precis a finding?"

"Hamid Mangin, who is Ayat Benkirane's second, appears to have much to do with a London-based law firm by the name of O'Connell and Hansen. In the past week, he has referred three clients to this firm."

"And how did you discover this?"

"I overheard him complaining about not being able to get headings to freeze on his Excel spreadsheet. So, I offered to show him how. Then I offered to show him a few other tricks. As a result, I got to see what he had on the spreadsheet. He has one sheet labelled O'Connell and Hansen. It lists many companies. Some I recognised as the ones we have already identified as shell companies using FSB to transact money."

"I don't suppose the beneficial owners were also listed?"

"Not as far as I could see. I didn't get a chance to study the spreadsheet properly, but I noted that he also keeps the information on a USB device rather than on the bank's system, so I can't even – er – 'accidentally' come across it on the bank system."

"Any idea where he keeps this USB?"

"It was attached to a lanyard. Once I finished showing him how to freeze the header, he removed the USB and put it in his pocket."

## 29

### A CHILD AT THE BANK

"You had a pleasant weekend?" M. Benkirane asked as he pushed an office chair to the conference table in his office for Saskia to sit at.

Saskia huffed a small laugh as she sat and levered herself up to an appropriate height. "I did, actually. My mother, who is always trying to find me a husband, arranged for me to meet with the son of an acquaintance. I objected to this arrangement, but it turns out he's pretty good company."

"Your mother will be pleased." M. Benkirane sat on a chair next to hers.

"Well, perhaps not," Saskia chuckled, opening the laptop she'd brought into the room and set on the table. "The best part is that he's gay, which his father doesn't know, so my mother doesn't know either."

"But you spent the weekend with him?"

"Much of the weekend. He's a keen cyclist, so we hired bikes and toured Brussels for a few hours on Saturday. On Sunday, we joined a few of his friends in their car, and they showed us around the countryside. I've also signed up to join the gym he's a member of."

"He's a long-term resident of Brussels, then?"

"No. He's only been here a few weeks. He resigned from his job as a bankruptcy accountant and decided to do something very different. So, he's now a barista."

"A barista!"

Saskia laughed, her fingers on the laptop's keypad bringing its screen to life. "Yes. Quite a change. He came to Brussels because his friends were here. They're a fun lot. So, my mother did me a favour after all."

"I'm pleased for you." M. Benkirane's attention shifted to the graph on the screen, but he said, "Has anything further come about regarding the attempt with your computer?"

Saskia sobered. "This is the unpleasant part of the weekend. You know how the apartment security people were adamant that there was no evidence that someone was in my apartment? Well, I told Olivier what happened. In his past work he sometimes dealt with stuff that wasn't always – um – you know – very ethical. He suggested I get a security camera, which I did that afternoon. I was looking for place to put the camera and found a listening device attached to the backside of a wall hanging! Then I went on a hunt and found two more! One in the kitchen and another in the bedroom. I told the concierge about it, and she called security. They came and inspected the devices and took them away. But how they treated the affair made it pretty clear they thought I'd planted the devices myself."

"Did you tell them you intended to put in a camera?"

"No. I don't trust them."

"That's unfortunate. Would you like me to ask the security company FSB engages to have a look at your apartment's security?"

"Can you do that?"

"Of course. I'll organise it." He turned his attention to the laptop Saskia had placed on the meeting table between them. "Now, talk me through your findings thus far."

Saskia moved a finger on the laptop's trackpad to move the cursor to a line on the chart. "You asked me to find firms offering advice on international carbon offset schemes – "

The office door opened without warning. M. Benkirane's head

jerked up, and then he launched to his feet, sending his chair skidding away.

Saskia swung her chair around to face the doorway.

A tall, thin man, dressed in a blue suit, strode into the office. He had slicked-back black hair, greying at the temples, and a neatly trimmed moustache and beard, both cut close. Thick, shaped eyebrows and a prominent nose made his dark eyes look predatory.

"Ayat," he began, but cut himself off when his gaze fell upon Saskia. His eyebrows rose. "Ayat! Are you playing computer games with children now?" His voice was high-pitched, almost squeaky. He spoke French with a heavy Middle Eastern accent, though Saskia could not tell from which country. His overly white, overly even teeth flashed as his fleshy lips parted in a grin.

Unable to completely mask his disquiet, M. Benkirane said, "Azzam. An unexpected meeting."

"I was in the city and decided to deliver a personal invitation to my chief banker."

Two other men entered the office. One was thick set in an ill-fitting black suit and dark glasses who took up a position just inside the door and became immobile, though his large hands curled slightly as if ready to grip something and squeeze hard. The second man was perhaps in his early thirties. He was clean-shaven, had a slender build and sandy hair. He wore a business-regulation, slightly chequered suit, striped tie and polished black leather shoes with long pointy toes.

M. Benkirane ignored the thug but acknowledged the younger man. "Amir, I didn't realise you were in Brussels also."

"At my invitation," the thin man said in an off-hand way. He brushed past Ayat, shifted the chair vacated by M. Benkirane before Saskia and sat, leaning slightly towards her.

He said, "Who is this creature?"

Saskia resisted the urge to physically draw back or change her facial expression from mild interest to active distaste.

"May I – " M. Benkirane began, but the newcomer cut him off.

"Who are you?" he demanded of Saskia.

"Monsieur," Saskia responded politely. "My name is Saskia van Essen."

"It speaks!" The man chortled. "Stand up."

Saskia slipped off her chair. Out of the corner of her eye, she saw M. Benkirane step closer, his lips drawn into a thin line, hands balled into fists at his side. But he remained silent.

"How tall are you?'

"I have a height of one hundred and twenty-one centimetres."

"You are full grown?"

"I am, Monsieur."

"How old are you?"

"Twenty-eight, Monsieur."

The thin man collapsed back into his chair as if this information astounded him. "Why aren't you in a circus?"

"I applied, Monsieur, but the ringmaster said I was not pretty enough to make my bike tricks worthwhile. So, I am forced to find other employment."

The response brought a hoot of laughter. "You wanted to do bike tricks at a circus?"

"Oui, Monsieur."

"What sort of bike tricks do you do?"

Saskia retrieved her phone from the back pocket of her trousers, swiped into the photo albums and chose a video of her BMX bike stunts at a skate park.

He took the phone from her and re-ran the video. His eyes flicked up to look at her. "You have more like this?"

Saskia showed him a video of her somersaulting off a kicker on a mountain bike trail.

"Who are these people?" The thin man pointed at bystanders in the video. "Are these children?"

"Yes, Monsieur."

"Why are they looking at you?"

"They are my students, Monsieur. I was demonstrating a technique."

"You teach bike tricks?"

"I sometimes teach children and adults how to do tricks on BMX, scooters or mountain bikes, Monsieur."

He turned to M. Benkirane. "Is she a relative of yours, Ayat? I didn't know you had more fuzzy wuzzies in your family."

"Doctor van Essen is my chief research officer." M. Benzirane emphasised her title; his voice cold enough to frost the windows. "Dr van Essen, may I present to you Monsieur Azzam Touati."

"Enchantée," Saskia said, though she was anything but enchanted by this man.

"Research, eh?" M. Touati mused. "What sort of research do you do?"

"Mostly financial research, Monsieur."

"So, you are also smart?" he tapped the side of his head, a condescending smile on his lips.

"It depends on whom you ask, Monsieur."

"I'm asking you."

"Then it depends on the day and the task, Monsieur."

M. Touati chuckled. "I like you," he decided. "You will teach my son how to ride his new bike. He is interested in learning tricks."

"I charge for lessons, Monsieur."

The man's amusement increased, grin widening. He studied her, stroking his cheek. "I will give you ten thousand euros if you can teach my son how to ride his new bike and do tricks."

"I agree, but only if your son wants to do this and his bike is the right kind."

"Then, we are agreed," he laughed. "You will hear shortly about arrangements to come to my residence on Sunday."

Rising, he turned to M. Benkirane. "I am having a birthday party for Gadil in one month. You will come. Don't forget your wife. She will no doubt want to see the children." He jerked his head towards the bulky man. "Give him his invitation," he said peremptorily. "See you in one month, Ayat." And with that, he strode out of the room.

The bulky man took an envelope from his coat pocket and set it down on a side table near the door, then turned on his heel out of the door. The young man glanced at M. Benkirane, gave a slight shrug and hurried out.

Ayat Benkirane walked stiffly to the office door and closed it. The face he turned to Saskia was red with rage. "First, I must apologise for his behaviour," he said, his voice low and tight. "Next, I want to know why you agreed to his outrageous offer."

"Because I was extremely annoyed, Monsieur," Saskia replied evenly. "I don't like bullies."

M. Benkirane drew in a sharp breath and blinked a few times as he stared at her, the red of his face draining away. "And you believe I do?"

Saskia shrugged. "I didn't consider you, Monsieur. I was only reacting to his goading of me."

"He is an important client of this bank."

Saskia nodded non-committedly, though her mind was racing as she tried to remember whether she had ever come across the name Azzam Touati as a bank client. "And may I ask the interest of the other two gentlemen? The one by the door looked like a bodyguard."

"You may be correct. I have not seen him before. I know the other man as Amir Berber." He rubbed his forehead, clearly disturbed, his dark eyes searching her face. "I understand that you may have been reacting to his goading, Saskia, but it may not be a good idea for you to continue with the agreement to teach his son. Please reconsider."

Saskia tipped her head to one side, "No need, Monsieur. But is there something I should know about Monsieur Touati?"

The European bank chief hesitated so long that Saskia wondered if she would get an answer. "Azzam Touati is a very wealthy man and, like all such men, can be, shall I say, fickle."

"Yes, I got that. But I only agreed to teach his son if his son wants me to. If not, I'll just let it go."

"Does the prospect of ten thousand euros attract you?"

"I told a lie. I don't charge for teaching children, though I wouldn't be sorry to lighten Monsieur Touati's pockets. Nevertheless, when the opportunity presents itself, I will tell the monsieur that I have never applied to a circus, and I don't want his money."

"But you intend to teach his son on the bike?"

"If his son wants it, sure, I'll do it. I like teaching children, and I'm good at it."

M. Benkirane stood still a while, a worried frown on his brow. "Saskia, I implore you not to work for Monsieur Touati."

Saskia chose to misinterpret his worry. "Monsieur don't worry. I've taught lots of children, and I'm confident I can do it. It will be fun to be involved with children again. I haven't had a chance since being in Brussels."

*Mostly,* she thought, *I am truly curious about Monsieur Touati's relationship with the bank, and why you are so worried about him.*

## 30

## LUNCH

"You have created an interesting challenge for us," Olivier said. They were strolling down the middle of Grote Markt, the famous and vast square in the middle of old Brussels city. It was a relatively warm day, the feel of summer beginning to edge out spring's changeable temperature fluctuations. Olivier was on one side of Saskia, and Gerard, a man as tall and muscular as Olivier but with reddish hair and a much-freckled skin who had been introduced to Saskia the week before as Olivier's friend, was on her other side. Hanging off Gerard's arm was Angela, who used to be Isabelle but was now an English tourist who had taken a liking to Gerard and decided to stay in Brussels for a while. She had red-brown, curly hair, tattoos down her arms, hoop earrings and hazel eyes. She wore tight jeans, a partly tucked in loose hoodie and slightly grubby sandshoes. All four spoke English because Angela spoke neither French nor Dutch.

Olivier dipped his head to look down at Saskia. "There is now a frantic search for who Azzam Touati is and why his name is not among the list of the bank's clients that you have been passing on to us. I can tell you that the man accompanying him at FSB on the day, Amir Berber, is an employee of O'Connell and Hansen. He flew in from London two days ago. We've been back and forth with our English partners about O'Connell and Hansen. The law firm is known to them as one of the go-to firms for wealthy individuals who wish to conceal their true wealth from tax authorities."

"I found out that Messieurs Berber and Touati were at the bank to meet Hamid Mangin, who is Monsieur Benkirane's second," Saskia said. "He usually deals with the bank's most important clients. I thought I'd downloaded his client list, but it seems some of his clients are not listed –"

Olivier touched Saskia's shoulder, bringing her to a standstill. He pointed to the most imposing of the many imposing buildings surrounding Grote Markt. "I've walked through here several times over the past few weeks, but I haven't done the tourist thing yet. What can you tell me about that building, Gerard," he said, then in a much softer tone, his lips barely moving, "We are being tailed and filmed."

"That's our town hall," Gerard said. "It's had many remakes over the centuries."

"Look at all those statues!" Angela exclaimed in her Oxford English accent. "Were they real people?"

"Yep. They represent local nobility. They are mostly dukes and duchesses of Brabant and knights of the noble houses of Brussels. A few are saints and allegorical figures. The statues are reproductions, though. The ones that used to be there in the fifteenth century are in the Brussels City Museum." Gerard pivoted to point to a four-storey neo-Gothic building with a central tower. "That's the King's House, which houses the museum."

"Why are dukes and duchesses of Brabant featured in Brussels? Isn't Brabant in the Netherlands?" Angela asked.

Olivier chuckled. "We'll stand here all day if you want to get into the history of that word."

"In short," Gerard explained, "in geological terms, it is a structure or a massif that stretches from England to northern Germany. The word means lowlands. Brabant is also the name of the feudal duchy that covered modern-day Belgian Flemish Brabant, Walloon Brabant and Antwerp, the Brussels-Capital Region and most of the present-day

Dutch province of North Brabant. It was divided after the Eighty Years' War."

"Our tail has been replaced by a woman," Olivier said quietly, adjusting his glasses. "Let's move on." He gestured to the closely packed houses with sculptural decorations lining the square. "Gerard, do tell us some more about these places around us."

An hour later, they strolled into Brasserie Le Plattesteen and sat in a corner booth with a mirror along part of the wall that provided a view of the rest of the room. Saskia wondered whether the person who had been occupying the booth and stood to depart the moment they entered was part of Gerard's team. She also wondered whether the two people in the closest booths, who seemed in no hurry to leave, were also part of the team. But she didn't ask, knowing Olivier preferred to give her 'need to know' information only.

Up until they placed and received their drinks and lunch orders, Angela told them more stories about her travel adventures and her life in England. Olivier shared stories of his time as an accountant and Gerard complained that his life in Brussels was boring compared to everyone else's.

"Have you heard further from Mr Touati today, Saskia?" Olivier asked, once the waiter had delivered all drinks and food to the table.

"This morning." Saskia took her phone from her back pocket and swiped into her messages. "Doctor research officer," she read in French, "my driver will pick you up at your apartment building at eight in the morning on Sunday. Be ready. We will feed you, so bring only yourself. You will be returned to your apartment in the afternoon."

"The command delivered," Angela murmured, tossing a side salad.

"To tell you more about O'Connell and Hansen," Olivier said, forking part of a meatball dripping with tomato sauce into his mouth. "As I noted, it is a law firm specialising in setting up domestic and overseas legal entities. The firm sometimes acts as signature of sale nominees, and it purchases commercial and residential properties for clients through trust or client accounts in the UK and other countries. As is usual for law firms, they have strict client confidentiality protocols. Anything more you can find about the relationship between

# THE BANK

O'Connell and Hansen and FSB would be good, Saskia. Now, Angela, bring us up to speed about Azzam Touati."

Angela leaned forward slightly, noting that Azzam Touati's official place of birth was Algeria, though there was no detail about his background before purchasing a property on the outskirts of Algiers. Ten years ago, he had settled in a chateau in Lyon, France, together with his wife and three children, though he continued to maintain a heavily guarded estate in Algiers that he frequently visited. After five years, he received French citizenship and, soon after, moved into a renovated estate on the shores of the upper Scheldt River, about twenty kilometres from Ename, Belgium. He kept a low profile in Lyon. He owned several property development companies throughout east and western Europe. Income from these properties was his purported source of ongoing wealth, and that income was banked with Rabo Bank.

"It's a puzzle that Benkirane says he's an FSB customer," Angela continued. "We've run the numbers for the funds he holds with Rabo, and they don't adequately explain his obvious wealth. Rumour has it that Touati was a key figure in the turmoil that engulfed Algeria in the nineteen-eighties and nineties, and his original source of wealth came from his links with the Saudis, who engaged him to promote Sharia law in Algeria."

Angela had ordered a side salad and chicons au gratin. She pushed endives around her plate as she spoke. "The castle estate he lives in now was derelict, but the locals say it was purchased some dozen years ago and significantly renovated. The fourteen-hectare property is surrounded by a three-metre spear-topped palisade fence with security cameras mounted on poles at regular intervals. There are dog patrols of the perimeter on a regular basis. There's quite a bit of coming and going at the estate, but none of it has to do with the locals, who are generally curious about the place."

"River access, since it's on the shores of the river?" Saskia asked, wondering if she should also feign intense interest in her food.

Angela tipped her head from side to side, an out-of-context smile on her lips. "Yes and no. There's a landing place for boats and a large gate, but it's locked, and there are security cameras mounted on poles nearby. There's a moat, but it's only on three sides because it's linked to the river in a U shape. We believe the moat was built in the twelfth century when the original castle was built. At the two places where the palisade fence intersects the canal, steel bars go all the way to the bottom of the canal, blocking access. The fortifications facing the river are the strongest and tallest. We think it must have been the castle keep at one stage. The portcullis-covered archway is a few hundred metres from the water's edge. There's a tower with guards posted on it over the top of the portcullis."

As she spoke, Angela traced a U shape on the table and a line through the top of the U to show the fence line. She ran her finger through the fence line to indicate the location of the gate in the middle of the U. With the palm of her hand, she erased the faint marks of her sketch from the tabletop. "We're currently searching through historical records to find as much as we can about the castle."

"There's an official walking and bike path on the opposite riverbank," Gerard said. "People often stop to look at the castle. In reality, all they can see is the entry and exit point of the canal, the palisade fence, a green field and a huge archway in a stone wall with towers at each corner and the portcullis, which is mostly closed. Locals say they sometimes see children riding bikes and scooters around the green space. That's the only time they see the children."

Gerard skewered a piece of tomato on his plate. "There are more towers spaced around the walls. Our drone footage showed men walking along the top of the wall. We flew one of our drones too close, and it was fired on. Soon after, security guards left the castle and began searching for the drone operators. So, it's clear they don't muck around with taking security seriously."

The drone image captured was of a long main building with two wings, he continued. The wings butted up against the wall on either side of the portcullis. According to locals, most of what was inside the walls was in ruins, so the building there was new. The castle wall was about nine metres high. The main entrance was via a road through a forest to a heavily guarded gate, with a guardhouse and garages at the gate.

"It looks like all cars stay at the gate," Gerard said, waving a piece of baguette. "That entrance is about four hundred metres from the drawbridge through the castle wall. Transport from the gate is via electric carts that travel on a track to the drawbridge."

"Lots of levels of security," Angela murmured.

"The place was purchased by Fleetwood Incorporated ten years ago for six and a half million euros," Gerard said, smacking his lips as he chewed a chunk of beef steak.

Saskia frowned, pausing in the act of cutting her cheese croquette. "That's one of the accounts held by FSB in Lyon."

"We noticed," Olivier chortled.

"Surveillance shows us that all electronic devices are taken away from visitors at the gate, and almost all visitors are subjected to a scan. We suspect the devices taken are subjected to scrutiny." Gerard waved his fork around.

"That means, Saskia, when you go tomorrow, you'll take a replacement phone and watch. Angela has set both up to mirror yours in all but the extra capabilities we installed for you. After this meal, you will both go to the ladies' toilets and exchange the devices," Olivier said.

"May I, for one second, be an anxious mama," Angela said, her tourist out-for-a-good-time facade slipping. "From the moment you step into Azzam Touati's vehicle, please be extra careful. We don't know yet know what or who we are dealing with, but nothing about this man makes me feel comfortable."

# 31

## BIKE TRICKS

The car waiting for Saskia outside her apartment at eight in the morning was big, shiny and black, with tinted windows. A man wearing a dark suit, sunglasses and an earpiece stepped out of the front passenger side door and opened the back door for her.

"Merci," Saskia said.

He gave a miniscule nod of his head and indicated the seatbelt.

She strapped herself in and he closed the door, resuming his seat next to the driver, who was dressed almost identically. The car moved away from the apartment and joined traffic out of the city.

*Alright!* Saskia thought. *No introductions. So, I'm going to be very imaginative and call the first guy Escort, and the other guy Driver.*

After ten minutes of stony silence, and being too low in the seat to see much out of the smoky windows, Saskia pulled her phone out of her back pocket, intending to read the book she had downloaded.

Immediately, Escort turned, extending his hand between the two front seats towards her. "Give!" he commanded.

Saskia opened her mouth to protest, decided it would do no good and placed the phone in his hand. He then pointed to her wrist. "Watch. Give."

She unclipped her watch and handed it over. Escort made a show of putting both watch and phone into a ziplock plastic bag, which he deposited in the glovebox.

Saskia sighed and resigned herself to studying the tops of trees and the cloud-decorated sky. Each time the car's generally even pace slowed, she saw the roofs of houses, the spires of churches and, once, the ruined top of a castle tower. Finally, the car came to a complete stop. Escort opened the back door. Saskia exited the car. Yet another black-suited, dark bespectacled man confronted her. This one waved a wand over her body and then handed her something that looked like a watch. "Put on," he commanded, indicating her wrist.

"What is it?" Saskia asked.

He shook his head as if the question was irrelevant. "Put on!"

"No."

The man made to grab her wrist, but Escort stopped him.

"Follow," Escort said.

Saskia followed him around the back of the car to a guardhouse built into the palisade fence Angela had described. As they approached the guardhouse, a small gate in the fence line clicked open. Escort led Saskia through, silently invited her into the back seat of a waiting electric cart, shifted himself into the driver's seat and set the cart in motion along a thin concrete lane bordered by bright yellow daffodils towards the castle proper.

Despite Angela's description, Saskia gawked at the scale of the nine-metre castle wall that towered directly out of a wide moat. Much of the wall was black with age. She guessed that the lighter stonework showed repairs. The lighter shades were particularly prevalent on the castellated corner towers and raised section above the entrance arch.

Escort stopped the cart just shy of the drawbridge, alighted, opened the back door for Saskia and said, "Walk now."

Saskia hopped out and was further taken aback at the sight of Azzam Touati under the arch. He stood behind seven children, who were neatly arranged from tallest to smallest. Four boys wore grey suits, white shirts and shiny black shoes. Three girls wore white lace dresses and sparkling slipper-type shoes. The tallest girl wore a hijab. The other two had white ribbons in their long dark hair. They all wore the wrist device that the guard at the gate had attempted to secure to her.

Azzam Touati had swapped his three-piece suit for a brilliant white gandoura with gold embroidered trim around the neck, down the front and on the sleeve cuffs.

Saskia walked across the bridge.

"You have come to my home," M. Touati announced in his high voice as she drew near. "These are seven of my children." He placed a large hand, bedecked with a prominent jewelled ring on his third finger, on the tallest child's head. He was a handsome boy with bright blue eyes, sandy hair and full red lips. "Gadil. He is fourteen years old. We will celebrate his majority at the party. You will teach him bike skills."

The boy eyed Saskia sceptically but did not move nor return her polite greeting.

M. Touati placed his hand on the head of the next child. "My eldest daughter, Tehzib. She is thirteen years old." She had a darker complexion than her brother. Her brown eyes swept up and down Saskia. Like her brother, she remained unmoving and silent.

"My daughter, Amina. She is eleven years old," he continued, placing his hand on the next child in line. Her complexion was more like that of her older brother, and she had a bold glint in her hazel eyes. The next daughter, Mouna, was darker and nine years old. Then came Tarek, aged eight; Yasser, aged seven, whose brown hair was touched with red; and finally, Jamal, aged five.

"My other three children are too young to trust to be well-behaved," M. Touati declared.

"You have a large family, Monsieur. And your children are very handsome."

Her host seemed pleased by that observation, allowing a smile to twitch his lips. "Now, you may come into my home."

Still silent and formal, the children parted to let her pass, girls to one side, boys to the other.

Saskia gasped at the sight that opened up. "Monsieur, your home is magnificent!" Though the surrounding walls were medieval in style, an

Islamic-style 'palace' was a better description of the two-storey sandstone building. A grand staircase flanked by huge urns filled with blossoming small trees led to an elaborate doorway through a multi-foil arch. The grounds between the wall and the palace were covered in a crazy pattern of short, trimmed hedges dotted by flowering trees arranged in a geometric pattern.

"Yes," M. Touati said with an offhand shrug. "Come."

He led the way up the stairs, his gold babouche-clad feet whispering with each footfall. The doors opened as he drew near, revealing a spacious octagonal room with a vaulted ceiling adorned with intricate geometric patterns in gold leaf. Light streamed into the foyer through stained glass windows set high up near the ceiling. The foyer walls were covered in elaborate tile mosaics in blues, greens and turquoise overwritten in places by flowing Arabic script, occasionally interrupted by ornate arched doorways. Lush potted palms designated seating areas with low divans and embroidered cushions. Classical columns supported a galleried upper level accessed by two sweeping staircases.

M. Touati crossed the foyer to double doors at the far end. Two men, dressed in brilliant white thobes, opened the doors in synchronised moves as their master neared, giving access to a huge courtyard with garden beds, seating areas and more fountains. Across the courtyard was a wide, flat, concreted pad. "This is the area in which bike instructions will take place," M. Touati said.

It was a statement, not a question, but he looked at Saskia as if he expected a response.

Overwhelmed by the opulence of her surroundings, Saskia said, "Um – oui – er – perfect."

He pointed to a nearby table surrounded by chairs. "While my son changes into suitable clothes, you will sit there and have refreshments."

Gadil returned to the house. The other children sat on a bench, all still silent.

*Okay! Definitely a creepy place*, Saskia decided.

Two women wearing identical black dresses and lacy white pinafores appeared and placed trays on the table, one containing jugs of juice and water, a bowl of fruit and cupcakes, and the other holding a teapot and a French press, glasses, cups and saucers.

They poured a coffee for M. Touati first and asked Saskia what she would prefer. "Er – tea. Thank you." The children, who had still not said a word and sat like statues on the bench, were each served a glass of juice.

Gadil returned, dressed in a tee shirt and jeans. A white-robed man appeared with a BMX bike and a large sack. Gadil took the bike and waved aside the offered sack.

"Show the midget what you can do," his father said.

Gadil mounted his bike and demonstrated a series of bunny hops, nollies and peg manuals. He spun to a stop facing Saskia, expression almost impassive except for the faintest tightening of his lips.

Saskia had long ago learned that it was no use trying to start any instruction with children until she had established her credibility. Sometimes, this meant she had to demonstrate her expertise. Sometimes, it meant getting a child's trust in other ways. She was extremely reluctant to take the first course of action, because she guessed M. Touati wanted her to do that, and she disliked him more by the minute.

"That's great!" she told Gadil, smiling. "I can see you've done a lot of practice."

M. Touati snorted. "When not at his studies, he is here."

"Practising is the best way to learn." Saskia kept her attention on Gadil. "Have you had any instructions?"

"YouTube," his father said.

"Any particular ones?" Saskia continued to address Gadil.

When the question was not answered for him, Gadil glanced at his father, who jerked his head in what might have been a nod.

"Mick Snow," Gadil said.

Saskia put her teacup on to the table and clapped her hands, thinking, *Stroke of luck, Saskia; here's your in!* Aloud, she said. "He's the best. I've had some great rides with him."

Gadil frowned, and his father pushed his fat lips into an exaggerated upside-down U shape. "You know him?"

"Oh, yes. I helped him with demonstrations on some of the videos."

M. Touati inspected her with his coal-coloured eyes. "You are on some of these YouTube videos?"

"I am."

He said something in Arabic to the white-robed man, who set down the sack and hurried away.

"Finish your tea. Gadil, you may have another juice."

The woman serving drinks put a glass of juice in Gadil's hand. Silence descended on the courtyard until the man returned and handed M. Touati an iPad. He clicked it to life, fiddled to obtain internet reception and handed it to Saskia. "Show!"

Saskia entered the address for the required YouTube series. She selected one that showed her doing various tricks on the flat. M. Touati viewed it and then called Gadil look at it.

"You will teach Gadil these now," he commanded.

"Sure." Saskia slipped off her chair. "So, Gadil, let's start by making sure the foundations of BMX riding are solid and automatic." She walked to the sack and looked inside. As she suspected, it was filled with safety equipment. She took out the helmet. "Rule number one. Never ride without a helmet. Is this yours?"

"I don't need it," Gadil declared, though he glanced at his father as if uncertain.

"It is an ornament," M. Touati said.

Saskia shrugged. "Then the lesson with me is over." She dropped the helmet back in the sack and turned to her host. "Please arrange for me to be taken back to Brussels. Or if you return my phone to me, I'll call my friends to come and pick me up."

M. Touati frowned and huffed, "Very good, Dr Midget." He turned to his son. "Wear the helmet."

Gadil jammed the helmet on his head, chin strap loose. Saskia indicated she wanted it tightened. With a glance at his father, Gadil clipped the strap into place. Saskia walked into the middle of the pad. As she'd hoped, there were expansion joints. She pointed to the longest one. "I want you to ride exactly next to that joint without weaving even a centimetre from it."

From mastering the straight line, Saskia required Gadil to move his body from side to side without wavering from the straight line, then to ride with one foot out, then the other foot out.

Time slipped by. M. Touati dismissed the other children, who looked back longingly as they walked away. Tehzib, especially, seemed crestfallen. An umbrella appeared to shade M. Touati, who took several calls on his phone while he watched his son. Saskia had to hand it to Gadil; he was strong, tireless and eager, having lost his surliness once he accepted Saskia knew what she was talking about.

Servants carried out a sumptuous lunch. The children reappeared, now dressed more casually. Silently, they sat at the table with their father and Saskia. Servants filled their plates with food. M. Touati indicated to Saskia that she could fill her plate with whatever took her fancy from the platters of cheeses, breads, fruits, vol-au-vonts, sliced meats and dips. He took more calls on his phone, mostly speaking in guttural Arabic.

After lunch, it was back to bike tricks, with the children allowed to stay and watch. "Would anyone else like to learn bike tricks? Saskia asked.

The children immediately stiffened, eyes wide, as if Saskia had said something dangerous.

M. Touati glowered. "For what benefit?"

"Well, they might enjoy it. And, maybe, they could put on a bit of a show with Gadil."

"A show?" He looked calculatingly at his children. "You can teach all of them?"

"Yes. While one is practising a technique, I can work with another."

"Girls too?"

"Sure. I'm a girl."

M. Touati turned to the white-thobed man who held the iPad and had hardly moved from his station. "Show her the bikes," he said, and then stood. "I have work to do, but I will observe from my office."

## 32

## THE WHOLE WEEK

More surveillance of Saskia's movements started the day after her visit to Azzam Touati's estate.

Mario alerted her to the tedious imposition. He slipped her a note when she returned from the bank on Monday evening.

> *Dr van Essen*
> *This morning, a man he talk to me and about you. I say him I not know much about you but you work at the bank and live here. I tell him you upset when someone try for your computer and you look for bugs in apartment. He say me his phone number and say if I tell him information about you, he pay me good money.*

The next day, when she saw Mario in the foyer, she discreetly slipped him a note thanking him for the information and suggested that if he found her doing something suspicious, he should call the phone number but first ensure he had the good money. She'd finished her note with a smiley face, reflecting that had this incident occurred six months ago, she would not have felt so relaxed about it. *How strange!*

On Tuesday evening, a man parked a car opposite the apartment building and sat there all night. The next night, a different car parked outside the building with a different man inside. Olivier told her the back entrance to the apartment complex was under similar surveillance.

"Do you think it's something to do with Azzam Touati?" Saskia had asked.

Olivier shrugged. "We don't know yet. We've taken photos of the people in the cars and we're running the images through databases to determine whether any are known to us."

More intriguing to Saskia was M. Benkirane's horror when she asked him to sign off on a week's leave so that she could spend the time exclusively with Azzam Touati's children.

"You have made a good impression, then," he said, a tremor in his voice.

Saskia tipped her head to one side questioningly. "You appear disconcerted, Monsieur. Would my week's leave inconvenience you?"

"No. Not at all. It's – just – that – he does not usually allow strangers into his place. But you must have earned his – trust."

"I don't know about that, but I did demonstrate that I can teach his children how to ride their bikes and scooters."

"All the children?"

"Yes." Saskia smiled. "Even the girls. I think the girls were quite surprised he agreed to let me teach them."

"You found them well?"

"The children? I did. They were very quiet while their father was about. But when he left, they loosened up and we had good fun. Monsieur Touati seems to intimidate them. At the same time, he gives them lots of toys. The bike shed contains every outdoor toy and game you can imagine. I suggested the BMX riding would be more exciting if there was a pump track to ride on. Once I explained what that was and showed him a loop design, he surprised me by saying he would have such a track built and ready for when I return next week."

"The children enjoyed themselves with you?"

## THE BANK

Saskia resisted the temptation to tilt her head again in wonder at M. Benkirane's intense interest in the children.

"I believe so. Jamal and Yasser were most comfortable on scooters, so I had them careening around the edge of the square, learning bunny hops, stopping very fast and weaving in and out of one another without crashing. The other children all wanted to use their BMX bikes. Gadil's obviously practised a lot, but Tehzib's the one with talent."

"And Basem?"

"Basem? Is that the nickname of one of the children?"

M. Benkirane hesitated. He took a deep breath and shook his head. "Ah, I misremembered. Forgive my curiosity. It has been a while since I have met with Azzam's family."

She mentioned the European bank chief's curious questioning and behaviour to Olivier the following morning as she perched on a stool in Petit Café, watching him prepare her breakfast. "He seems, on the one hand, to be uneasy about Monsieur Touati, and, on the other hand, resigned."

Olivier shunted a mug of coffee across the counter to her. "Did you feel threatened at all when you were at Touati's place, Saskia?"

"No. I mean, I think the atmosphere of the place is unpleasant, and they tried to get me to wear a wristband, which you think might be a listening device. The man reeks of wealth and vanity. I got that from the moment I laid eyes on him, though, from how he dresses, does his hair and trims his beard and eyebrows. He treats his children and household as if they're just there to enhance his greatness. I wouldn't be surprised if his staff are slave labour. The only ones that don't look intimidated are the security thugs."

Saskia wrapped her hands around the warm mug and took a sip. "And I know I'm just a pawn to push around to get him more kudos. I think he wants to show off how great he is to people he wants to impress at that birthday party he's organising. I mean, I think that one of the things he wants to show off is that he can produce talented and beautiful children. But I feel sorry for the children. I don't think there's much fun in their lives. That place is so much like a prison, and they are clearly frightened of him. So, I like seeing them smile. I've agreed to work with them for their sake, not his."

A thoughtful crease formed between Olivier's eyebrows. "Saskia, you've made a lot of observations in that statement. The more I get to know about this man, the less I feel comfortable about you getting closer to him."

"It's alright, Olivier. I won't do anything dangerous. I mean, I won't try to steal information or something like that. But I have a strong feeling he might be the breakthrough we need for this case. I know you think so, too. It would be great if we could turn up more than just disparate data points that show an increasing tangle of transactions through trusts, shell companies and offshore banks. It'd be even better if you could arrest more than bunches of minor criminals who won't or can't tell your team who the big boss is. What if he's one of the bosses?"

"Saskia – "

Saskia held up her hand. "Don't worry! I will only observe. Nothing more. And look! I don't think he would dare do anything to me. He might run a fiefdom inside his palace, but he can't completely ignore the laws of this land. I know that if something happens to me, he'll have law enforcement at his gates. I've told him I'll only agree to stay for the week if I have free access to a mobile phone and can call friends and family without restrictions on a daily basis. So, I'll be able to report in."

A man walked into the café and to the counter. Saskia recognised him. She'd seen him in the car parked outside the apartment complex that morning when she walked past on her way to the café. He looked tired and grumpy.

*Well, serves you right for being up all night*, Saskia thought unsympathetically.

The dishevelled man approached the counter. Saskia said, "I like it at the bank. I work mostly independently, but the staff always make a point of including me in conversations if I'm around. And I get invited to join them for drinks after work."

"Good to hear," Olivier said. He turned to his second customer of the morning. "Bonjour, Monsieur. How may I help?"

"Coffee. Black. Hot," the man growled. He glanced at Saskia as she slid off the stool and took her coffee to the corner table she preferred. Sun streamed in through the window, warming her back as she extracted her laptop from its backpack pouch. Minutes later, the man sat at the table next to hers, leaning back in his chair, perhaps to get a better view of her laptop screen. She ignored him. Even if he could see her screen, he would only see her scrolling through Reddit chats and answering personal emails.

Olivier delivered coffee to the growly man and placed a warm croissant and a pot of jam before Saskia.

"By the way, I'll be away all next week," Saskia said, as if Olivier didn't already know.

"Anywhere nice?"

"You know that guy I went to see on Sunday? He wants me to spend the week at his estate with his kids," Saskia continued, partly to give the growly man something he could report and partly because she felt mischievous.

"Oh! You're calling his place an estate? What's it like?"

"Over the top! Security everywhere. Get this. They took away my watch and phone and did a body scan when I first came and then wanted me to wear this wrist thing that I suspect is some sort of tracking device or something. That wasn't so bad. What really ticked me off was that when they returned my watch and phone, I found they'd inserted a bug in the phone's casing."

"How did you find that?"

"Since I found those cameras in my apartment, I've been doing regular checks on all my devices."

"What did you do when you found the bug?"

"I told whoever was listening that I'd found it, and I didn't appreciate my stuff being tampered with. Then I removed it and put it in a glass of water."

"And your watch?"

"My watch seems okay."

"Are you safe in that place, Saskia?"

"I don't feel unsafe."

"Why the surveillance, then?"

"I think the family's just very rich, and people like that probably need to be careful about their safety."

"What's the place like?"

"Inside, I've only seen the foyer. It's impressive. I was mostly in a courtyard with the children."

"And the children?"

"Nice. They know how to listen to instructions more than most kids."

"When are you leaving for your week away?"

"A car's picking me up at eight on Saturday morning."

"Are you still going to the gym for your exercise session on Friday afternoon?"

"Yes."

"Well, I'll see you there."

Saskia chuckled. "No. You'll see me for breakfast tomorrow."

Olivier grinned as he turned away. "Ah, yes. You've become such a regular. I think of you as my first cup of coffee."

*An apt simile, given the colour of my skin*, smiled Saskia, returning her attention to the laptop screen. She studiously avoided looking at M. Growly, hoping the lengthy exchange between herself and Olivier had provided him with more useful information than the rest of the night had. She especially wanted to convey she was innocent, naïve and trustworthy.

In the women's changeroom on Friday after their usual gym workout, Angela swapped over Saskia's phone and watch. She took two blouses out of her duffle bag. "Everything about Azzam Touati makes me feel uncomfortable, Saskia," Angela said. "Please don't take any chances. We've found a place where we can monitor what goes on in the estate's open spaces, including the courtyard." She held up one blouse. "This shirt has a green collar, sleeves and buttons. Put it on when you think the threat level is increasing." She held up the second blouse. "This blouse has a red collar, sleeves and buttons. Put it on when you need to be extracted." Angela then took different coloured hair ribbons out of the duffle bag. "You like to wear ribbons in your hair. Wear a different coloured ribbon every day. Only use the red and the green ribbons when sending us a message. Accent the blouses with green and red ribbons in your hair."

"How do you intend to extract me if I need to be extracted?"

Angela shook her head. "Need to know, Saskia," she cautioned. "It's good you negotiated access to a phone and informed Touati that your family and friends will become alarmed if you don't call daily."

"I'm pretty sure it won't be a smartphone."

"No matter, as long as you can make those daily calls. Just make sure you call your parents or Hans every day. Make it your routine from day one. Azzam Touati's security detail will probably be listening in to your conversations, so be careful. We'll listen in to your parents' and Hans's phones, so we'll know when you're making the calls, and we will listen carefully. Use the codes we've set up. Do you remember them?"

"If there are no issues of concern, I need to finish the call with, 'Love you heaps' in English. If the situation has taken a turn for the worse, I need to say at some point in the conversation, 'I'm wondering whether you've thought of getting a pet'. If I need to get out, I need to say, 'I didn't sleep a wink last night'."

Isabelle nodded. "We'll also listen carefully in case you're trying to send us some other sorts of messages. You're clever, so I don't need to remind you not to make those messages obvious." Angela crouched down until she was face-to-face with Saskia. She put her hands on Saskia's shoulders. "I repeat, Saskia. Do not put yourself in danger in any way. Not by word or by action."

# 33

## STAND-OFF

A man dressed in camouflage pants and shirt, the strap of a long black gun slung over his shoulder, pulled open a plastic ziplock bag and thrust it in front of Saskia. She undid her wristwatch and extracted her phone from the back pocket of her trousers. "This time, don't tamper with my stuff," Saskia said, looking up into the man's heavily bearded face. She held her devices suspended over the bag. "I expect to get them back without bugs."

The man frowned uncomprehendingly at her, then turned and said something in Arabic to a second man, who was searching through Saskia's suitcase.

The second man turned his dark eyes on Saskia. "Next time you leave bug in," he said.

Saskia shook her head. "That's not going to happen. You leave my stuff alone, or I go home."

"Not go home. Leave bug in! You wear this." He picked up a wristband from the table and held it out to her.

Saskia returned her phone to her back pocket and slung the band of her watch over her wrist. "I will not wear that. Please close the suitcase and return it to me. I'll go home now."

At this point, the man who had driven her to the palace entered the guard house. Saskia said to him, "Please tell these people that I have cancelled my stay of the week and will return to Brussels. If you don't take me, I'll call my friends to pick me up."

The driver's eyebrows rose. He spoke in Arabic to the two security guards. What seemed like an argument among the men erupted, culminating in the driver picking up a phone receiver secured to the top of a table. More guttural Arabic ensued.

The driver replaced the receiver. "Wait," he said.

Saskia leaned against the doorway, crossing one ankle over the other while she fastened her wristwatch band. The man searching her suitcase continued rummaging through the clothes she had packed neatly that morning. Finishing his inspection, he unzipped the suitcase's outside pocket and removed a paperback novel and a notebook with an attached pencil. He flicked through both, dropped the novel on top of her clothes and frowned at the notebook's contents.

"What is?" he demanded, showing her a page of sketches.

"Lesson plans for the children." Saskia had spent hours preparing the plans, drawing stick figures performing tricks on bikes and scooters. She'd used arrows and notations to describe the parts she wanted the children to concentrate on. The three men examined the notebook in minute detail and then threw it on top of the novel, closing the suitcase lid over the mess they had created.

Annoyed, Saskia stepped to the table and refolded and packed her clothes. She was zipping the bag closed when yet another man walked into the guard house. Saskia managed – just – not to startle. The heavily muscled, entirely bald man with a red beard was head of the same security firm that FSB employed. She had never met him personally, but recognised him from a photo in the bank's personnel files.

He spoke briefly in Arabic with the driver and two guards, then turned to Saskia. "Mademoiselle, my name is François. I am head of security for Monsieur Touati. We need all people working for him to be monitored at all times," he stated in good but heavily accented French. *Canadian*, Saskia decided.

He towered over her, making himself bigger by sticking his elbows out as he rested his wrists on the butts of pistols stuck into holders on his belt.

"Enchantée, François. But you are mistaken. I don't work for Monsieur Touati. I understand that you would want to ensure I don't bring anything into his home that might impact his safety, but I do not agree to my privacy being impacted once I'm away from here. Nor do I agree to being invasively monitored while I am here." Saskia pointed to the listening device she'd been told she needed to wear. She waved a hand at the security guards. "I noted last time I was here that there are sufficient eyes on me to make sure I behave."

"By coming here, you agree to work for Monsieur Touati."

"No. I do not. If my presence here creates an unacceptable risk, I have no problem returning to Brussels."

"He is paying you money."

"He is not. I have told him I will not take his money. I don't teach children for money. I teach children because I like to do it."

"I was told you agreed to accept a substantial sum from him in Ayat Benkirane's office."

*Did you now?* thought Saskia. Aloud, she said, "It would appear that you did not hear a subsequent conversation where I told him I was not interested in accepting money for teaching his children bike tricks."

"Why did you negotiate the original terms?"

Saskia straightened her shoulders and glared up into his icy blue eyes. "Because I was indignant that he made fun of my height and appearance. Has he ever suggested to you that the muscles of your arms, your bald head and your beard make you look like a good circus act?"

That seemed to give François pause, because he blinked, opened his mouth, worked it a little then closed it without saying anything.

"Look!" Saskia sighed. "I think this is all getting too complicated. I'll call my friends to come and pick me up. I'll go and sit under a tree over there by the road. It will probably take them an hour or so to get here." She pulled her suitcase off the table and turned to leave the guardhouse.

François engulfed her shoulder in a large, calloused, heavy hand.

"Wait!" He barked something in Arabic and the driver moved a chair towards her, indicating that she should sit. With yet another sigh, Saskia hitched up on to the chair. François strode out of the guardhouse, his mobile phone pressed to his ear as he paced back and forth in front of the gate, sporadically venting words.

Finally, he pocketed his phone and returned to the guardhouse. "Monsieur Touati agrees to your terms," he said shortly. "Give over your phone and wristwatch. Stand still while we carry out a body scan. Then you will be able to proceed."

## 34

### BASEM

A maid in black dress and white pinafore, her black hair pulled back into a tight bun, met Saskia in the magnificent foyer, took her suitcase from the driver and led her into the courtyard. She wore the wrist device.

Five men in the courtyard paused in their work to glance at Saskia and the maid. Two men were at a fountain, buckets at their feet and their long-sleeved shirts soaked. The others were tending flower beds. All wore wrist devices.

The maid led her diagonally across the courtyard towards a door at the far end of the left wing of the palace. She said something in Arabic.

Saskia shook her head. "I'm sorry," she said in French, "I don't speak that language."

The maid gave her a blank look and swallowed nervously. She was young; perhaps in her mid-teens, but already had stress lines around her eyes. Saskia guessed she might be Filipino, so she repeated her statement in English. "I'm sorry, I don't speak Arabic."

The girl's shoulders dropped with relief. "I speak English. I am learning Arabic."

"That's clever!"

"I said that we have prepared a room for you in the female wing," she said. "That is the male quarters." She pointed to the wing on the opposite side of the courtyard. "My name is Harmony. I am assigned to take care of you. You will please let me know if you need anything during your stay. I am in the dormitory on the opposite side of the hallway to your room. There will always be someone in the dormitory if I am not available. You just need to ring the bell I show you."

Harmony led the way through a small doorway into a long, brightly lit corridor, camera eyes prominent on the ceiling. There were two widely spaced doors on the right side of the hallway. Harmony explained they were the access to the two female dormitories the maids occupied. Her dormitory was through the first door. On the left-hand side of the hallway were fifteen evenly spaced doors. Harmony removed a key from her apron pocket and unlocked the third door.

"This is your room," she said, opening the door to a small chamber containing four items of furniture: a bed covered by a brown throw, a slim chest of drawers, a small white desk and a green plastic chair. Light spilled through a barred, rectangular window, the sill of which was at Saskia's head height. A surveillance camera attached to the ceiling faced the door and, doubtless, gave a wide-angled view of most of the room.

"You have your own bathroom." Harmony pointed to a door in the room.

Saskia walked into the bathroom. A bath towel, hand towel and washer sat neatly folded on a washstand, which was jammed between the shower recess and toilet. A surveillance camera was attached high up over the top of the washstand.

"Thank you," Saskia said. "Where is my telephone?"

Harmony's eyes widened a little, her shoulders stiffening. "Telephones are not permitted, Miss."

"I see."

Harmony pointed to a cord hanging next to the bed. "Please pull that if you need something,"

"I see."

"Miss, I am to inform you the children will be waiting for you in thirty minutes. I will come to collect you. I will have refreshments ready for you at that place."

"No need. I can find my way."

"Miss. I – you are not allowed to be on your own – except in this room."

"This is getting ridiculous!" Saskia muttered. She put her suitcase on the bed, unzipped it and picked out a pair of underpants and one of the ribbons Angela had given her. She shoved the desk and then the chair into the corner under the security camera, clambered up and secured the underpants over the eye of the camera with the ribbon. Harmony watched with wide, horror-filled eyes, hands over her mouth.

Ignoring Harmony's quick, frightened breaths, Saskia grabbed another pair of underpants and a ribbon and dragged the chair into the bathroom. She wedged it between the toilet and the wall, stood on the chair back and, with a grunt of effort, managed to block the second offending device.

"Right!" she said, moving the furniture back. "I'll be ready when you come to collect me."

In precisely thirty minutes, Saskia heard Harmony unlock the bedroom door and knock timidly. Saskia set aside the novel she was reading and followed Harmony out, expecting to return to the concrete pad in the courtyard. Instead, Harmony led her out of the courtyard and under the open portcullis on to the spacious grounds between the castle wall and the river. The children, lined up and holding bikes and scooters, stood before a new pump loop track. Two bike ramp kickers had been set up not far from the track.

Saskia smiled at the children, nodding approvingly when she noted that all wore helmets and Gadil had strapped on knee, elbow and ankle protectors, though she needed to force cheerfulness because she felt affronted on the children's behalf that they all wore wrist devices. *He's listening in to what his children say all the time. Bastard! Saskia, you'll need to be careful not to make their situation more precarious.*

"Amazing!" Saskia exclaimed, clapping her hands and causing the children's faces to relax into smiles. "We've got a pump track and a couple of bike-jump ramp kickers. We are going to have so much fun!"

# THE BANK

She invited the children to lay down their bikes and scooters and walk around the track with her to inspect it. She explained the construction and use of the berms, rollers and crossovers to them. It was a relatively small track, but it had a good flow and there were plenty of challenges for the children. Most pleasing was that the soil surface was hard-packed and smooth. Whoever had built the track knew what they were doing. The ramps were standard off-the-shelf, but perfect for beginners.

"May I offer you refreshments, Miss?" Harmony asked, interrupting the track examination. The maid stood next to a table set under an umbrella.

The man holding the bag of safety equipment stood immobile without head covering, his features so expressionless that Saskia worried his mind had fled.

"A glass of juice would be lovely."

Saskia hardly had the juice in hand when a gun-toting, black-suited security guard strode through the portcullis towards her.

Harmony shrank back, and the children hunched into themselves. The guard barked at Saskia, who sipped her drink and frowned uncomprehendingly up at him. "He wants you to follow him," Harmony translated quietly.

Saskia finished her juice, returning the guard's stare – though she took care not to add venom to it. The guard's right hand gripped the strap of his gun, his left hand clasped and unclasped as if ready to grab something. *Probably my arm to drag me with him. Or maybe my throat to crush my insolence.*

"Okay," Saskia said, giving Harmony her emptied glass.

The guard turned on his heel and led her into the foyer and through an arched doorway and an anteroom where six women, completely covered in black except for their eyes and hands, worked at computers. At the far end of the room, an old man with a long, straggly grey beard looked up from his desk. He removed a pair of thick spectacles, replacing them with another equally thick-lensed pair, stood up and waved his hand for Saskia to approach and follow him. He led her through a massive, intricately carved black door, and into a spacious lounge room furnished with richly covered couches, armchairs, thick oriental rugs and low tables to yet another door. Glancing down, perhaps to ensure Saskia was still at his side, the man knocked.

Something that sounded like, "Ya!" caused the man to open the door, revealing – on the other side of more lounges and low tables – Azzam Touati seated behind a highly polished desk. François stood beside him.

Determinedly, Saskia walked to the desk, pushing away the feeling that she'd been called to the school principal's office to be reprimanded, though she fully expected this meeting was all about reprimanding her.

M. Touati glared at her. "In my home, I demand that you follow the security protocols I have put in place."

"Monsieur, I offer my services willingly, but if it means I must give up my freedom and privacy with that offer, then I withdraw it. I will close up my suitcase, return to the gatehouse for my devices and call my friends to pick me up."

"That is not an option."

"Oh?" Saskia posed the question and waited.

M. Touati's face reddened, anger narrowing his eyes.

François said, "Dr van Essen. As I explained to you before, it is vital that we maintain strict security protocols on these premises."

"That's fine. I've given up my devices. I don't mind being locked into a room in the servants' quarters. I'll accept not wandering around without a staff member accompanying me. But I will not wear a security bracelet or have the privacy of my room compromised. You also promised me access to a phone, and my offer remains conditional on you either returning my own phone or giving me one I can use while I am here."

"Why?" François demanded.

"Because my family and friends are worried about my being here and because I am in the habit of being in regular contact with them."

"Why are they worried?"

"Monsieur, why not? This place is a fortress and secretive. It is beyond their experience – or mine, for that matter."

When both men simply stared at her, she uttered a small sigh. "I repeat. You are not obligated to accept my services. If my presence here causes you discomfort, then I lose nothing by leaving."

François opened his mouth to say something, but M. Touati held up a hand for silence. He leaned over his desk and glared at Saskia over his hawk nose for what felt like several minutes. She met his stare, ensuring her own expression remained neutral.

Finally, M. Touati nodded slowly. He sat back in his chair. "If I offer you twenty thousand euros, will you comply?"

"As I have explained before, Monsieur, I am not interested in accepting money to train your children."

"Fifty thousand euros?"

Saskia shook her head.

A calculating smile drifted over M. Touati's lips. He nodded. "Very well, Dr Midget Researcher. I accept your terms. In return, I have two further demands." He paused. "Excuse me." His apology was acidic. "The word I should use is 'requests'. I would like" – he said the word 'like' as if it hurt – "you to be part of the bike demonstration you are teaching the children, and I would like you to include another child. That child is disabled and physically incompetent."

"No to the first request, but to the second request, I will do my best."

Lips tightening, M. Touati glared at her again, then gave a single nod. He reached forward and pressed a button on an intercom arrangement on his desk. He barked something in Arabic, then turned his attention to the paperwork before him.

François stayed unmoving beside the desk, eyes on Saskia, so she assumed she should remain where she stood. She let her gaze drift around the room. On the wall behind the desk hung a chequerboard arrangement of black-framed paintings of geometrical shapes in red, gold and black. Two elaborately worked copper disks hung on either side of a window overlooking the courtyard. Three framed photos hung on the wall closest to Saskia. She was tempted to study the photos, but allowed her eyes dwell on them only for as long as they'd dwelt on the other wall adornments, before returning her attention to the top of M. Touati's head.

It occurred to her that usually such photos were haram for Muslims. *Strange, given that everything else about him seems to adhere to Islam...*

*Well, no! Islam teaches that life is sacred and believers have a duty to uphold truth and justice. You, Monsieur Touati, take only those pieces of the Quran that feed your ego.*

The office door opened. M. Touatti glanced up. "Basem is the one I spoke of."

Saskia turned.

Basem had the characteristics of disproportionate dwarfism.

## 35

### UNIQUE PROPORTIONS

Saskia walked out of Azzam Touati's office with Basem at her side. He was clearly the oldest of the children, with facial hair beginning to darken his chin. The scowling security guard strode behind them. Neither Saskia nor Basem spoke as they crossed the courtyard, though each inspected the other from the corners of their eyes.

Saskia's main interest in observing Basem was to assess the physical characteristics she would need to consider in her lessons. He had short, thick arms that he held out at the elbows, indicating he may have restricted joint movements, and he had a rolling gait, though his legs were relatively long and straight.

The manservant spotted them and hurried to fetch Basem's bike. The children, still standing where Saskia had left them, stared at Basem. He smiled and gave a single nod as if to reassure them.

*Impressive! So, they respect you*, Saskia thought.

The manservant returned with a bike and held it while Saskia bent to examine it. It had a low step-through, narrow handlebar, short-reach brake levers and a different crank and wheel version to standard bikes. Saskia had seen this unique bike among the stable of bikes in the shed and been puzzled by its design, which now made sense. It was custom-made to take account of Basem's short arms and legs. That Azzam had purchased this specialised bike for his son might have increased Saskia's opinion of the man had he not called his son "disabled and physically incompetent".

"I see plenty of scratch marks on the bike. So, I'm guessing you do a fair bit of riding," Saskia said, straightening and addressing Basem for the first time.

"We are allowed to ride our bikes on a daily basis," he said.

"What sort of riding do you usually do?"

"We ride around the perimeter of this estate."

"Have you practised on the concrete pad like Gadil does?"

"No. I only ride the bike around and around."

Saskia studied the boy for some seconds. He had inherited his father's coal black eyes and black hair, though his head was large for his size, and his brow was heavy. He looked at her with more direct interest than the other children had at their first meeting with her. She glanced at his wrist. Like everyone, except for the security personnel, he wore the security device.

Basem startled Saskia by acknowledging her glance with a slight raising of his wrist, while his other hand touched his ear. Then he winked.

*He actually winked!*

Saskia blinked, eyes widening as she stared at him.

Gadil dropped his head forward, though, from her shortened vantage point, Saskia saw the boy's lips twitch into a smile.

"Er – would you like to learn some of the tricks you can do on a bike?" Saskia asked.

"It is what my father wishes for me."

Saskia scanned the faces of the children. None had moved. All were waiting for further instructions. She looked around. Harmony stood next to the refreshment table, ready to receive orders for drinks or bites to eat. The manservant stood next to sacks of equipment, vacant expression in place. Security guards with guns looked down from the two towers on either side of the portcullis. By the palisade perimeter fence, two guards patrolled with a black dog on a leash, pausing to inspect three hikers passing on the opposite side of the river. The hikers waved, but the security guards didn't wave back.

Saskia felt a wave of rage. *Azzam Touati is a monster!*

"Okay, Basem. Let's have a look at your style. Jump on your bike. All I want you to do is ride to the palisade across the lawn, turn in a wide arc and come back. I don't want you to go fast or slow. I want you to just ride for the enjoyment of being on the bike."

She turned to the other children. "Okay, the rest of you. Sorry it's taken so long for us to make a start today. Let's go on from where we left off last week and start having some fun on the pump track.

Saskia taught the children in rotation, giving each an opportunity to rest and sometimes to learn vicariously. If one or another obviously did not want to rest, she would set them to racing around the lawn or perfecting the basics on the concrete pad in the internal courtyard. Never apparently taking her attention off the children, Saskia continued to note the security patrols around the palisade perimeter of the estate and the walkers and cyclists who stopped on the far side of the river to stare for a while before moving on. A few times, a canoe paddled up or down the river.

She was delighted by Basem's competence on the bike and told him so. He quickly mastered the balance basics she required and surprised himself when he mastered his first bunny hop. She was even more delighted when she heard Yasser and Jamel laughing after she instructed them to chase one another across the lawn.

By mid-afternoon, Saskia declared everyone had done enough. The ever-vigilant manservant stepped forward to collect helmets, other safety gear, bikes and scooters. With a significant show of reluctance, the children trudged through the courtyard and disappeared into the main house.

## 36

## PROGRESS

Saskia followed Harmony back to her allocated room in the female servants' wing, and thanked the girl for her attention all day.

Harmony closed the bedroom door and locked it. Saskia looked up at the location of the security camera, nodding when she saw wires dangling from where it had been attached. On the desk were a small mobile phone and charger and the two underpants and ribbons she had used to obstruct the view of the security cameras.

There was also a note. Saskia picked it up.

*Did you have to use underpants?*
*F.*

Saskia grinned. She assumed 'F' stood for François, and hoped he'd had to dismantle the cameras himself because the other security guards refused to touch her underwear.

She showered, changed into clean clothes and then sat at her desk to work on ideas for choreographing the children's show. Now that she understood the layout of the pump track and had a better knowledge of the children's talents, ideas for what could be done were beginning to flow. She wondered whether she could also organise music.

The click of a lock releasing and a soft knock on the door disturbed her a few hours later.

Harmony handed her a tray containing her evening meal. "I hope it is to your liking. It is a goat stew with salad and couscous. I hope it is sufficient," she said. "Please let me know if you require anything further. I will collect the tray in one hour and a half."

"It looks wonderful. Thank you, Harmony."

Saskia sat at her desk and studied her drawings, but her thoughts had drifted to an idea of how to pass on information to Olivier and Angela during the week. She turned to a fresh page of her notebook and began to craft a story.

The stew had gone cold by the time she returned her attention to it. She screwed up her face as she ate the now congealed meal, finishing it just as Harmony knocked on the door.

She brushed her teeth and lay back on the bed, phone in hand. It was a dumb phone, only capable of making outbounds, though she was sure that it contained a listening device.

No matter.

She pressed in her parents' phone number. Her mother answered.

"Hello, Mama. It is Saskia."

"So, you are now in another place again, Saskia?"

"I am, Mama."

"Is nice?"

"Yes, Mama. It is very grand, and my room is comfortable."

"You teach children but not do banking things?"

"Just for a week, Mama. How is your knee? It was very sore when I spoke to you last time."

That was all that was required to head her mother off from asking more questions. Twenty minutes later, Saskia had been brought up to speed with the doings of the restaurant and her parents' niggly health concerns. She ended the call with, "I love you heaps," in English.

She then tapped out Hans's phone number.

"Hello? Is this you, Saskia? You said you'd probably call me from an unknown number."

"Yes. It's me."

"How's it going?" Hans asked.

"Not bad. I'm beginning to sort things out with the children."

"I've been waiting for you to call. I'm bursting to tell you the good news."

"Oh?"

"It's about Melanie. She contacted me. She's in a rehab place in Paris. Did you know that?"

"After leaving my apartment in Lyon, she hasn't contacted me again. How is she?"

"We had a long talk. She said she'd understand if I never wanted to see her again. But of course I want to see her. I don't think she can believe I'm still crazy about her. She says she's in the hands of some good counsellors who can speak Dutch. I'm going to Paris in two weeks to see her."

"That is so good!"

"I know. But there's something else. She wanted me to tell you she's very sorry she tried to steal your laptop. She said she wasn't thinking straight when the people she got involved with said they'd trade her drugs for the laptop."

"Poor Melanie. Tell her I understand. It's no matter. I'm happy she's now in a good place."

"Yes. But Saskia, it got me thinking. Are you in some sort of trouble? Why would someone recruit her to try to steal your laptop?"

"The police are looking into that, Hans. It's bizarre. I hope Melanie can tell them everything she knows. I hope she doesn't associate with those drug people anymore."

"Well, that's why she got out of Lyon and Rotterdam. She said she doesn't really remember how she got back on to the drugs, and the guys just kept giving her more, and then they took her to Lyon."

Saskia winced, guilt causing her heart to skip faster. Doubtless she had been the real target of the people manipulating Melanie.

"Poor Melanie. I hope it doesn't happen to her again. Please give her my best, and I look forward to catching up with her again. I think she's sweet."

"I'll do that."

"Listen, I wanted to ask a favour."

"Ask away."

"So, where I am now, I'm basically stuck in my room without company unless I'm out with the children."

"That's bad!"

"No. Not really. I don't mind. I don't think I have much in common with the people here, so it's okay. But listen, I only brought one book to read, and I'm pretty much done with it. So, do you remember that computer game we started designing a few years back? Do you still have it?"

"Sure. I've also still got the Unity Twenty Nineteen and the game maker we played around with loaded."

"Great! Well, I was hoping I could schedule you to make time for me at around about this hour for the rest of the week?"

"For you, my first love, I will move mountains."

"You are a wonderful romantic," Saskia laughed. She sat up against the wall, scrunching the single pillow to buffer her back, notebook on her lap. "Here's the basic concept. I want to change what we originally had, which was a sort of space odyssey idea, to a more earth-bound, ancient theme based on the ancient Roman city of Lugdunum. We could even call the game Lugdunum."

"You mean like the place we visited in Lyon?"

"Yes."

"Okay." Hans said the word slowly as if his thoughts were catching up with the idea. "I'm not sure it would be my first choice, but let's run with it for a while. I may be able to persuade you to add space odyssey into the mix. How do you want to do this? Are you thinking of creating a game that is something like *Civilization*, or something more like *Dungeons and Dragons*?"

"I'm thinking we'll be flexible. Maybe fall between those two stools. But to start with, I want you to recreate the ancient city in the game app. Maybe there are pictures on the internet that'll give you ideas of what to include."

"Hmmm. Let's see. Let me pull up some images."

For some time, Saskia only heard the click of keyboard strokes and mutters.

"I'm not getting anything that's complete online. But I remember when I was in that Lyon Rome museum, I took some photos of what the ancient city might have looked like. I'll dig those up and see what I can do. What's your story concept?"

"Well." Saskia took a deep breath. Now, she had to be very careful. "I'm thinking we'll set it up so that gamers have to build the Roman city based roughly on the history of how Lugdunum was actually built and then destroyed. So, we'll have gamers choose to be certain characters. We'll have three central characters and develop others around their adventures."

Referring to her notes, Saskia provided names and tasks for the various characters. Her real idea was that the setting of Lugdunum on the river would mimic the river setting of Azzam Touati's estate. She hoped Olivier and Angela would grasp that she was matching characters in the game with characters who were part of the investigation.

In particular, Saskia wanted Angela and Olivier to research whether there was a familial or pre-banking relationship between Antoine Aubert, Ayat Benkirane and Azzam Touati, because she had seen all three standing together in apparent friendship in one of the photos hanging in M. Touati's office.

"So, we have Lucius Manatius Plancus. He's the person who establishes the city. But it's really the Roman Senate who told him to establish it. I don't know who in particular in the Senate came up with the idea, but for the sake of the game, let's say it was a single Senator, and he was an economic genius who could see the potential of the site of Lugdunum as a trading centre. He can also be some sort of relative to Lucius, so he has an extra incentive to give Lucius the job. If I remember the history of Lugdunum correctly, it was initially occupied by refugees expelled from another place by the Gauls. Let's say the leader of these refugees was also connected somehow to Lucius. Or he could just be a Roman desperate to escape being killed by the Gauls. The game can start with this triumvirate and then be about these three people building the city and the Gauls then trying to destroy it."

"Mmmm," Hans still sounded doubtful. "Sounds a bit all over the place. How about you work some more on the storyline and I'll develop the design of the set and dream up what the characters might look like."

## 37

### THE PRICE

Day four.

The morning was cool and the weather unsettled, but rain did not seem imminent.

Basem stood next to Saskia, leaning over the handlebars of his bike as they watched Tarek, Yasser and Jamel bunny hop in figures of eight on the concrete pad. "May I ask how you started training children?"

Saskia turned to meet Basem's dark eyes. He was the only child that occasionally engaged her in conversation that did not directly involve the task at hand. Thus far, however, he had restricted his interests to remarks to the weather, how food served by Harmony was prepared, the way the servants kept the grounds beautiful and details of the construction of the pump track, the kickers and fountains.

"I sort of fell into it, so to speak. Some older children at the park I used to visit started teaching me and then when I picked up a skill, I showed others. Usually, at skate parks and such like, that's what we do. We trade our expertise."

Basem tilted his head slightly, intrigued. "Does that mean you don't do this full-time?"

"No," Saskia laughed. "I work in finance and IT. I muck around on bikes and a bit on scooters for recreation. Mostly, these days, I go mountain bike riding with friends."

"What sort of work is finance and IT?"

"Well, at present, I work for a bank. I research the finance market for them, looking at trends and likely opportunities."

"Does that involve IT?"

"What doesn't involve IT these days? My speciality is looking at how IT can help or hinder the finance industry."

"Are all your biking friends also interested in IT?"

"No. I have biking friends and, separately, IT friends. My IT friends are mostly white hats – I mean, they look for vulnerabilities in IT systems. Some of them are also game developers. Have you got an interest in IT?"

"I am learning about computing. My father has determined –" he paused. "So, why are you here?"

She smiled. "Well, it started because I was miffed that your father made fun of my small size and, because I'm not good at keeping my mouth shut, I revealed that I knew a thing or two about acrobatic biking. He challenged me to teach his children. I couldn't resist. I quite like working with children."

Reluctant to stop the conversation, but mindful of her duties to the other children, Saskia held up her hand to stop the boys. "Okay, that's enough," she called out. "I want you to stand in a line over there, lift the front wheels with brakes on for scooters and practise spinning the bar like I taught you yesterday." Turning back to Basem, she said, "If you're feeling rested enough, please practise straight lining and leaning to the left and right again."

After a break for lunch, she was mildly surprised to find Basem once again parking himself close by, this time as she watched Gadil practising on the pump track.

"You are patient," he said.

"You children are amazingly attentive," Saskia returned with a smile.

Basem looked around as if checking whether anyone was close by.

Then, he leaned over the handlebars of his bike, his arms crossing over at the wrists.

"You would be too if your father had left as many whipmark-scars on your back for so-called disobedience," he said softly. He uncrossed his wrists, uncovering the listening device. "My brother Gadil is a serious person," he said in a normal tone.

Saskia looked from the listening device to Basem's face.

He winked – again, and sat back on his bike seat. "He is very good, isn't he?" He crossed his arms, again covering the listening device. "We only dare cover it for very short periods. We then pretend we were conversing about something else and covered the device accidentally." He uncrossed his arms. "Do you think I can do manuals on the pump track? Could you teach me?"

"Umm –" Saskia stumbled, mind racing to take in what Basem had just revealed. "I'd like to see how you can get speed up on the track first."

"I think my father would be pleased if I could learn manuals." He recrossed his arms, covering the device. "We despise him," he whispered.

"Er – yes! Umm – you are full of surprises, and I admire your pluck."

"We are enjoying ourselves with you. It's good to see the young ones laughing." He lifted his chin, motioning it towards where Tarek and Yasser were racing scooters across the lawn on to the ramps, trying to outdo each other's time holding up the front wheels in tyre taps.

"You're small, but you don't look like a dwarf," Basem continued.

"Er – well – there are many types of dwarfism. I had a growth hormone deficiency."

"I have Achondroplasia. You probably know that it's the most common type. I've had eighteen operations on my legs to lengthen and straighten them. I've also had injections of Vosoritide."

"That explains your height. I bet you ache, though."

"Yes. Sometimes. Especially when I'm cold or if I've been in one position for a long time. My joints get stiff."

"That's the problem you'll have on the pump track. It will be hard on your joints. Let's continue to practise on the concrete pad and the lawn first. When we feel you're comfortable with manuals on the flat, you can start on the pump track."

Gadil finished his turn on the track. Jamel leapt up from his spot under the shade of the umbrella, where he had been sipping a drink and eating a snack, to take his turn.

He froze mid-step.

Gadil also stopped mid-stride.

Saskia and Basem turned to see what had caught the boys' attention.

It was Azzam Touati, white thobe swishing with each quick step toward them, François at his side.

"Show me the progress you have made with my children," M. Touati commanded, coming to a standstill a pace away from Saskia. He clasped his bejewelled hands behind his back.

*And good day to you, too! We haven't missed you!* Saskia thought, turning her back on him to face the children. "Certainly, Monsieur. Let's start with Tarek and Yasser. They have been practising tyre taps. We're thinking it might be fun to do synchronised tyre taps with high front wheel lifts and spins as part of a demonstration of skills." To the boys, who had both fallen from the kickers and sat on the ground staring at their father, she said, "Up you get. Line up at the mark I made and scoot to the kicker, then one tyre tap and one bar spin. Just like you've been practising."

The boys executed the moves perfectly. Their father nodded but did not comment. He pointed to Gadil. "Him?"

"Gadil, please do a couple of rounds on the pump track to get up some speed. Then I want you to do a manual over half the loop and just one air over the gap. That's it. Don't overdo it."

Gadil had practised each of these manoeuvres over and over, and he did her proud.

M. Touati nodded again, turning to look at Basem. "Him?"

"We were about to learn manuals – that's pulling the front wheel up and keeping it up. I'm still learning about Basem's range of skills. We can return to the concrete pad to look at what he's achieved, and you can look at the girls too."

"No need," M. Touati dismissed. "You will come with me now." He strode back towards the main house and Francois indicated with a jerk of his head that Saskia should follow.

"Er – take a break and then practise what we've been doing," Saskia told the children over her shoulder as she hurried after the men. "Gadil, perhaps you could take charge?"

François closed the office door and pointed to a position in front of the desk where Saskia should stand. M. Touati sat behind the desk and François stood next to him.

*Back in the principal's office!* Saskia thought with an inward sigh.

"My children," M. Touati began, "are being taken away from their normal duties because of your insistence on being with us for only a short time."

"Er – Monsieur, I thought you wanted to have them ready for a party, which is now only two weeks away."

"That is the case for Gadil. It has no importance for the others. I have permitted their involvement as an indulgence. I may revoke that excess. But I do not want to speak of them further. They are not your concern. I have learned you have uses beyond teaching these children. So, once again, Dr Researcher, I am offering you a substantial reward if you accept payment for your services."

"Thank you, Monsieur, but I don't want payment."

"Why?"

"I have no interest in the money."

"But it could be useful. You could give it to your parents to help them. They have always struggled to make a reasonable living from their business."

Saskia's stomach clenched. Why mention her parents? And what did he mean by 'other uses'? Keeping her voice even, she replied, "Monsieur, my parents are not your concern."

M. Touati's perfectly clipped, black, thick eyebrows rose.

"Oh? You don't think so? Why is money of no interest to you?"

"I have always taught children for pleasure, Monsieur. I have no desire to change that."

"There are more than children at stake here, Doctor Researcher. As I said, I have discovered you have other uses."

Saskia allowed several seconds to elapse in silence. "Why do you push me on this, Monsieur?"

"First, you are to perform at the party."

"If you want skilled riders to perform at the party, Monsieur, I can give you the names of friends who would gladly put on a significant performance and accept payment for it."

"Why not you?"

"It is not what I want to do."

"Why?"

"For me, playing with bikes and scooters is purely a hobby. I don't want to turn them into anything else."

Azzam Touati bent over the desk, leaning over his forearms.

"Because people would laugh at how clever a midget you are if you displayed yourself publicly?"

Saskia's reply was immediate and delivered without a change in her even tone. "I don't need to be mounted on a bike or ride a scooter for that to occur."

M. Touati sat back slowly, nostrils flaring. François's head tipped slightly, his eyes alight with interest.

"You have insulted me for the last time, Doctor Midget!" M. Touati snapped. Saskia thought his high-pitched voice somewhat marred the commanding tone he wished to convey. "It is time to bring you to heel."

François unfolded his arms, picked a large envelope up off the desk and extracted several A4-size photos. He laid them before Saskia. The images were of her parents, her brother Jan, and the café. "We have uncovered that the café is a pickup point for illicit drugs distributed by your brother," François said, tapping a forefinger on a photo of Jan placing something in the hands of a man Saskia did not recognise. "This person is a regular visitor to the café and tells us Jan is his main supplier. You can be sure he will testify such when law enforcement begins to make enquiries about why drugs have suddenly become more available in Delft."

The allegation was so clearly fabricated that Saskia's jaw dropped slightly. She stared at François in disbelief.

"I can see you appreciate the gravity of the serious crime your brother is perpetrating. Indeed, imagine further how unviable your parents' livelihood would become if your mother's sore knee should suddenly become worse because of an accident on the uneven stones of the city. But let me move on to another issue that should concern you."

The photos François now laid before Saskia were of Melanie. One showed her inserting a needle into her arm, another showed her working in a kitchen, and another showed her sitting in the shade of a tree reading a book.

"I believe you have had several interactions with this woman. She is in Paris in a rehabilitation centre." François tapped the picture of Melanie in the kitchen and then of her reading. "She is beloved of a past lover of yours, Hans. He is very concerned for her health and well-being. You are still on good terms with Hans. It would cause him significant grief if she regressed once more. It takes very little for people like her not to revert to old habits."

Saskia looked from François to Azzam Touati. The latter watched her with evident pleasure.

With a growing sense of horror, Saskia realised that, despite all the warnings Olivier and Angela had given her and the subtext of Ayat Benkirane's foreboding, she had precipitated this situation by stubbornly rejecting every attempt by Azzam Touati to control her. She should have realised that a man like him would become obsessed with finding the means to thwart her independence. Touati saw his multitude of servants, his immaculate and opulent home, his children and those who managed his money – she was increasingly convinced that two primary handlers were Ayat Benkirane and Antoine Aubert – as demonstrations of his control and power.

Azzam Touati leaned forward again. "Dr Midget, this is what you will do. You will wear the wrist device that everyone in my home must wear. You will contact Ayat Benkirane on the phone you have been using to entertain yourself in the evenings and tell him you will be busy here until the time of the birthday party. You will perform at the birthday party. You will remember that if you reveal the substance of this conversation in your phone conversations, your family and friends will suffer. Your cooperation now and into the future is all that will keep your family and friends safe now and into the future. We will speak further about other tasks you can perform for me at another time."

## 38

## INFORMATION

Saskia did not notice the expressions of dismay passing among the children as she rejoined them at the refreshment table, or that Basem nodded for Harmony to offer Saskia a drink. The glass rattled against her teeth when the act of bringing it to her lips brought the monitoring device strapped to her wrist into her field of vision. She gulped the liquid and retched as her clenched diaphragm restricted her throat. She hunched forward, dropping the glass.

*Think, Saskia! This is not helping anyone!* She pressed her hands on to her bent knees, tightening her jaw.

Taking a deep breath, she picked up the glass and handed it to Harmony. "Apologies. That was very clumsy of me," she said. Harmony took the glass. There were tears in her brown eyes.

Saskia had avoided riding the bikes or scooters to demonstrate the moves she wanted the children to perform. Mostly, her intent had been to thwart any ideas Touati might harbour about making her part of the show. Now, it didn't matter.

Mouna's bike was the best fit for her.

"Excuse me while I borrow this," she said to Mouna, taking the bike out of the girl's grasp. "I just need to let off a bit of steam so I can think again."

## THE BANK

It took two loops of the track for her to get a proper feel for the bike, and then she began to pump, pushing in and out of the berm and using manuals and jumps to increase her speed. After five times around, her brain started to focus on other things than her hatred of Azzam Touati. She lifted the front wheel and performed a manual over the longest straight of the track. She performed the tricks she'd been patiently showing the children, manualling the bike over half the loop, taking a run up on to the edge of the berm to leap from one part of the loop to the other, getting height and spinning the bike under her. Two more fast loops and, with her legs feeling leaden, she stopped, spinning to face the children. She leaned over the handlebars, heaving air into her lungs.

When she had enough breath to speak again, and having somewhat sorted the muddle in her brain, she raised her head. The children, Harmony and the manservant – why had she never asked his name? – were staring open-mouthed at her.

"Alright," she said, wheeling the bike back to Mouna. "What did I do wrong?"

No one said a word.

She held up two fingers. Crooking the first finger, she said, "I was not wearing a helmet. That is a huge no-no. Don't ever do it." She crooked the second finger. "I was upset. Don't do dangerous things when you are upset. Your judgement goes out of the window, and you can do yourself serious damage."

She clapped her hands. "Alright! Where were we? Let's get back to practice and get in a bit more before Harmony brings us lunch."

When Harmony finally walked her back to her room, Saskia's carefully controlled distress had lodged into a pounding tension headache. She lay back on the bed and stared at the surveillance camera that had been rewired into a corner of the room. Before this morning, her emotions had been of discomfort with Azzam Touati's unsavoury treatment of his family and servants. Now, her emotions bounced between rage and dread.

She closed her eyes, concentrating on her breathing.

"This listening device," François had told her as he strapped it on to her wrist, "will pick up sounds you make. It also picks up your heartbeat." He grinned mirthlessly. "Should you have a heart attack, we will be immediately to your aid. It is waterproof, so do not remove it even when you bathe. The battery lasts twenty-four hours. You will receive a newly charged device every twenty-four hours."

Saskia squeezed her eyelids together and then relaxed them. She tightened her jaw and then relaxed it. She shrugged up her shoulders and then relaxed them. Tightening and relaxing, she worked through the parts of her body until she lay fully relaxed on the bed. Then she imagined sitting at the base of a tree, forest plants gently moving in a soft, fresh breeze. Her imagination took her to examine the petals of a dandelion, the smooth texture of blades of grass, the structure of mushrooms and the smell of the earth.

The click of a lock and a soft knock brought her out of her meditation.

It took her a moment to re-orient herself to the room.

Another soft knock and, "Miss, I have your dinner."

Saskia slipped off the bed. She opened the door to take the tray from Harmony.

Goat stew again.

"Thank you, Harmony."

Sitting at the desk, Saskia considered how best to change the choreography of the children's show to include herself. She flipped through her sketches, adding ideas. She toyed with the thought of dressing Basem and herself up as clowns and introducing dark humour, but dismissed the idea. She had a hunch that Touati would probably hide Basem – his imperfect creation – rather than display him at the party.

Saskia's lips curled. *You called him disabled and physically incompetent, but he's got more worth than the nail on your manicured little finger, you bastard!*

Saskia sat back and considered. If her hunch proved correct, then it was likely that only Gadil and herself would be part of the show. She needed to plan for that.

An hour later, she showered, wondering if security guards were gathered around a screen gawking at her nakedness. She resisted the temptation to give them a show.

From the pocket of her trousers, she took out the piece of paper on which Touati had written Ayat Benkirane's private phone number. Taking her notebook with her, she sat on the bed and leaned back against the wall with the pillow providing a thin buffer.

Without prelude, Saskia spoke as soon as M. Benkirane answered. "Monsieur, this is Saskia. My apologies for calling you on your private number. I need to let you know that I must extend my stay with Monsieur Touati."

"Saskia?" Ayat sounded surprised. Then, after a pause, he continued, "Is there a problem?"

*Lots!* "Monsieur Touati believes it would be best if I stayed for another couple of weeks."

Another long pause. "How are you?"

"I am well." *Get the message! Things are not well!*

"And the children?"

*Why are you interested in the children? And you knew about Basem.* "The children are well." *But the situation here is really fucked up, and what is your hand in all of this?* "I hope that my staying here for another couple of weeks does not inconvenience you. I will probably see you next at Gadil's birthday party."

Another very long pause. "Thank you for letting me know, Saskia. Take care."

"Bye."

Saskia rang off. Very aware that the security camera was focused on her every move, she did not drop her face into her hands or throw the phone hard at the wall or show rage. But she did take a few deep breaths before tapping out the next number.

"Hey, Saskia, you're calling a bit early. I'm still eating my dinner."

"Hi, Hans. I decided not to call my parents tonight. I don't quite have the energy to listen to gossip."

Hans laughed. "I love your relationship with your parents. I don't think they quite know what to make of you."

"I love them just the way they are."

"You're just their little girl."

"It's true. But hey, I've been wondering, have you thought of getting a pet?" *Are you listening, Olivier and Angela? Did you hear me?*

"What? No. I couldn't bear the responsibility. You sound a bit off. Are you feeling a bit grumpy? You do grumpy very well."

"I am a bit grumpy. I've just learnt that I'll be here for another couple of weeks."

"Really? Why's that?"

"To get the children well and truly ready for the birthday party."

"Are you happy about staying another week?"

"It will be good for the children."

"This guy's serious about making a good show, isn't he. I'm looking forward to hearing all the details when you get out."

"Don't look forward to it too much. I haven't seen or experienced anything more than the backyard and the courtyard of this place. Anyway, privacy is obviously a big thing here. So, I'll respect that."

Waves of cold and hot emotions washed through Saskia. *Did you hear that?* she thought to her invisible castle spies. *Believe it Touati! Cut me some slack!* But in reality, she feared the worst. After today's conversation, Saskia was quite certain Touati would find a way to ensure she never had a chance to leave this fortress alive. And what had he meant when he said he had other uses for her? Did he want to use her computing skills? Had Benkirane talked to him about that or Aubert? What was their association?

Saskia looked down at the notebook spread on her lap. "I'm quite pleased with the routine I've developed for the children. There are a few more things I'll need to iron out, though."

"Are they enjoying themselves?"

"Hugely. I'm not even getting a fuss when they crash."

"You've always been good with kids."

"Which is a nice segue into this game we're developing. Should we introduce some children in the mix?"

"Give me a break, Saskia! I'm obsessed enough with this game. I can hardly concentrate on my real work, and now Nicolaas has got involved, and I talked to Claasen about it. She thinks you might have a saleable twist mixing the game genres. She's offered to help with the images and soundtracks, and we can run the whole thing through her systems when you're back on board. Anyway, I think I've got the look of the three main characters perfected."

Saskia smiled. Hans had been unable to resist introducing cyber and mythical features to the characters. He'd fitted Lucius Manatius Plancus with high-performance armour. A second hero called Vercingetorix had the capacity to summon an eidolon, which, in Greek mythology was a spirit image of a living or dead person. Last night they'd spent an amusing half-hour debating the form of the eidolon since such a concept was not part of the ancient Roman culture. They decided that Vercingetorix, being a Gaul in their made-up narrative who had a Roman father, would be more comfortable with an eagle ghost than a human ghost since eagles were associated with Jupiter and victory by the Romans. The third hero, whom they'd decided to call Publius Acilius Attianus, had the power to persuade others to do his bidding simply by speaking to them. Saskia had argued they needed to put a few caveats around this gift. They had decided to work out the details about caveats later.

"Have you had more ideas you want to flesh out tonight?"

"I've got some more ideas about the set-up. There was a huge amphitheatre on the opposite side of the river. We didn't visit it when you and Melanie were in Lyon. There's not much left of it, but at one stage, it was huge. The story goes that some Christians were martyred there. I thought it would be a good idea to recreate that theatre precinct. It'd make a wonderful arena for some of the contests we'll get the characters engaged in."

Hans groaned. "Saskia! We don't need another setting. Gamers are going to be challenged enough building the old city with the two smaller theatres on Fourvière Hill, especially when they need to compete with one another. "

"I think the amphitheatre idea is crucial. It became a hub for all the major Lugdunum events. I wish Isabelle were part of this discussion. Do you remember Isabelle?"

"Of course, I remember Isabelle."

"Well, she was heavily into Roman history, especially of Lugdunum. It would be good if she could explain how it all worked. She was great at telling the story of it all."

"Maybe she could send me some images. Have you got her contact?"

"On my phone. I don't have it in my head. Anyway, she's on some high seas adventure at present."

*Did you hear me, Angela and Olivier? You need to contact Hans and tell him what I'm doing! Trust him!*

## 39

### NUMBER SERIES

Day five.

The day was cool, and rain threatened. Ordinarily, Saskia would have pulled on a coat to keep herself warm, but, this morning, she needed to display her green-trimmed blouse. She mixed the message with a red ribbon around her ponytail, hoping it conveyed that she was in deep trouble, but extraction was not an option at this time.

She followed Harmony to the concrete pad in the courtyard. The children were lined up, helmets on heads and bikes or scooters in hand. They watched her approaching in silence, different from the other mornings when they had grinned and wished her a good morning while fiddling with their bikes and scooters, eager to start the day's lessons.

The difference in behaviour was due to the presence of their father, with a bodyguard at his back. Touati wore casual slacks and a woollen cardigan over a polo top; a picture of sartorial elegance as he leaned back in a chair, one leg crossed over the other, showing off moccasin-clad feet.

"Bonjour, Monsieur," Saskia greeted in her politest voice.

"You intend to use this surface?" he asked, indicating the concrete pad with a jerk of his chin.

"It is a good surface."

"Show me."

"Certainly, Monsieur. But first, the children will need to warm up their muscles. If they don't, they could hurt themselves." She turned to the children, giving Touati no time to respond to her imperative. The portcullis was closed, so she had to warm the children up around the courtyard. "On your bikes and scooters, please. I want you to do three rounds of the courtyard – first one slow and the next two fast. Gadil and Tehzib, you go four rounds. On the fourth round, do a series of bunny hops along the concrete paths and one bar spin. Basem, I want you to slide into a stop. Do a track stand, then cycle back easy." She clapped her hands. "Off you go."

She kept her back deliberately turned to Touati as she watched the children follow her directions. Then she instructed each to demonstrate what they had learnt to do on the concrete pad, leaving off the tricks each had still to master comfortably.

"Now you," Touati said, making no indication he was impressed by any of the children's accomplishments.

Saskia had expected this. She asked Mouna if she could borrow her bike and performed a series of tricks that were showy but not hard. She returned the bike to Mouna, saying, "Merci," as she did so.

Azzam rose. "I saw you on that track outside yesterday. You may continue to teach my children. I have no further use for them just now." He waved an indolent hand in the direction of the portcullis as he turned to leave. With a creak and a groan, the portcullis began to lift, giving access to the area beyond the castle wall, the pump track and ramps.

The children were as attentive and quiet as they had been on the first day, casting anxious glances at her as if guarding against something Saskia might say and do. Saskia tried to behave in the same cheerful and encouraging way she had on previous days, but anger and dread kept tying up her emotions, not helped by the weather, which blew increasingly cool. Thunder rumbled threateningly from dark clouds that flashed periodically with lightning. The sky gave every indication that the day's lessons would need be cut short.

This would probably be for the better, Saskia reflected. She was finding it impossible to turn her mind to adapting the choreography she had developed with the children to inserting herself, especially since Touati's behaviour this morning had intensified her belief that, come the date of the party, he would likely only display the prowess of his son and hide his other children – or, at best, only briefly display them wearing their finest livery.

He would probably hide Basem altogether.

As if drawn by her dark thoughts, Basem walked his bike over to her. "Saskia, I believe there is something amiss with the pedal of this bike," he said.

Saskia crouched to inspect the pedal. Indeed, blades of grass had wound around the spindle in the gap between the crank and the body. "You must have got this gummed up when riding through the long grass near the palisade fence," she said, beginning to pick at the blades to loosen them.

Basem leaned forward to look and stumbled, landing awkwardly on top of her. His mouth close to her ear, he whispered, "Tell your friends the app Father uses is called anom with a zero." He pushed himself to his feet. "I am very, very sorry," he flustered loudly, righting his bike. "Have I hurt you! I am sorry."

"Er – umm – I'm fine. I'm fine. Did you hurt yourself?"

*Anom with a zero! What on earth is he talking about?*

A while later, Gadil gave her a meaningful look while tapping the crossbar on his bike. "Why can't I get up as much speed as you on the pump track?" he asked.

"Er – umm –" *What are you children up to?* "Okay, let me demonstrate."

Tehzib was next to engage her, casually pointing to three tiny black numbers on the underside of the bike's crossbar. When the opportunity presented itself, she looked and found three more numbers on the crossbar of Basem's bike. On Gadil's bike, she saw two numbers separated by a period.

Saskia had time to sneak another look at the numbers to commit them to memory before rain burst from the black clouds, drenching everyone before they had time to reach cover.

## 40

## MESSAGE DELIVERED

Harmony took Saskia to her room. "Please, Miss, I will come and collect your wet clothes in an hour? and I will see they are dried."

"Thank you. Could I also ask you to do some washing for me. It seems I will be staying a while longer, and I didn't bring enough clothes to cover more than week."

Harmony glanced at the listening device on Saskia's wrist. "Yes, Miss. Please just give them to me with your wet clothes."

Saskia warmed up under the shower, mentally repeating the information the children had provided. The numbers, she thought, could be an IP address – perhaps for a server? Maybe Basem was hoping she could contact the white hat friends she had mentioned to him. Maybe he thought they could somehow mount a cyber assault on his father's fortress and free them.

The poor children!

But Saskia was desperate enough to pass on any crumb of information that might help Angela and Olivier extract her from the mess she'd created for herself. Her position had moved beyond retrieving information to help Project Archane.

Towelling her hair dry, she sat at the little desk and stared at the sketches she'd made to support the computer game she and Hans were developing. Particularly, she stared at sketches of the three amphitheatres: the two small ones on the western side of the Saône and the large one between the Saône and Rhône.

What did Basem mean by 'the app father uses is anom with a zero'?

Harmony brought her dinner – goat meat stew again – and a fully charged replacement monitoring device.

When the digital display on the dumb phone indicated her family would be settled for the evening, she rang their number. Jan answered. Her parents, he explained, were visiting Tante Alice who had just had an operation.

"You were not called upon to drive them?"

"No. Oom Anton picked them up. I'm here with Marietta. We're having a quiet evening."

"Oh, well. I won't delay you, then. I only called to say hello. I've nothing much to report except I'll be staying at this place for another couple of weeks so Mama and Papa still can't call me."

"Why so long? Is it so nice there?"

"An anomaly with zero chance of changing has come up."

"What do you mean by that?"

"Only that I didn't anticipate the change, but I've cleared it with my boss at the bank, so all is moving along. Say hi to Marietta for me."

"Will do."

Saskia took her notebook, pencil and phone to the bed, set herself up against the wall and called Hans.

She was calling earlier than usual again but he answered immediately. "Hey, Saskia! What have you got for me this time?"

"Phew! Hans! You're eager tonight."

"You have no idea! I'm totally into this game now. So is Nicolaas. I've got you on speaker phone."

"Hey, Saskia," Nicolaas said. "How are you?"

"I'm well. A short day today. It's started to rain."

"Right. Well, we now have a lot more information on Lugdunum,"

Hans said. "I didn't realise that such a decisive Roman battle was carried out there."

"Also, many early Christians were martyred there," Nicolaas added.

"How did you get the information?" Saskia asked.

"It turns out that our library here in Rotterdam had quite a lot," Nicolaas said. There was a pause, then he continued, "We got the help of quite an angelic researcher."

*Angela! Are you with them listening in to this conversation? Is this why both of you sound wound up?*

"That's perfect," Saskia said. "I've been working on two possible story lines. One that should take place in one of the smaller amphitheatres and another in the large one. In the smaller one, it should be something to do with arguments by the senators and magistrates and maybe the company of boatmen to do with trade. If we go with the larger one, maybe we go with something to do with the persecution of Christians. Which one do you want?"

"Give us a moment," Hans said. "I'll just put you on mute."

Sometime later, Hans returned with, "If we're going to keep to the characters we've already developed – you know, the triumvirate – we should stick to the earlier period of Lugdunum's history before Christians."

Saskia laughed. "Give over, Hans! Surely we're not going to try to be historically accurate when you've got people in techno-advanced armour."

"Eh! Oh – you're probably right. So, which one do you want to start with?"

"For the sake of simplicity, let's flesh out a story around a trial of some Christians. Let's make the real baddy Caligula. He was a particularly nasty piece of work."

"How does the triumvirate fit into this?"

"Well, I'm thinking we could start by having Caligula insisting on putting the Christians to death by horrible means. Let's have Vercirgetorix bringing the Christians to Caligula, Publius standing by as judge and Lucius readying his fighting forces because he knows that those who are supporting the Christians will mount a battle to rescue the prisoners."

"Who are the Christians?"

"Some anom – " Saskia cleared her throat. "'Scuse me. Some anonymous people with no chance – zero chance – of escaping."

"Just a minute. I'm going to put you on mute again. Someone's at the door."

The silence was long. Eventually, Hans came back online. "Talk about Christians. We just had a couple call to try and convince us to go to bible classes," he said. "Sorry for leaving you on hold. While I was fending them off, Nicolaas has been working on the idea. You should see this place, there are books about the history of Lugdunum all over the place. Some of it is in French, some in Dutch, some in English and there's even a few in Spanish."

"How are you going with the Spanish ones?" Saskia forced another laugh.

"We are struggling. Anyway. For simplicity's sake, let's call the Christians Mark, Luke and John."

"Good Christian names, but I'm thinking we should have more than just three." Saskia took a deep breath. This part was very important to get right, and she hope that whoever was listening from Azzam Touati's group was either not very familiar with internet protocols or stupid – preferably both. "So, we've got four sets of people involved in this part of the game. Point one is Caligula. Then there's the Christians, say we have one hundred and sixteen of them. Another point is the triumvirate. Then there's also the, let's call them rebels, let's say there's two hundred and two of them."

"Odd sort of numbers."

"Hey! I'm trying to make it realistic!"

She heard both men laugh. "This game is going ballistic!" Nicolaas said. "You do realise that when you get out of that place, you are going to have to take up all the rest of your vacation time and finish this with us."

"That would be the best type of vacation," Saskia said. She squeezed her eyes shut. What she wanted to do now was turn the phone off, crawl between the bed sheets and put the pillow over her head so that no one of the invisible watchers would notice that she was shuddering with tension. She had delivered two messages and could not know whether either had been delivered successfully. What's more, she now had zero interest in developing the story any further.

But, of course, all those things were impossible. So, Saskia took a deep breath, referred to her notes and enthusiastically continued to flesh out the story with two of her most trusted friends and, she was sure, several of the Project Archane team.

## 41

### RAIN

The rain persisted throughout the next day. Harmony delivered breakfast.

"Miss, do you have a raincoat for today's lesson?"

"Harmony. Until the weather clears, I will not be giving lessons unless there's an indoor space to do it in."

"Oh, Miss. We haven't been given instructions for anything like that, and we've been told the children will be ready as always."

"Please tell whoever is giving you instructions that it is too dangerous to continue with lessons when the surfaces are wet and slippery. I will not put the children in danger."

Saskia next saw Harmony when she delivered a lunch of dates, bread rolls and cheese. Saskia had spent the morning filling her notebook with further story ideas – a burden since creating a story was neither an interest nor a skill of hers. After lunch, Saskia turned her mind to something of greater interest, a database app she'd had in mind for some time.

Harmony delivered dinner and clean, dry and pressed clothes.

Saskia reviewed her notes about the story and rang Hans.

She need not have sweated over the storyline because Hans and Nicolaas had involved Claasen, and the three had done wonders with the bones of Saskia's ideas. Saskia had little to do but listen to sound effects, descriptions of imagery and the developing storyline. The eidolon Hans had initially given to Vercingetorix had become a dog. At one stage, Hans asked her whether she'd ever thought of getting her own dog. Saskia stumbled in her answer, realising Hans had been tipped off about the code phrase. "Umm – yes – sometimes – but I – er – probably not for a little while."

She heard Nicolaas yawn. "Oh, sorry, getting a bit tired," he said. "How have you been sleeping, by the way?" The question dispelled any doubt Saskia might have held that the two men had not been briefed about her situation.

"Er – I'm managing. It's – umm – a little disturbing being shut up in my room all day. It's still raining."

She wondered whether Claasen had also been briefed. Given the enthusiasm of the three, she guessed that was the case.

The next day, intermittent rain still made the grounds too slippery and wet for lessons. Saskia asked Harmony to bring her extra notepaper since her own store had been used up.

Instead of returning with notepapers, Harmony returned to tell her that M. Touati wanted to speak with her and that she needed to bring her notebook with her.

Nerves crawling over her skin at the thought that maybe her carefully coded messages to her friends had not been secure enough, Saskia followed a security guard through the rain-soaked courtyard into the main house. A guard stopped her at the entrance to the main office, where the burka-clad women and the elderly man with the straggly beard were still silently attending to their work. The security guard pointed to the listening device on Saskia's wrist. "Take off."

Saskia handed the despicable device to him. He pointed her to the ornate door on the other side of the room, which three bodyguards barred. One of them knocked and pushed open the door as she approached, letting her into Touati's ostentatious ante-lounge.

He sat in an armchair, posing as if the seat were a throne. With him, also seated in armchairs, were two other men, dressed casually in shirts and dress slacks. One was middle-aged, clean-shaven, slender and fair of complexion, with sandy-coloured hair cut short. The other was large, heavily muscled, black-bearded and bald. The fair slender one looked at her with interest, one eyebrow rising as Saskia entered the room. The large bald one smirked, the tip of his tongue coming out between his plump lips and making tiny movements from side to side.

*Ugh!*

The door to the lounge closed, and Saskia stood alone, facing the three men.

Touati held out his hand.

Saskia approached, handed him her notebook, and then stepped back, her hands clasped loosely in front.

Touati flipped idly through the notebook, briefly studying the stick figure choreography sketches and frowning over her notes about the computer game. The two men shifted their gaze between Touati and Saskia, who kept her attention on her notebook.

"What is this?" Azzam Touati demanded, speaking in heavily accented English. He held up the notebook, showing the page of code.

"Code for an app I'm developing," she replied in French.

"Speak English!"

She repeated her response in English.

"You develop apps?" Touati barked the question.

"It passes the time."

The big man said something in a rough voice in a language Saskia did not understand. Balkan origin, perhaps? Neither of the other men reacted to what he said. Saskia wondered if they had understood him. Perhaps their common language was English.

Touati lifted a sheaf of papers off a low table next to his armchair and held them out to her. "What are these?"

Saskia needed to go no further than the first page to know what the papers were. She took her time to go through all ten reports, though, sending messages to her knees not to buckle and her brain to stop racing from one terrifying scenario to another, all of them centred on how Azzam had obtained these reports and why he was showing them to her.

"These are reports I have written for FSB, Monsieur."

"How you come for information in report," Touati demanded. His accented English caused her to pause as she translated what she heard, "How you come for information in report?" he repeated impatiently.

"By analysing bank data, Monsieur."

"How you got data?"

"I am a bank employee, Monsieur. I have such access."

"Who give you access?"

"I was employed in the risk management section of the bank to assess the bank's risk exposure to money laundering and terrorism financing. My job came with clearance to access the bank's data and identify the risk areas. This clearance is from the headquarters in New York. These reports," Saskia held the documents up, "are part of the output of my job."

"Who you send?"

"In the first instance, they were passed on to my then superior, Madame Le Fèvre."

"What Madame do with them?"

"I am not privy to that information, Monsieur."

"Why write in English language?"

"English is the language used for any report that might be going to the bank's New York Headquarters."

"So these go there?"

"I am not privy to such information, Monsieur."

"You still do this work?"

"Soon after Madame Le Fèvre's promotion, I was given a training position and then moved to Brussels to work with Monsieur Benkirane."

"You done more these report?"

"Not since I changed my work, Monsieur."

The slender man held out his hand for the documents. Saskia looked to Touati for permission, and then, keeping as much distance as she could from the bald man, held the reports out so that her hand would not touch the receiving ones.

The slender man grinned, looked her up and down, and then turned his attention to the documents. "Give her the other ones," he said, not looking up. He also spoke English with a marked accent, but she couldn't quite place it. Perhaps Russian?

Azzam picked up another sheaf of papers and handed them to Saskia. "What these?"

Saskia spent less time looking through the new document. "These are part of the Panama Papers."

"How people find information for Panama Paper?"

"I don't know, Monsieur. Rumour is that users could see the directory structure. It would seem that the network architecture was weak, and the email and web servers were not segmented from the client database. I believe that the Mossack Fonseca organisation had weak data security. Hackers could have found their way into the system. There might also have been leaks from the firm itself."

The three men gawked at her. She wondered whether they understood even half of her explanation.

"You use the Panama Papers to make these your reports?" the slender man asked.

*Yes, Russian,* Saskia decided.

"Not directly, Monsieur. But I have studied them. I have also studied the Luxembourg Leaks, Paradise Papers, Pandora Papers and others."

"Why?"

"It was part of my academic work, Monsieur."

"Ah! A klever leetle leetle gerrrl. She go-ing akademik," the bald man said, his voice so deep it seemed to come from inside the cavity of his broad chest. He leered at her, tongue now stroking his top lip.

*Ugh!*

"You say in report bank is laundering money." The slender man held up her reports. "Why?"

"Tractfin in France requires suspicious transactions to be reported to it. My research indicated the bank was not doing so consistently and I reported my suspicions."

"Hoo Tracfin?" the bald man demanded

"France's finance regulator."

"Why you suspicious?" Touati asked.

"The financial regulator defines suspicious transactions, Monsieur." Saskia knew the details by heart, so she began to quote them. "They include money remittances carried out through a cash or e-money transfer that exceeds one thousand euros or an aggregate amount for the same client over one calendar month that exceeds two thousand euros. As well as cash deposits or withdrawals –"

"Stop!" the bald man snapped. He glared from Azzam Touati to the slender man. "No more! Tell her go. She too dangerous to leave alone. We talk."

Touati glared at the man. The slender man sat forward slightly, anticipation bordering on delight tugging at his features as his gaze flicked from Touati to the large bald man. All Saskia's instincts told her to run. There was no love lost between these men. Something had brought them together, and she had little doubt that they had identified her in their search for whatever had disturbed them.

When Touati flicked his hand at her to leave the room, Saskia turned away, her legs almost too weak to carry her to the door.

## 42

## CODE RED

"Hoi, Papa. Hoe gaat het met jullie?" (How are things with you all?)

"Saskia! Waroom beld ye niet gisteren?" (Why didn't you ring yesterday?)

Saskia took a deep breath. It was so good to hear her father's voice and, mostly, to hear the familiar note of complaint about her violation of expectations. It was also good to speak the language of her childhood. Doing so helped to settle the mush and panic that had consumed her brain in the hours since returning to her room and waiting for the time she usually made her evening calls.

"I became distracted, Papa. I was playing a computer game with my friends."

"Tch! Saskia. I had to put up with your mother's complaints for hours. She wants to know when you will get your own phone back so we can call you."

"Maybe another week, Papa. But tell me, how is Mama's knee? Is it still all red and swollen?"

"It didn't become red and swollen. It was just stiff. She is a hypochondriac." Saskia heard her mother screech in the background, and her father chuckled. "Uh oh! I think I am in trouble. Here she is."

"If he has sore knee, complain, complain, complain," her mother protested.

Saskia laughed. "Did it get red and swollen?" she asked.

"Not red. Thick a bit."

"Well, if it goes red, be sure to see a doctor. Otherwise it might stop you from sleeping a wink at night." *Are you listening, Angela and Olivier? Red! Red! Red! And no sleep! Look out for my family!*

"It is raining, raining, raining here," Saskia said.

"Also bad weather in Holland." Her mother then launched into an extended session, with her father occasionally providing details, on the ailments of Tante Alice, who was still in hospital.

Saskia revelled in the minutia of her parents' concerns; they were normal, wholesome, connected and very, very far removed from the tangle she was in.

A knock on the bedroom door caused Saskia to end the call.

Harmony, who had come to remove Saskia's dinner tray, frowned worriedly at the largely untouched stew.

"I'll just keep the bread roll, Harmony. I wasn't very hungry tonight because I've just been lying in bed."

Locked into her room again, Saskia resumed her position on the bed and pressed the numbers to connect to Hans. He answered immediately. "Hi, Saskia! You're on speaker again. We've moved to the café."

"The – the café?"

"Ya. Saskia," Nicolaas said. "We talked to the gang and decided we missed having you around, so we're doing a group thing."

"Well – ummm – that's nice."

A cacophony of greetings sounded in the background, causing moisture to well into Saskia's eyes.

"I'm going to take control of the talking on the phone," Nicolaas said. "Just to keep things in a bit of order."

"I'm – er – flattered by all this attention."

"You are our Saskia," Nicolaas said firmly. There was a pause, and then he continued with, "By the way, how are your parents?"

"Umm – I was just speaking with them. They are fine."

"I'll be going to Delft soon, and I'll take over a bunch of your mother's favourite red roses."

A shudder ran through Saskia. *Message received!* "That's very kind of you."

"Did you do more bike things today?"

"No. It is still raining, but I think the weather is clearing, so hopefully I'll be outside again tomorrow. I'm getting a little sick of being in this room."

"What can you see from your room?"

"Not much. I have to stand on a chair to properly see out of the window." Then, thinking that maybe Angela or Olivier was nearby and wanting further information, she continued. "Umm – er – my room's the third one along the – er – west wing, so I can only see the biggest fountain in the centre of the courtyard and a bit of the other wing of the palace. I can see some of the concrete pad the children practise on. But the courtyard's pretty so it's nice to look at. Umm – the whole place is amazingly well looked after." Saskia cleared her throat, loosening her grip on the phone because the phone's edges were biting into her fingers, and hoping her reply raised no alarm bells for security personnel.

"Are you doing a lot of sleeping while you're in your room?"

Saskia sat forward. Nicolaas was asking for the code sentence. "Umm – I didn't sleep a wink last night." Then, because she was afraid that the resultant silence might trigger caution among security, she hastily added. "But listen, amuse me with what you guys have dreamed up. I'm at a bit of a disadvantage just now. I was talking to Monsieur Touati and he wanted to look at my notebook, so he – er – he's still got it."

There was a pause and a background of murmurs, and then Nicolaas said, "I'll hand you over to Claasen. She'll tell you what we've put together. See if you can make sense of it."

Saskia could make little sense of what Claasen told her in overly technical details about software programs the group were using to construct segments of the game, synchronised sound effects and sequences for gamers to work their way through. Saskia listened with only part of her attention, wondering how she could get Hans to mention Melanie so she could also say something red about her.

But, as Claasen talked on, occasionally interrupted by Hans and input from Nicolaas, Saskia gleaned that the team working on the game design had decided that the Christians, as a result of yesterday's game embellishment, were about to be freed by a rebel army.

"Jezus!" Saskia exclaimed, snapping into complete focus.

"We've thought about using Lyon's traboules as escape routes," Hans said. "Remember, we did a tour of them with you in Lyon. Melanie loved them. I remember they've been used over the centuries in revolts and escapes. The French resistance used the network to evade the Nazis."

"But traboules weren't around in the Roman times," Saskia blurted and then felt stupid because she'd been the one to point out that nothing about this game was time-bound. More importantly, Hans had given her the opening she'd hoped for. "Er – Melanie was impressed by them. And I remember how her red dress looked all dark every time we ducked into another passage."

"Red dress?" Hans sounded puzzled.

Saskia plunged on. "I really liked that dress. It had a red collar and red buttons. But I'm going off-topic. You guys are doing amazing things." She forced a laugh. "Claasen, I can only understand half of what you're saying, but I think I'm getting the idea."

## 43

## ARMOURED VEST

Saskia's fitful sleep was full of armour-enhanced heroes mounted on rabid ghost dogs running through tunnels with ornate traboules doorways. Each time she jerked out of another confusing dream, she tried to work out what message Claasen had been sending about traboules … or was there a message at all?

Saskia imagined Angela and Olivier taking on yet another personality and role, coming to the gates and, perhaps, posing as gangsters or tradesmen with some story about gas leaks they were investigating. Or maybe they would come in a canoe that tipped over, and swim to the gate and plead for help. There was also the possibility of smuggling her out in a laundry basket as sometimes happened in movies … except she hadn't seen laundry baskets being used in the castle precinct!

*Clutching at straws*!

No scenario Saskia could think of would work. Touati lived in a fortress, and short of a military intervention, there was no way to access the fortress without his permission.

Belgium was a democracy where law enforcement needed to show legitimate cause to invade a person's private property. Saskia doubted that Angela–Isabelle and Olivier–Simon could persuade a judge to allow a forced entry to rescue a person who had voluntarily walked into the 'lion's den'.

Although he had effectively kidnapped her and blackmailed her with threats against her own person, family and friends, she had no way of telling law enforcement officers these facts. Even if the Belgian authorities suspected he was keeping his family and staff like slaves, which, surely, was against the law, it would not precipitate a military-style assault on a castle. There'd be enquiries and lawyers would become involved and time would slip by … enough time for her family, Melanie and herself to meet with 'unfortunate accidents'.

Or maybe she would be blackmailed into staying in the fortress with the threat of 'unfortunate accidents' to family and friends keeping her as a slave to Touati's whims … and maybe the whims of the other men.

She shuddered, remembering the way the big bald man had moved his tongue over his wet lips.

Saskia pressed her lips together to stop a groan escaping.

Who, Saskia asked herself for the thousandth time, were the men who'd been with Azzam Touati? And why were they concerned about the reports she had put together?

The reports must have come from Antoine Aubert.

Or perhaps from Ayat Benkirane.

Who were the Christians that Claasen had talked about being rescued? Was it her parents? Was it Melanie?

Saskia hoped so.

She scrubbed her face with her hands. Around and around the thoughts cycled. She buried her face in the pillow and forced herself to think of what she would do with the children the next day, telling herself that, at the very least, Touati would want to keep her alive until after the party, and perhaps there would be enough time for Angela and Olivier to find ways of protecting her parents and Melanie…

*I think Olivier and Angela will work out how to come as guests to the party, and they'll somehow smuggle me out. That's how it's done in thriller movies.*

*Stop it, Saskia! Go to sleep.*

Saskia put the pillow over her head and began her relaxation meditation routine.

Something pressed hard on the pillow, then jerked it from her grasp. A gloved hand closed over her mouth, cutting off her cry.

A shadowy figure leaned close. Warm breath touched her ear. "Calmly! It's Olivier!"

A shudder passed through Saskia's body as she stared wide-eyed at the black silhouette bending over her.

"It's Olivier." This time, the whisper was a little louder.

Saskia nodded.

The hand over her mouth released its pressure, but another hand pressed gently against her chest to keep her from sitting up. The warm breath came close to her ear again. Saskia shook her head. "Shh," she hissed. She groped around, found the gloved hand on her chest and brought it to cover the listening device on her wrist. She touched her ear and then pointed to the ceiling where the camera was located.

"Camera dismantled," Olivier whispered. "Take off the wristband."

Saskia tore it off.

Olivier helped her sit up, legs over the side of the bed. "Put these on," he breathed, helping her slip arms through a body armour vest then placing a helmet on her head.

Clumsy in the darkness, Saskia fumbled straps across her chest to close the vest and clip together the chin strap of the helmet. Both were too big. Olivier slipped shoes on her feet and tied the laces.

"I'm going to carry you," he whispered, checking the fastening of her body armour and helmet. He wrapped one arm around her back and slid the other under her knees. She put her arms around his neck as he lifted her. He walked to the closed bedroom door and paused.

Saskia stiffened as shouting, gunfire and light erupted in the courtyard, chasing shadows into the room. Dogs began to bark. Olivier crouched, pulling Saskia tight against the hard casing of his body armour. She stared up into his face. His cheeks were smeared with black stripes, and he wore dark goggles and a helmet. He gave her a tight, reassuring smile and pursed his lips. "Shh." He stayed still, listening. Saskia flinched again when loud explosions assaulted her hearing. Men and women screamed in panic. Olivier didn't move. Heavy, running steps pounded along the hallway outside the bedroom, disturbing the line of light leaking in through the gap under the door. Olivier shifted his position, settling Saskia on to one knee and freeing one of his arms. In a millisecond, his freed hand held a gun.

Something landed heavily against the door, followed by the sound of a hard-fought scuffle. Outside, the barking of dogs, shouting and gunfire continued.

Another deafening explosion came, shattering the room's window. Olivier flinched at the sound, but the hand holding the gun remained steadily pointed at the door.

All light winked out.

For a long second there was absolute silence, then the shouting began again, most of it in Arabic, some in French. Saskia thought she heard the high-pitched voice of Azzam Touati.

Olivier holstered his gun and cradled Saskia in both arms again.

He stood. "Hold tight!" he murmured.

The bedroom door swung open.

"Go!" said a female voice.

Olivier bolted through the doorway, down the hallway and out into the courtyard. Saskia clung to his neck, trying to make herself as easy to carry as possible.

The portcullis had a huge hole blown into it. Olivier leapt through the hole, hardly breaking his stride. He raced past a kicker ramp, and was level with the pump track when "Crack! Crack! Crack! Crack!" the rapid, sharp, percussive sound of an automatic rifle split the air. Grass and dirt sprang in small clumps around Olivier. Dull thuds indicated bullets were finding their mark on his armoured vest. Saskia's head jerked as a bullet glanced against her helmet.

Then Olivier stumbled and fell, throwing Saskia clear from himself.

"Run!" he gasped, rolling on to his back, a gun in his hands. He began shooting at a figure on the castle wall, who ducked out of sight.

Saskia stared at the wall, breath coming in short gasps, expecting more bullets to fly in her direction.

"Run, damn you!" Olivier yelled. "There's a boat waiting for you at the landing. The gate's open. Run!"

Saskia scrambled to her feet and stumbled forward. The too-big-armoured vest knocked against her thighs. The too-big helmet slipped over her forehead.

"Crack! Crack! Crack!" Dirt exploded around Saskia. She bleated a tiny, terrified gasp and hunched forward but the movement caused the vest to knock against her thighs and she stumbled, almost falling.

Olivier's gun sounded again. Then many guns sounded in deafening unison.

Saskia tried desperately to increase her stride, pushing up the helmet with one hand and hauling up the vest with the other, her breath coming in sobs. She squealed when arms caught her up. "It's Angela. Hold on!"

Saskia grabbed the straps of Angela's armoured vest, lifting her legs up to keep them out of the way of Angela's pumping thighs. Angela surged between the twisted bars of the river gate and dumped Saskia into a waiting boat. "Get her away!"

## 44

## NATALIE

A smiling, older woman dressed in a police uniform pressed a warm mug of hot chocolate into Saskia's hands. "Here now," she said, settling a soft blanket over Saskia's shoulders and tucking it around her thighs. "My name is Alexa. You're all safe now, so let's help you stop shivering."

"Olivier was shot," Saskia said. "What's happening back there? There are children. Are the children going to be safe?"

"We know about the children, Saskia, and about their mother. Word is that the team is wrapping things up. Olivier's being treated. We're going to take you back to your apartment now and someone will be along to answer all your questions. Alright? Now, you drink up that hot chocolate and don't worry any more. Alright?"

*Don't worry anymore?* Saskia blinked at the woman. *I've got so many questions and worries my head's about to explode. In fact, I've got a dreadful headache.*

"Umm – would you have some paracetamol?"

"Yes. Yes, I do. Your helmet took a hit." Alexa ran a gentle hand over Saskia's head. "Anything feel bruised here?"

Saskia shook her head.

"You've a few scrapes on your thigh and elbow. Do they hurt?"

Saskia shook her head again. "No. I've just got a bit of a headache."

Alexa sat with Saskia in the back seat of a police car, which had picked them up from wherever the boat had stopped. The driver introduced himself as Bruno. Alexa kept up a not-unpleasant murmur during the journey into the gathering dawn. She commented on how she'd been born in this part of Belgium and, although she'd travelled a bit, it was her favourite area. She also talked about her children and grandchildren. Occasionally, Bruno would add a comment. Saskia assumed that the non-consequential dialogue was to help calm her jittery nerves. It worked to a degree. By the time the car eased into the Brussels' morning traffic, Saskia was almost asleep. However, she was sufficiently together to feel embarrassed about entering the foyer of her apartment block with a blanket over her shoulders, wearing grass and mud-stained pyjamas, shoes without socks.

And her hair must look like an unruly bird's nest!

"Er – I don't have my keycard to get into my apartment," she told an astonished Annalise at reception.

"Of course," Annalise said, her black plaits falling about her face as she busily created another card, all the while shooting uncertain glances at the impassive, uniformed Alexa.

"I hope you don't mind, but I'll stay with you till I get the all-clear," Alexa said as they took the lift up to Saskia's apartment. "Bruno will park the car and stay in the foyer."

Saskia didn't mind. She didn't care. She showered, put on clean clothes and considered breakfast because she could smell coffee brewing and bread toasting. Instead, she brushed her teeth and climbed into bed.

When she woke, it was to see the smiling face of Angela – or was it Isabelle – sitting in the green suede armchair near the window and studying her with a mischievous twinkle in her pale blue eyes. She wore ripped jeans and a tee shirt. Her hair was now an indeterminate colour, the redness having all but leached out, and it was straight and tied back in an untidy ponytail. Her eyebrows were almost white, and no makeup adorned the Nordic fair skin of her face.

"Natalie," she said. "That's my real name. Just in case you're wondering."

"How many personas do you have?" Saskia sat up slowly, pushing her hair back off her face. "Is it all over then?"

Natalie grinned. "It is for us. It's just up to the big brass now. We will fade back into obscurity."

"And Olivier – er – Simon?"

"Whose real name is Claude. Well, he's one of the big brass. He's going to be busy with a lot of paperwork and doing interrogation of baddies for quite a while."

"But is he alright?"

"He's okay. Grumbling a lot about catching a bullet in his thigh, but he'll be alright."

"Oh!" Saskia put a hand over her mouth. "He was shot in the leg! Is he really going to be okay?"

Natalie's grin widened. She nodded. "He's tough. He'll get by."

Saskia sat up, leaning forward over her legs, frowning gaze on Natalie's relaxed features. "Is it really all over. I mean is everything … I mean –"

Natalie stood up. "How about you get yourself dressed and come out and have something to eat. Alexa has got us some nice food. I'll fill you in on everything."

Alexa and Natalie were watching a television news show when Saskia joined them. Three men wearing Belgian police uniforms stood facing a camera. One of them, with a rectangular rank insignia of three gold crowns on his left jacket pocket, was speaking:

"… a multi-year investigation involving our partners from Europol and Interpol. It has uncovered a trail of drug and child trafficking and money laundering that reached into many parts of Europe. Principals in a prominent law firm in London and a United States bank with branches throughout Europe have been taken into custody. They are charged with several offences, including dealing in the proceeds of crime. Three underworld figures on the Interpol Red List have been apprehended. Further arrests are underway."

Natalie switched off the television. "Ya-di-ya-di-ya," she said carelessly. "He'll go on to tell everyone what a wonderful job they did, and that anyone thinking of stepping outside the bounds of the law should think twice. Let's eat. I'm hungry. Alexa has got us a meal of breakfast and lunch all rolled into one. Yum!"

"Who are the underworld figures he's talking about?" Saskia asked, levering up her chair to table height.

Natalie waved a finger from side to side at Saskia. "No. First you. I want you to give us a blow-by-blow of what happened in that castle."

Alexa placed a neatly folded cheese omelette in front of Saskia, who nibbled at it while she gave an account of her interactions with Azzam Touati, François, other security personnel, the children and servants.

Natalie asked questions until she was satisfied with the details, and then, between mouthfuls of her own portion of omelette that disappeared without the decorum either Angela or Isabelle had shown, she said, "Well, first things first. The three characters whom you faced yesterday –" she glanced at her watch. "Yes, it was yesterday. The two Red List figures the General Commissioner was talking about on the television are nasty characters we've been after for years. Not only do they move around with high personal security, but they also constantly change their identity. The Russian is Vladimir Antonovich Ivanov, a particularly unsavoury oligarch who runs several highly dubious enterprises in Eastern Europe."

Saskia figured Natalie was talking about the fair slender man.

"The second man," Natalie continued, "is Dion Prifti. His gangs have terrorised refugee communities from northern Africa who had settled in Europe. You were right to feel very nervous of these men."

Natalie shook her head, mouth twisting. "The third is the nasty Azzam Touati. I'm happy to report that all three are in police custody. Monsieur Touati seems to be particularly affronted by the audacity of being imprisoned. He has been threatening legal action, war and the wrath of every god he can persuade to listen to his prayers."

"I do not like that man," Saskia muttered. "I'm surprised he's calling on god; I'm sure he'd feel more at home speaking to someone from the underworld."

Natalie smirked and waved a fork at Saskia. "Now, this will particularly interest you. Your Monsieur Touati's original name was Ahmed Bakkali. He was born in Casablanca, and was in the Moroccan army for a while but disappeared, which is why we couldn't find much on him."

The oven timer beeped. Alexa rose from the table, donned oven gloves and brought a casserole to the table. Natalie leaned over the dish when Alexa lifted the lid and inhaled.

"Ooh, Moroccan chicken stew. Perfect!" She held out her plate – scraped clean of all traces of the omelette – for Alexa to serve her then returned her attention to Saskia.

"But let me lay out the picture for you in sequence. Let's go back to how you first became involved. Our theory holds that Amin Aziz released the ransomware infection you thwarted at FSB. We believe he needed money to pay for a promised passage of members of his family, who are languishing in a refugee camp in southern Lebanon. The money was to be paid to Monsieur Antoine Aubert, who promised to arrange the passage. The unfortunate outcome of your actions was the death of Amin and his family because Aubert was afraid that follow-up of the scam might lead to him."

"But there wasn't any effort to follow up on the scam!" Saskia protested. "I didn't and it wasn't reported to the police."

Natalie shrugged. "Perhaps it's the nature of the devils Aubert got into bed with. We're still questioning him. He's not being very cooperative so far."

"So, Antoine Aubert? Is he – "

Natalie waved her fork again. "Let me get to all of that. We suspect that Aubert figured that the probability that law enforcement authorities would investigate FSB's lax money-laundering protocols increased because of Amin's failed scam. This was especially the case after Amin's wife attacked you in the market, drawing even further attention to FSB."

"Oh! Mon dieu! How awful."

Natalie nodded, continuing to fork food into her mouth as she spoke. "Such is the nature of the devils we run after. All that surveillance you were put under initially was orchestrated by Ayat and Antoine and involved your Mister François, who ran a nice racket employing skilled, if ethically challenged, spies, even if I do say so myself. We had a devil of a time trying to find out who was keeping tabs on you!"

Saskia glanced down at the chicken stew Alexa set before her and told herself it was very different from goat stew.

"As you know, Azzam Touati was a new entity to us," Natalie said. "Belgian police were aware of him, of course, but he was just another rich man, and they had no reason to suspect him of any criminal activity. When you told us to have a look at the association between Antoine Aubert, Ayat Benkirane and Azzam Touati –"

"You understood what I meant?"

Natalie chucked. "Yes. Eventually. You made us scratch our heads for a bit, but then our Moroccan colleagues, via Interpol, turned up a photo of the three of them together in the army. At that point, we could start to unravel the careers and connections of the three men."

Natalie scraped up the last of the chicken and pushed her emptied plate away. She leaned her elbows on the table. "When you talked about Isabelle in your conversation with Hans, and you followed by talking about getting pets, we went into overdrive. We decided to tell Hans and Nicolaas what was going on. So, I travelled in one huge hurry to Rotterdam. I can't say I quite expected their reaction." She grinned, revealing her beautifully even white teeth.

"Which was?" Saskia prompted.

"They were furious that we'd put you in harm's way. They wanted to know everything you'd been doing, and despite my vehement objections and even threats, they got the rest of your nerdy friends involved. Unsurprisingly, their modus operandi was to completely ignore the letter of the law, and they began hacking into the computer network of FSB, O'Connell and Hansen and the private accounts of Antoine Aubert and Ayat Benkirane. They looked for a way to get into Touati's fortress, but it wasn't till you sent that IP address that they managed that."

"Oh! I was right. It was an IP address. The children gave me those numbers. I was afraid I hadn't communicated them in a way you'd understand."

Natalie huffed. "It took your nerdy friends a nanosecond to figure out what you meant by the numbers. It took them a few more nanoseconds employing their dubious tactics to help tie the knots of that data you've been gathering for us over the months. We got hash CaseIt Ten involved. She's a whizz at sorting stuff, and there's a lot to sort through now. Your database application is a godsend. The data guys will be busy for a long time, and I have no doubt there are a lot of very nervous crooks out there right now."

"Man! That is such good news!"

Natalie chuckled. "But your repeated anom zero references had us totally bamboozled."

"It had me bamboozled. It was obviously important to Basem, but I had no idea what he meant. I thought I'd try and pass it on anyway."

"He is one clever lad. I doubt even he knows the significance of the information he provided. He probably thought it was an app like Messenger or Messages. In fact, it's something the US FBI and the Australian AFP had designed by a renegade criminal who was clever at those sorts of apps. The FBI and AFP managed to sell the app into the criminal underworld as an exclusive, encrypted messaging vehicle. Certain police units worldwide have thus been listening in on criminal transactions for years, and making the occasional swoop. One of our Archane team members knew about the app and figured out the clue you gave us. The app's name is spelt A N Zero M. Once we worked that out, the people keeping tabs on AN0M cooperated and segmented the messages from Ahmed Bakkali, which was the name Touati used for his criminal activities."

Natalie put a forefinger to her lips. "But please. Information about AN0M doesn't go further than this room. Okay?"

Saskia and Alexa nodded.

"By this stage of the saga," Natalie continued, "I was holed up in a café with all your nerdy friends. Nice pizzas, by the way, and not bad coffee. They'd moved monitors in and had the place wired up like the best of IT centres. They'd been hacking and reading code for more than twenty-four hours. Do they ever sleep?"

This was probably a rhetorical question, but Saskia shrugged one shoulder and waggled her hand in a gesture of 'sometimes, and sometimes not'.

Natalie huffed a grunt. "They kept muttering to one another in what I can only describe as tongues. Every now and then, they'd cluster around one or other computer and get excited. When you came online last night," Natalie glanced at her watch again and murmured, "Yes, it was last night. No wonder I feel like shit!" She took a deep breath. "When you came online, they were all there staring at the phone. I thought for sure you'd hear the heavy breathing. As I said, it took them nanoseconds to work out you were giving them an IP address and only a few more – after you left off the call – to work out the arrangement of numbers that gave them access to the one connection Touati had to his castle-base internet. I'm pretty good with computing stuff, but your friends left me for dead. They managed to connect to the internal network of the castle and see what was going on. Not only that, they took control of the network. Nice work. It was invaluable when we started planning our assault on the castle. They disabled the network so that castle security became blind."

Saskia punched the air. "On you team!" she laughed. "I'm going to have to get them a special chocolate pizza."

"I don't think your friends need more unhealthy stuff. Some of them are seriously health deficient!"

"Don't judge my friends," Saskia chided.

"You know they think you belong to them. They kept muttering things like, 'Got you, you bastard! No one mucks around with our Saskia'."

Saskia laughed. "I think they'd say that about anyone in that group. But what about Touati's children? Are they safe? I don't think they've had much of a life in that place."

"Yes, they are safe. I'll get to them. Let me tell you about Ayat Benkirane."

"I'm sad he turned out not to be a good man."

"Reserve your judgement." Natalie sat back in her chair, crossing her arms. "By the time you called Ayat to tell him you were staying an extra week, Belgium DJC – that's the General Directorate of Judicial Police in Belgium – were fully briefed about Project Archane." Natalie reconsidered. "Well, almost fully briefed," she amended. "So, when Ayat called the DJC and told them he had significant crime information for them, he was funnelled straight to the right people."

"Ayat called the police?"

Natalie nodded. "Much of the information we now have on O'Connell and Hansen and FSB, and our increased ability to properly make sense of all the data you've been helping us collect, comes from what Ayat has revealed.

"He told us that he, Antoine and Ahmed started with smallish scam ideas while in the army. Ayat had the senior rank – a colonel or something – because he had a university education. Antoine also had a good education. But it was Ahmed who was the real brains behind the scams. After a time in the army, Ayat and Antoine found themselves jobs in the finance industry. When FSB wanted to set up a branch in Morocco, the three of them could see that controlling a bank would be useful.

"On the back of the profitable way Ayat managed the Moroccan branch – profits gained on the back of handling dirty money – sources that FSB HQ never questioned – Ayat was promoted to the position of chief manager of FSB Europe. Antoine landed the manager's job in Lyon.

"These promotions were perfect for Ahmed who, by that time, was deep into scamming the carbon trading scene and needed to move money quickly from Europe into save havens overseas. Ayat and Antoine set up the banking systems to ensure safe passage for that money, involving O'Connell and Hansen to set up shell companies and trusts and scam signatories. At first, it was just for Ahmed but quickly they were moving money for other criminals and terrorist groups.

"When, the French government and other European governments wised up to the carbon credit scams and changed the system to squeeze out the scammers, Ahmed and other criminal networks concentrated on growing their other activities, especially drugs and weapons smuggling. They used the now well-oiled method of laundering money set up during their carbon trading period. Ayat and Antoine collected margins from moving dirty money, O'Connell and Hansen collected their fees and the bank profited from the money flow. It was a neat arrangement."

"This sort of stuff makes me so upset!" Saskia railed. "It's an abuse of the system. I mean the carbon trading scheme was supposed to benefit society as a whole. Instead, short-sighted already-well-off people and criminals use it to benefit themselves."

"You don't have to convince me," Natalie returned, eyebrows rising.

"Well, it's just that the well-off people complain when less well-off people advocate for change, but it's because it's the little people who are being constantly squeezed!"

Natalie pursed her lips. "Do we want a discussion on the consequences of unethical behaviour by the powerful on the general welfare of society, or shall I continue?"

"Eh? Oh! – um – sorry." Saskia took a deep breath. "I'm sorry about Monsieur Benkirane, though. He just seemed like a nice man. I suspected he must be involved in bad stuff, but it was hard for me to believe it. Why did he eventually go to the police?"

Natalie sat back in her chair, rolling her shoulders then rubbing her face. For the first time showing signs of fatigue.

"Your call did it," she said. "You see, things began to unravel for Ayat about sixteen years ago. Ahmed married one of Ayat's daughters. Apparently, Ahmed can be very charming, and that was the side that Ayat chose to focus on – his words, not mine. Ayat's daughter went to Algiers to live on Ahmed's estate. Pretty quickly, she reported that Ahmed was anything but charming. Things became very bad when she gave birth to Basem. Ahmed was furious she'd delivered him a deformed son. He threatened to murder both mother and son. Ayat managed to talk him out of that, saying there were treatments for dwarfism in Europe. Ayat offered to adopt Basem, but Ahmed doesn't give up any of his possessions, even those he despises. He struck a deal with Ayat. If Ayat gave up his second daughter, Ahmed would give Basem the best treatment he could. Ayat folded."

"And the daughter agreed? Is she the mother of all the other children?"

Natalie nodded. "Seven children, a babe in arms and another on the way. All perfect little specimens and, apparently, to Ahmed's satisfaction. I don't think she necessarily agreed. She did as she was told."

Saskia scrunched up her face. "Poor woman."

"As I noted, your arrival on the scene was the last straw for Ayat. He'd brooded over the fate of his daughters and grandchildren and Ahmed's increasing brutality, not only against his family but in his criminal activities. Ayat began to hear of tactics, such as the deployment of unaccompanied minors to sell drugs, which was the focus of Project Archane. He suspected they were directly linked to Ahmed. In addition, Ahmed progressively cut off all Ayat's communication with his daughters and grandchildren."

Alexa extended a hand to Saskia's plate, asking a silent question with a lift of her eyebrows if Saskia had finished eating. "Merci," Saskia said, lifting the plate for Alexa to take. Alexa gathered all the plates and took them to the sink.

"Ayat was in a bind. He had a history of wrongdoing, and his daughters and grandchildren were in the hands of an increasingly tyrannical criminal. His only occasional contact with his grandchildren was through Basem, whom he managed to see during Basem's frequent trips to hospital for operations and to deal with the other complications of his condition."

"Touati called Basem disabled and physically incompetent," Saskia growled.

"Ayat believes that Basem's clever enough to know how not to draw attention to himself. Given what you've told me about Basem, I think Ahmed clearly underestimated him. Ayat said the other children looked up to him. On the rare occasions when Ayat was allowed to speak to his daughter, she told him that Basem was a major reason they all kept sane. He made a game of bypassing the surveillance system and was clever enough not to be caught."

"Mon dieu! That poor child. Those poor children. What happens to them and their mothers?"

Natalie wagged her finger. "Patience. Let me tell my story. When Ayat first read your reports, he quickly realised that you and Madame Le Fèvre were well on the way to uncovering the bank systems that criminals and the bank profited from. By this stage, he had lost his stomach for more hardcore criminal activity, so he decided to move you both into positions where you would have your focus elsewhere. But then he realised that you just kept on digging."

Alexa served coffee; white for Saskia, black for Natalie.

"By the way. Ayat organised the attempted theft of your laptop from your hotel room."

"François?"

"Yep."

"And what about involving Melanie? Getting her on drugs again?"

"Ayat knew about that, but it was cooked up by Aubert and François, who, incidentally, is currently in hospital. He didn't come off unscathed in the castle assault. Claude's had a chat with him. He's not cooperative, but when Claude mentioned your name, he apparently smiled. He said he thought you had a lot of pluck and he could never figure out whether you were as innocent as you seemed."

"Pluck!" Saskia scoffed. "He put that horrid listening device on my wrist. I'm going to have nightmares about that thing for the rest of my life. It was worse than having people watching me sitting on the toilet!"

Natalie chuckled. "He asked whether you were working with us."

"What did you tell him?"

"That Ayat alerted us to your imprisonment by Touati, and told us he'd had a hand in having you watched."

"So, no one knows I was working with you?"

"Only the Project Archane team. But let's get back to Ayat. When he discovered you were still fiddling around uncovering systems even after moving you out of your original bank position, he moved you again. This time to work directly with him in Brussels. And," Natalie leaned forward to pat Saskia on her hand, "he increasingly found himself in the awkward position of liking you and wanting to protect you. He was horrified when you agreed to Touati's proposal to teach his children. He was terrified when you further agreed to stay a week at Touati's establishment. When you rang to say you'd be there another couple of weeks, he feared Ahmed would create an unfortunate accident and you would never leave the place." Natalie held up her fingers in quotation marks when she said 'unfortunate'. "That was the straw that broke the camel's back, so to speak."

Saskia took a deep breath. "So, all this was happening while I was drawing stick figures and teaching bike and scooter tricks?"

"Is there any interest in dessert?" Alexa asked. "I bought lovely Belgian chocolate ice cream."

"Sounds divine," Natalie said. She stood up and stretched her arms up to the ceiling, bending from side to side. "Have you had enough of this story, or shall I go on? My throat's getting pretty dry."

"There's more? Oh, yes! The children. Where are they?"

"Over the past couple of days, the powers that be have come to several conclusions. Please do not repeat this information further." Natalie held up her hand, fingers splayed. "Ayat has been extremely cooperative." She crooked her forefinger. "He would last maybe five seconds if placed in jail, given the extensive reach of the criminal masterminds he has exposed." Another finger crooked. "His daughters, his wife and his grandchildren need him." Another finger crooked. Natalie balled her hand into a fist. "That family, including Ayat, have disappeared."

"What do you mean, disappeared?"

"Figure it out, Saskia." Natalie moved her head from side to side, rolling her shoulders again. She nodded to the bowl of ice cream Alexa had set in front of Saskia. "I'd advise you not to put on too much weight if you want people to rush to your rescue." Natalie leaned back, hands pressing into the small of her back. "I'm still suffering from lifting you. I'm going to bill a massage treatment to management."

"Umm – the vest and helmet made it awkward."

"They were the smallest we could find! Anyway, do you want to know how we got into the castle?"

"I think I need another headache tablet," Saskia groaned. "Of course, I want to know."

Natalie turned her chair and sat astride the seat with her arms over the back to pick up her bowl of ice cream. She spooned the dessert into her mouth and continued.

"One of the things the team – not your nerdy team, the Project Archane team – started to do as soon as you decided to go into the lion's den was to search for every scrap of information about that castle. It was quite something in its day. A particularly interesting feature we discovered was a labyrinth of underground passages where the castle inhabitants could retreat to or escape through when sieges got a bit too awkward. Our friend, Ahmed, found this feature particularly attractive. He renovated some of the tunnels and used them to store weapons and drugs, and – well, we're still going through his store. Unbelievable the stuff that's in there!" Natalie set down the bowl, freeing a hand to trace invisible lines on the tabletop to illustrate her description.

"There's only one entry and one exit to the tunnels. One is in the forest about a kilometre from the castle. It's at the site of a rather nice little hunting cottage that just happens to have furniture that can be moved to reveal a stairwell. The other exit or entry, depending on your point of view, is into the tower near the drawbridge."

"Oh! That's why you all started talking about traboules and using them as an escape route."

Natalie frowned. "I take it you are only now realising that we were giving you vital information."

"I missed it completely."

Natalie shook her head in mock disappointment. "I am particularly put out you didn't figure out our carefully crafted message after forcing us to decode your cryptic ones."

"I was under stress," Saskia protested, finishing her dessert. "You'd better get on with your story. I'm listening."

Natalie heaved a sigh. "So, to continue. We knew about this access to the castle even before you decided to walk into that place and stay for a whole week. We'd been keeping an eye on the hunting lodge in case we had to use it. We got ready to use our knowledge after you displayed the green blouse. Then, when we found out about the AN0M app and talked to the guys monitoring the feed from the app, they told us they'd intercepted messages that two men were going to meet with Ahmed at the castle. Wonder of wonders! Who should turn up at the cottage disguised as hunters with a contingent of protective thugs, but Vlad and Dion. Belgian police were very happy to nab them on their way back out after the meeting with Ahmed. It was quite a satisfying haul, but had to be kept very secret because by then you'd made a phone call in which you said 'red' so often and complained about not having any sleep that we knew we didn't have time for finessing any plan." Natalie's eyes glazed over momentarily as she recounted the story.

"Nevertheless, in a perfectly coordinated operation with your nerdy team and the Project Archane team, plus a whole lot of us more active types, we mounted our rescue. Your nerdy team mucked around with the castle's security cameras to confuse the enemy. Claude and I – I might point out that I rushed from being with your nerdy team to being part of the active types – Claude and I and others snuck through the tunnels, disabled a few unsuspecting guards and made sure there was no one around to operate the drawbridge. Other active types hoisted an explosive at the gates across the river to blow them up, while, at the same time, a third team assaulted the main gates."

Natalie manoeuvred an extra-large spoonful of ice cream into her mouth. "Well," she said, smacking her lips together, "you sort of know the rest. It always gets messy when we do these active bits, and you don't have to know those details."

"But what about the children? I mean, this whole operation was about stopping all that horrible stuff from happening to the migrant children."

Natalie nodded. "Well, we have had one significant win. There's no easy solution to the problems of the abuse of people, the flow of drugs, the laundering of money and the financing of terrorism, but today, we've had a significant win. This is not a war that ends, Saskia. It's one where law enforcement has some wins, the criminals regroup, and we just try to beat them back again." She set down the bowl, leaning her forearms over the back of the chair. "Yes, it's exhausting." She smiled. "And you've helped a lot. Tell me, would you like a medal or some form of recognition for helping with this operation?"

Saskia jerked back in horror. "Absolutely not! I just want to go back to my little apartment in Lyon and to my backroom job at the bank and never mention all of this to anyone ever again."

"Ah yes. Madame Claire and Rufus will look forward to that."

# 45

## LYON

Saskia sat in her favourite corner in her favourite café, breaking off pieces of a croissant and enjoying her first coffee of the day. She scanned through news items and the chats she liked to keep tabs on, but her mind was elsewhere. She smiled when she recalled the conversation with her parents last night. They were still confused and excited about the sudden influx of police to the café two weeks ago. "And then, the next day, the police just disappeared," her father said. "No explanation. Nothing! We think there must have been something happening in Delft, but we haven't heard a word."

Saskia wondered what sort of tale would be woven to fill the vacuum of information about police behaviour.

Hans reported he had bought Melanie a red dress and that he was more in love than ever. Saskia wished with all her heart that all would go well with the couple. She promised to visit Rotterdam as soon as possible and bring that chocolate pizza.

Madame Claire and Rufus had been warmly welcoming. They'd had a good holiday but were happy to be back in their home. They all missed the company of the beautiful and enigmatic Isabelle.

Her croissant and coffee finished, Saskia packed away her laptop, waved goodbye to the café's proprietor, collected her bike and cycled the rest of the way to her job at the FSB.

The past two weeks had been confusing for the bank, with two executives suddenly plucked out of the management team. In fact, Saskia had walked into chaos when she arrived at the Brussels offices, innocently returning to her research portfolio. She looked suitably horrified to hear that law enforcement authorities were investigating the bank, and that Ayat Benkirane and his family had disappeared. Along with other bank staff, she had been subjected to questioning – though that was just for show. Claude, his leg obviously uncomfortably sore, and a fellow officer had spent the time with her planning how they could meet up again to delve further into the information on her app.

Mme Le Fèvre had rung, explaining that she'd been asked to take over management of the Lyon branch, and would Saskia return and work with her. Saskia had accepted the invitation with alacrity.

She locked her bike into a stand and entered the bank's doors. It was like coming home.

"Hi, Saskia!" greeted the receptionist. "It's good to see you again. Please go to Madame Le Fèvre's office. She's waiting for you. It's Monsieur Aubert's old office."

Mme Le Fèvre opened the door to Saskia's knock. Her lips were pressed tightly together and she glared at Saskia as if she was furious with her.

Saskia startled back.

Mme Le Fèvre jerked her head to indicate Saskia should enter the office and then banged the door shut harder than necessary.

"Meet Luca Ittimani," she said in English. Another jerk of her head indicated the black-suited man perched on the edge of a seat. Mme Le Fèvre leaned back against the desk, her arms crossed. She glared at the man she had just insultingly introduced.

Saskia knew who Luca Ittimani was, of course. He was FSB's Chief Executive Officer. He was the highest-ranked executive in the bank's global hierarchy and resided in New York. She'd seen his photo in the brochures about the bank.

Saskia's first thought was that he was in Lyon to help sort out the bank's current chaos.

But that would not explain Mme Le Fèvre's obvious displeasure and the way that Mr Ittimani stood, seemed embarrassed about towering over Saskia, and sat again.

He balanced awkwardly on the very edge of his seat and leant forward towards Saskia, his elbows on his knees.

"Dr van Essen, as chief executive of this bank, I am sometimes called upon to do rather unpleasant things. Let me begin by saying that your work is exemplary, and should you require me or any of the executives of this bank to give you a reference, we will do so in the most glowing terms. However..."

Saskia's jaw dropped and she stared at Mr Ittimani, seeing his lips still moving but not hearing what he said.

*Am I being fired?*

Saskia pulled herself together. "Umm – sorry – what were you saying?"

Mr Ittimani pulled a face, pushing dark-rimmed glasses further up the bridge of his nose.

*He is nicely dressed. Hair well-cut and greying at the temples, but thinning. Shiny black shoes. Rather than looking profoundly embarrassed, he should be sitting back in his chair, his legs crossed and the toe of those shiny black shoes swinging idly.* Saskia's thoughts scattered, grabbing at inconsequential details as she waited for Mr Ittimani to gather himself to start again.

"Your work has been exemplary. We know that you forewarned the bank of lax controls. Unfortunately, many employees of the bank are also aware that the penalties they now face result from your exposure of their shortcomings. We cannot afford at this uncertain time for the bank to have more discord. Rather, we have come to a decision that the better course of action is for those who are blameless, such as Madame Le Fèvre, to rectify the situation."

Arms still folded across her chest, Mme Le Fèvre emitted a derisive huff.

"Madame Le Fèvre fervently opposes our decision and has herself threatened to resign over this issue. This would be a grave loss to the bank. We hope that you will agree to a compromise. We have put together a very handsome severance package – "

Saskia turned on her heel, walked stiffly to the door and let herself out.

She was almost to the reception area when Mme Le Fèvre caught hold of her shoulder. "Wait, Saskia," she said gently. "Come in here, and let's talk." She drew Saskia into a nearby meeting room and closed the door.

"I will resign over this," Mme Le Févre said, kneeling before Saskia. "This is beyond unfair. He only told me of the board's decision this morning."

Saskia took a deep breath. She put her hand on Mme Le Fèvre's soft cheek. Her favourite supervisor smelled faintly of a very nice perfume. Her eyebrows, though drawn together in consternation, were still perfect.

"You know," Saskia said. "I'm suddenly very exhausted. I'm going to find some friends to go on a mountain biking holiday and explore the Alps. In some ways, he's right. People know I dug around looking for stuff. It might get uncomfortable for me to work here. People might jump, thinking I'm police or something. You should not resign. You'll do great things with this bank. Maybe we'll have a chance to work together in the future."

Mme Le Fèvre drew Saskia into a hug. "You're a rare one, Saskia. I'll make very sure your severance pay is enormous."

# AFTERWORD

I hope you enjoyed 'The Bank'. If so, *please leave a rating and a review* to help others find the tale.

I was moved to write 'The Bank' by an article in *The Guardian* newspaper, titled 'Beaten and tortured: the north African children paying a bloody price for Europe's insatiable appetite for cocaine' (https://www.theguardian.com/global-development/ng-interactive/2024/jun/11/north-african-children-beaten-tortured-europe-cocaine-gangs). It brought to stark reality the incredibly difficult task of law enforcement authorities trying to track down criminals who cleverly use the loopholes in legal systems that benefit the powerful and wealthy.

I worked a number of issues into this story that are based in real events, even if the events didn't occur in the sequence as described in this story. Scams are, of course, part of parcel of our daily lives. Saskia's nerdy friends arose from information about scam baiters (https://www.theguardian.com/technology/2021/oct/03/who-scams-the-scammers-meet-the-amateur-scambaiters-taking-on-the-crooks) and, of course, the work of white hats. Global systems, such as those set up in good faith to ameliorate climate change, and stop money laundering and the financing of terrorism, are repeatedly abused by criminals and

*Afterword*

the ethically challenged in society. The abuse of the Carbon Credit scheme cost the France billions of euros … and, yes, the government was very slow to act! (https://www.france24.com/en/20180129-france-trial-carbon-credits-fraud-paris-crime-emissions-scam-melgrani-marseille) And AN0M really does (did) exist.

The presence of Interpol's HQ in Lyon was my initial motivation for the book's setting. But then, I fell in love with the city and let Saskia enjoy it, too. Lyon has a rich history that I shamelessly exploit in 'The Bank'. From its extraordinary murals to its wonderful food, setting at the confluence of two rivers, modern and ancient architecture, parks and surrounding landscape, the city has much to offer tourists and residents alike.

Perhaps you'd like to know what Saskia does after being fired from FSB. Join my newsletter (https://dl.bookfunnel.com/xvfkcvhvfj) and receive a short story about her next career move. Or you can jump straight into the next book in the Saskia van Essen series, 'The Forest'. I've included an excerpt over the page.

# CHAPTER EXCERPT

**Chapter 1,** *The Forest*

Saskia jumped her bicycle off the roadway and onto the footpath to avoid a car that had swerved too close. Hardly breaking speed, she bumped back into the morning traffic flow and wove in and out between slow-moving vehicles.

Her attention was only partially on the road chaos. She had often navigated it on her way to the office of International Financial Services – IFS, the company she owned with her three partners, Claude, Natalie and Clarissa.

A vibration in the pocket of her jacket caused her to touch her earbud.

"Are you on your way?" It was Clarissa, sounding uncharacteristically nervous.

"I'm on my way."

"Ms Rowland said she would be here at ten, and I know she'll be on time. Natalie and Claude are already here. You're running late."

"I'll see you soon." Saskia touched off.

Clarissa was IFS's Administrator. Without her, IFS would likely be a tangled mess rather than a highly efficient, sought-after service. Clarissa also owned and lived in the house from which IFS operated.

*Chapter excerpt*

She spoke four languages fluently – including her native Jamaican Patois – and with such cultured tones that the people she interacted with on the phone would never guess she slopped around the office in slippers and a tent-like dress. Nor would they guess she was agoraphobic and disliked dealing face-to-face with strangers.

Tania Rowland was no stranger to IFS. She was the United Nations Rapporteur into Criminal Activity in the Global Timber Industry, and the IFS team had been working with her for the past eight months, helping to gather data for the first of two reports she would submit to the United Nations General Assembly. It was not in Saskia's nature to be intimidated by people, even given that her small stature meant she needed to look up when she spoke to most adults. But she'd been overawed by Tania's intensity and then by her quick mind. It had taken a few days to realise that under Tania's serious focus was a friendly, thoughtful and sympathetic nature.

Three days ago, Saskia had been sitting with Tania in her temporary office at the New York UN headquarters when Tania asked if IFS would be interested in taking on a private assignment. Saskia was sufficiently intrigued to discuss it with her partners. Tania had offered to travel to Lyon to provide a more thorough brief about the assignment, and Natalie had invited her to the IFS office. Admittedly, it was the only way to include Clarissa in the face-to-face conversation, but the phone call just now revealed that Clarissa was filled with anxiety.

Saskia slid around a corner, one foot off a pedal to catch a slip, into a quieter, rough-paved street, then around another corner into an alleyway made narrow by high stone walls that enclosed the small backyards of two-storey terrace houses. She skidded to a stop at a wooden gate, punched a code into a keypad to unlock a latch and walked her bike on to a path bordered by carefully tended flower and vegetable gardens. The gate sprung closed behind her.

Another keypad code let her through a back door into a small mudroom. She leaned her bike against a wall and hung her helmet on a hook set lower than the rest to accommodate her diminutive size. Tzutsi and Malta, Clarissa's two small dogs, burst through a doggie

*Chapter excerpt*

door separating the kitchen from the mud room, jumped up eagerly to greet her, then rushed back through their doorway, barking excitedly.

Their behaviour forewarned Saskia that Tania had arrived and Clarissa was trying to confine her pets to the kitchen. "Dat gaat niet werken," Saskia murmured. Like each of the IFS partners, she was a proficient speaker of languages, but often reverted to her Dutch roots when she spoke to herself.

Sure enough, she entered the kitchen to find both dogs barking and hurling themselves at the door into the lounge – or, as Clarissa called it, "IFS Reception". Three cats sat on a kitchen bench, tails flicking disapprovingly.

Saskia pursed her lips, wondering how she could get through the door and not release the pets from the prison that so aggrieved them.

The door handle turned, and the door began to open. Tzutsi and Malta rushed through the widening gap, still barking noisily. The cats followed the dogs at a statelier pace.

Claude stood in the doorway. He bowed to Saskia, a bemused smile playing on his lips. "And may I invite you in as well?"

Saskia raised an eyebrow in question while indicating the room beyond with a tilt of her chin.

"Tania says she would be most pleased to meet the animals and doesn't think they should be deprived of their usual run of the house," Claude said with a chuckle. "Come. Join us. Clarissa's cleared the dining table for our meeting."

Clarissa's living area-cum-IFS reception was a long room with armchairs at the far end facing a huge television screen in front of heavily curtained windows. A tall bookcase, crammed with books and magazines, lined the wall shared by the next house. Close to the front door and at the foot of the stairs was a large desk, the top dominated by a computer screen and two monitors. The door had double locks and was barely used – though it must have been unlocked to admit Tania. Downlights brightened the room, and ducted air conditioning freshened the air. In every corner of the room and hanging from the uprights of the stair railings were pot plants, their leaves and flowers giving the illusion of being in a conservatory. Close to the kitchen door was a round dining table covered with a floral tablecloth. In the centre of the table was a plate of small pastries, a French press full of coffee, five mugs and plates, a small jug of milk and a sugar bowl.

Natalie, Clarissa and Tania were seated at the table, though Clarissa launched from her chair, almost knocking it over, when the dogs burst into the room, making for Tania. "No! Malta! Tzutsi!" she cried.

But Tania seemed unperturbed by the animal assault. "Hello. I'm pleased to meet you too," she said, bending sideways to pat the dogs as they scrabbled at her leg.

"Should – should I take them away?" Clarissa asked. She stood frozen, half in and half out of her chair. Saskia noticed she had made an effort to look business-like, wearing a dark blue suit dress. *That must have been ordered online in a hurry*, Saskia thought.

Tania shook her head, the layered waves of her salt-and-pepper hair barely shifting. Her face was slightly askew, with faint scars marking its left side. Saskia envied Tania's well-behaved hairstyle. Her own black, frizzy hair needed to be pulled back into a ponytail to achieve a semblance of control. But then, most details about Tania seemed well-behaved. She was tall and slim, wore tailored clothing, always looked neat, and enunciated her words carefully; her control was particularly impressive since she was a partial quadriplegic, the result of an accident some thirty years before.

"I'd love them to stay. I'm sure they'll settle in a bit," Tania said.

Saskia picked up Malta. "I've learnt that if you put Malta on your lap and scratch Tzutsi between the ears for a bit longer, they'll settle," she advised.

"Then, by all means, put Malta on my lap, and I'll give Tzutsi a bit more of a scratch between the ears," Tania said.

"But they'll put hair all over you," Clarissa fussed. "It might be better if I put them in my bedroom out of the way."

"It's only hair," Tania assured as she eased back a little in her seat to accommodate Malta on her lap, holding the dog in place with her clumsy right hand as she leaned sideways again to fondle Tzutsi's ears.

Clarissa plonked into her chair, uncertainty or distress writ large in the set of her upturned brows and tension of her mouth.

*Chapter excerpt*

Saskia hitched herself onto an office chair that she could raise to a comfortable height.

With a mischievous grin that indicated she was enjoying the show, Natalie said, "Now that we've got that sorted, what's the agenda, Tania?" She reached forward as she spoke and poured coffee into the five mugs. "All Saskia's told us is that you've got something that's a bit left field but might interest us." She pushed steaming mugs in front of each person. "Help yourselves to milk, sugar and pastries."

Tzutsi rested his head onto one of Tania's feet, seemingly content to stay there. Tania straightened. "Thank you for the coffee," she said. "My agenda is I want IFS to help me uncover criminal activity in my family's organisation in Australia."

"You want IFS to help you uncover criminal activity in your family's organisation?" Claude said, doubt in his tone.

Tania nodded. "Specifically, I hope IFS will agree to help me restructure my family's organisation and, in the process, discover the nature of criminal activity within the organisation. I propose that my organisation contract Saskia to join the company as a consultant and for the rest of the IFS team to back her up as required."

"You want Saskia to go undercover in your family's organisation in Australia to uncover criminal activity?" Claude said.

"Claude, stop sounding like a broken echo," Natalie complained. "Tania, you'd better say why you want IFS and why Saskia." She sat back in her chair, causing the bump of her pregnancy to show. Natalie's expertise was cyber security, the dark net and computer languages. Her dress code rarely strayed beyond ripped denims, tee shirts and slip-on shoes. She had pale blue eyes, thin pink lips, and eyebrows and lashes that were almost white. Her appearance contrasted sharply with that of her husband, Claude, who had dark hair and beard and was almost always fashionably attired and carefully groomed.

Tania opened her mouth to answer Natalie's question, just as Clarissa's oversized ginger cat leapt onto the table and glowered challengingly down at Malta. Clarissa swept him off the table with a mortified gasp, almost overturning the filled coffee mugs the cat had expertly avoided. "Moté! Naughty! I'm so sorry! I don't know what's got into these animals."

"I think they're lovely," Tania said. Her deep blue eyes studied Clarissa as she wrestled the cat into her lap. Saskia had worked long enough with Tania to guess that she was assessing the nature of Clarissa's discomfort. "Please don't be concerned," Tania said, returning her attention to Natalie. "Why IFS? Because I have come to trust the integrity of IFS –"

"What sort of criminal activity are we talking about?" Claude interrupted.

Tania hesitated, more, Saskia thought, to re-orient her thoughts than because she was uncertain. "I'm not sure. I suspect money laundering but I don't know what the source of the funds are."

"And you don't want to go to the law enforcement authorities?" he asked.

"Not yet. Partly because I don't have anything concrete to take to them, and partly because I'm concerned for the welfare of employees and my family. I'd prefer to minimise disruption."

"So, what grounds for your suspicions?" Claude sat forward, helping himself to a pastry.

"Basically, I cannot believe our profits can be so high, given our expenses. I cannot find errors in the accounting, but I don't believe the numbers. There may be a simple explanation."

"Is anyone acting suspiciously?" Natalie asked.

"This is one of my biggest problems. Although I am nominally head of the organisation, I'm not as familiar with the personnel as I should be."

"My impression is," Clarissa said, seeming to finally relax enough to become part of the discussion, "that this is not a new problem you've discovered. So, I'm curious why you're only now worrying about it?"

"I've only recently taken over management of Rowland Enterprises." Tania paused. She briefly studied each face, then, as if coming to a decision, said, "It may be useful if I give you a little background about Rowland Enterprises."

*Chapter excerpt*

"Good idea." Claude took his coffee mug in his hands and leaned back.

"Rowland Enterprises was started by my grandfather and his brother in the nineteen twenties. Over a few decades, he grew the organisation to comprise a forest in the southwest of Western Australia, and a large forest on the eastern part of Australia near a town called Arwon. Associated with that forest in the east is a timbermill and a village called Timbertown. Rowland Enterprises owns both. It is this eastern forest and its dealings that I am concerned about. When my grandfather died some four decades ago, my father took over management of the organisation and expanded it to include other activities, mainly carpentry, framing and flooring sections."

"Why?" Saskia asked.

"The timber industry in Australia has been in long-term decline, facing steep competition from imported woods. Diversification into value-adding businesses was a sensible move. Rowland Enterprises now also uses imported woods to supplement its output."

"So, you don't produce enough timber from your forest?" Claude asked.

"No. And not the sort of timber customers now wanted in the quantities that would be profitable."

"Before we get hung up on the financial details, let's get back to talking about the company's background," Natalie said.

Tania nodded, took a sip of her coffee, and continued, "My father suffered an illness a few years ago, and my cousin, who is Chief Financial Officer, stepped in as acting General Manager. My father returned to that position last year but then suffered a stroke at the beginning of this year. He is still unwell and not likely to recover. I've taken over management."

"Not your cousin again?" Natalie asked. "Why?"

"No." Tania looked down at Malta, pushing hair back off her forehead then smoothing it down again. With the slightest sigh of regret, she continued, "Already before my father's first illness, I began to notice the mismatch between expenses and profits. After my father returned to work, I discussed it with him. He told me he trusted Josh –

the Chief Financial Officer – but he'd look into it. Although he tried to shrug off my concern, it worried him. It still worries him, and rather than have my cousin take over the company, he – or, more accurately, my mother – asked me to step in and determine whether I have a cause for concern."

"I get the impression you're not part of the organisation but somehow know all about it," Clarissa puzzled.

Tania nodded. "Yes. My position is somewhat complex. Until recently, I was not employed by or receiving income from the organisation. But I have always had an interest in its welfare. I know the circumstances of many families who are long-term employees and live in either Arwon or Timbertown. Over the years, my father and I have often discussed aspects of the company."

"What's the revenue of this organisation?" Claude asked.

"Upwards of a hundred million a year."

"Number of employees?"

"About two hundred and fifty, counting those in Western Australia."

"Okay. So, we're not exactly talking about a small organisation here," Claude said.

"Do you think your cousin is involved in criminal activity?" Saskia asked.

"Maybe. He has always been a competent financial controller, and I find it strange that in the last five years or so, especially, many of the financial systems have deteriorated rather than improved."

"Did you ask him?" Natalie asked.

"I did. His explanation was the pressure of managing the organisation in my father's absence."

"You don't believe him?" Natalie pressed.

"He went on to tell me that to relieve the pressure, he needed to rely more on others in the organisation. He pointed to improvements in the organisation's balance sheet due to his decisions to delegate."

"And you want Saskia to work out whether he's become a criminal?" Natalie asked.

"Partly. My analysis of the organisation since my greater involve-

*Chapter excerpt*

ment is that it will not survive unless we make better use of our assets and restructure. I want to engage IFS to help me in that task and, in doing so, investigate whether there's a basis for my suspicions."

"How do you see this working?" Saskia asked.

"Ideally, you would agree to live in the Rowland family home, which is large enough to accommodate you and give you privacy. You would work predominantly with my nephew, Peter Allessander, to whom I have given the major task of seeking new opportunities for the organisation."

"Would Peter know the dual nature of my task?"

Tania nodded. "Yes. I discussed the appointment of IFS with Peter and my mother, Dianne. It was she who suggested you stay at the family home. Doing so would strongly signal that you have the backing of the Rowland family for your project."

"You don't think your nephew, Peter, is involved in any criminal activity?" Clarissa asked.

Tania shook her head. "No. Peter is not involved in whatever criminal activity might be occurring," she stated adamantly. "I trust him, and IFS should also trust him. The same goes for my mother."

"No one else knows about the undercover work except your mother and nephew?"

"No one else. I don't know whom I should suspect, so the fewer people alerted to the investigation, the better. I am also hoping my suspicions are baseless. In which case, the investigation need never come to light."

The three members of the IFS team turned to Saskia just as Moté decided to launch himself from Clarissa's lap into Saskia's arms.

"What do you think, Saskia?" Claude asked, only acknowledging Moté's new focus with a slight raise of one eyebrow.

"Er," Saskia said, pushing the cat out of her face. "Yes. It sounds interesting. I'd – er – have you got a timeline and what further information would we get about this matter?"

"Of course," Tania said. "I propose a start date in two months. Say, towards the end of January next year. In the meantime, I'll provide IFS with Rowland Enterprises reports, financials and personnel data."

# OTHER BOOKS BY MIRIAM VERBEEK

The Forest (book 2) The Website (book 3)

Skyseeker's Princess (book 1) Cryptal's Champion (book 2) Si'Empra's Queen (book 3)

If you want to read all books in one hit, download the boxset: 'Songs of Si'Empra' available at www.miriamverbeek.com

To receive updates and news, subscribe to Miriam's newsletters: www.miriamverbeek.com

Printed in Great Britain
by Amazon

57805285R00169